A Long Time Burning is the second book in the
Nell Montague Mystery Series.
The first book, *Finding Ruby*, was a
Page Turner Book Award winner in 2021.

A Long Time Burning

To Amanda

Many thanks

J A HIGGINS

First paperback edition October 2022

Cover design by riverdesignbooks.com

ISBN 979-8-8315-6164-7 (paperback)

DEDICATION

I would like to dedicate this book to my parents,
Nora and Eric who gave me so many wonderful
Christmas memories.

Unfortunately, not everyone is so fortunate, and many
face Christmas with sadness or dread. May the magic of
this season find you and bring you the gift of hope.

ACKNOWLEDGMENTS

Thank you to everyone who has supported and believed in this story. Special thanks go to Sarah A; to my beta readers Sarah, Pat, and Ann; and to all my generous Kickstarter campaign supporters.

I would also like to thank my editor Jenny, of Write Into The Woods for her patience, and to riverdesignbooks.com for my beautiful cover.

Thank you to CTS Logistics for allowing me to use their strapline 'Dangerous, Delicate, Difficult', and to the staff of SilverWood Books who continue to offer me their guidance and support.

PROLOGUE

Ric shuddered; the hanging tree was long dead, but its limbs still stretched out towards the full moon like bleached coral reaching for a distant sun. Clouds stirred to block out the light, and as the wind increased, a small bunch of herbs protruding from a rotting knothole shuddered, then fell to the cold grass below. Ric flicked up her collar and wished again that she had accepted the offered lift home. Rummaging in her bag, she found one black glove and a beanie hat. She frowned for a second, not recognising the hat, and slowly bringing it to her nose she sniffed. A small smile sketched across her face; it was Seb's.

Just ten more minutes and she would be home. Quicker if she went across the field. She hesitated and glanced at the sentinel standing guard in the centre. The hanging tree was rumoured to be over 500 years old and the source of much superstitious interest. All nonsense, of course, but somehow even as she thought this, Ric felt a little less sure than usual. But no, it was all nonsense; it was just an old oak that had stood in the middle of a field for far too long.

It was certainly a cold night, though. The wind felt angry, outraged, and the first snowfall of the winter had been forecast. Should she chance walking across the field? It was so exposed and she'd be in the direct path of the wind. No chance; she would go the longer, but more comfortable way home. Then, as if flicking on a switch, the clouds were swept aside, the cold light returned, and the moon had centre stage again. Its glow gave the hanging tree a menacing glamour so Ric locked her eyes defiantly on the path in front, the path that would lead her safely home. Why was she so nervous tonight? She did this more nights than not, liking the calmness of her walk home after the drama of the restaurant where she worked. But something felt off and had for a couple of nights now. Like something was starting. Or had started already. She smiled. Perhaps it was the approaching midwinter solstice. The small town of North Chase was one of the few places in the country that still celebrated the pagan festivals, but Ric didn't really buy into any of it. It was alright for the tourists it attracted, and more than one local entrepreneur had cashed in, but it just didn't make sense to Ric. She didn't particularly have any religious beliefs and blamed her mother for that. She had been dragged to Sunday school and church before she was old enough to protest, or have a mind of her own, but now purposefully shied away from anything even remotely religious. It was one of the few subjects they argued about. But she liked Christmas and would hang a wreath on her front door, put up a tree, and decorate the porch with lights. It always made the cottage look pretty, and cheered her up in these gloomy winter months. And at the moment, she needed that.

The wind picked up and brought her the threads of nearby laughter. Someone was having a jolly time, she thought. But as the laughter continued, Ric realised it was just one voice. One person laughing by themselves. Odd. She turned her head, trying to get a sense of where it was coming from. But apart from a skittish black cat that mounted a wall and then disappeared, there was no one else in sight.

Grabbing her phone, she stabbed a number.

'Seb, you bastard. Pick up.'

She paused, expecting to see he was ringing back. He must be asleep already. Now she was looking at that damn tree again. It certainly looked creepy tonight. She considered taking a photo, wondering if her phone would do it justice. She could send it to Seb. Raising her mobile, she took one shot then the phone was back in her bag. It was too cold to stand about taking stupid photos of dead trees. But that was a lie. She was merely aware that as she stared at the tree, it seemed to be staring back at her. She picked up speed and hurried home.

Later, in the warmth of her bed, she tried to rationalise what had happened next. The sudden howling of a storm in the field, though no wind stirred the wisps of hair sticking out from under Seb's hat. The loud sharp crack as a huge white limb split from the trunk and crashed to the cold ground below. And the shadow which must have been waiting by the tree the whole time she had been walking, the shadow which she had assumed was part of the tree trunk until it had moved away and walked swiftly across the field just after the limb fell. Just an old tree losing a branch in the wind and her eyes playing tricks. But as she tried to turn her mind off after a busy night there was one thought that she could not shake off. She had seen something that she should not have seen. More worrying, that *something* had also seen her.

1

5 November – 7.30p.m.

The bonfire spat and crackled as it sent glowing embers into the night sky. The old wood collapsed, new wood dropped, and red and yellow flames struck out in anger. Shivering, Nell thrust her gloveless hands further into her pockets and shuffled closer. But although the fire scorched her face her back was slammed by the icy wind which raced over the sea and onto the cliff where she stood. Now a series of fireworks ripped open the sky and blossomed with a bright palette of colours and noise. Look at me, she thought, being all sociable at the local firework display. But although she had waved hello to a few familiar faces and returned the smiles of some of the families she recognised from her walks, her enjoyment was as fleeting as the rockets that after a few seconds of sound and light left the sky dark and cold again.

Fake it until you make it, she attempted, reminding herself that she had lived here only nine weeks so was making good progress. In many ways it felt like she had lived here forever, but also like only last week that she had attended the funeral of her grandmother, been beaten up by her boyfriend, and escaped here. Now late summer had turned to autumn, the leaves were falling, and the year was heading to its end.

As she listened to the bonfire roar, she made a conscious effort to gather all that she had endured over the past year and to mentally throw her pain into the flames. She was trying to get past this, trying hard. Doing everything the self-help books and websites suggested. Her friend Max had introduced her to the five stages of grieving. She had successfully got past the *denial* stage, but had now made herself a blockade of *anger*, *bargaining* and *depression*, under which she seemed unable to emerge. Perhaps she should just accept that she was damaged beyond repair, would be alone for the rest of her life, and was quite probably going mad.

There was something peaceful about watching flames. Unapologetically destructive and dangerous, but at the same time so cheerful and beautiful. They danced in the unrelenting wind and licked defiantly at the night sky. *Cathartic*: that was the word, and amid the destruction and noise she finally felt her body settle. Twisting and turning, the fire's bright glow tired her eyes and her lids flickered and then closed. Peace filled her head for the first time in weeks, as the flames warmed her aching limbs, brushing against her exposed skin. Suddenly, the loudest fireworks yet erupted and a small boy began to wail in protest. Nell's eyes snapped open; invisible hands had grabbed her arms and she was being dragged forward. Dragged towards the fire. Panic erupted like a Catherine wheel and she began to struggle, began to scream. Then she was in the fire itself, looking out to the huddled crowd. A wave of heat hit her, as if she was burning from inside out. Scolding blood raced to her face and beads of sweat erupted on the nape of her neck. Twisting ropes of fire blurred in front of her as she gasped for air, tears streaming down her face. Thick smoke blinded her as she gasped and coughed, and then she was standing firmly back on the wet grass again.

Shaken, she turned to see if anyone was looking but their eyes were fixed on the sky above. A hallucination? She hadn't been sleeping well so was probably exhausted. Actually she *had* slept but the nightmares were back, leaving her fatigued in the morning and in a trance like state for the rest of the day. Her nana used to call it 'away with the fairies,' when somehow she felt on the verge of falling into a dream all day. And now she had just imagined herself in the middle of the bonfire. Just as she thought; she was going crazy, bonkers, mad.

More fireworks erupted, but this time the smile on her face was genuine. Perhaps it took a frazzled, over-stimulated imagination to fully appreciate just how beautiful they were as more colour bloomed over the inky sky. The small boy began to wail again, louder this time. Nell felt her own arms ache as she watched his mother scoop him up. Arms around her neck, he pushed his face into her long hair.

'Don't be silly. Mummy's not going to let those noisy fireworks get you.' As she moved him away she gave Nell a faint smile. Yes, Nell thought, she was here on her own, but she was still included in the crowd. It had been a good idea to come. But the intimate moment between mother and son had woken in her a longing to hold her own child, to feel small fingers seek sanctuary around her neck and in her hair. Soft footsteps to patter across her floor, and squeals and giggles to fill her silent apartment. Loneliness raised its head again and began gnawing at her ribs; being acknowledged in a crowd did not replace being here with someone, with friends or family, or even a partner standing by her side. Maybe next year things would be better. The only people in Nell's life now were Austin, a private detective, and Max; two people whom she had not known a few months ago. And out there somewhere was her estranged father, the only blood family she had left, and who, until recently, she had assumed was dead.

The display was over and her feet and face numb with cold so, turning away, she headed back to her beautiful penthouse apartment, which perched proudly on a cliff overlooking the beach and surf. Walking into the wind, she tucked her head further into her collar and picked up speed.

'Well, that's tonight over with. It will be Christmas next.' Nell froze. The words spoken in jest, between two family groups, made her feel like she was being dragged into the fire again. The year was disappearing fast and the holiday that Nell was dreading most was creeping closer. Christmas: like a flamboyant dame waiting in the wings, tonight would no sooner have taken its final bow before Christmas would come rushing on. Loud, bright, over cheerful, and literally taking over the whole stage. *One day at a time*, she reminded herself, and tomorrow was 6th November so there was plenty of time before she needed to panic about how to face Christmas.

There was just her car in the car park now. A few weeks ago, an unexpected bout of warmer weather had seen the return of some of the part-time inhabitants. But rain the following week had flushed them back to their city homes. Not that she knew them very well. She had just begun to know Leon, late owner of the village surf shack, but he had left when summer ended and a for-sale sign displayed in his window informed the world that he would not be returning.

The one problem with living on the top floor was the number of stairs you needed to trudge up. Although there was a fully functioning lift, now she was the only person in the building Nell worried it would break down and she would get stuck. And there were only three floors so she shouldn't be so lazy. As she dragged herself up the final set of stairs she felt the burning start up again and this time there was no roaring fire to blame. She shed her coat as she entered her apartment and was just pulling one arm out of her sweater when she met the central heating. Perhaps the temperature contrast, from outside to inside, was making her flush. At the word flush, another thought arrived with malice; she had just turned thirty years old, surely she was too young for hot flushes. Hidden deep in her heart there was a secret wish that she would meet the someone meant for her and perhaps start a family. But not if her body was going to betray her with an early menopause.

There had to still be time for her, after all those wasted years with Gary. Was she now being punished for being too scared to leave him? She had always been waiting for the right moment, and somehow the perfect storm had been Nana's passing followed by a night in the short stay emergency unit after a particularly violent beating when she hadn't said yes quickly enough to Gary's proposal. Nana's gift of money and this apartment had allowed her to escape. No, she was too young for the menopause and she seriously had to stop jumping to the most horrific conclusions every time she had a headache, or a fever. Or a reoccurring nightmare.

Perhaps it was something else? She glanced across to her laptop. Max had warned her of the dangers of Googling every symptom instead of getting real support. And that support had been Max for a while, but lately she was turning more and more to Austin. She was lucky to have two people in her life, but also acknowledged that she had known them both for a very short time. Her eyes drifted to the newspaper cutting that she had stuck on her fridge weeks ago. Words and phrases flew out at her. 'Missing teen found shackled in local hero's basement. A local man has been arrested and charged with the kidnap of thirteen-year-old Emily Blake following a tip off from a member of the public …' And then further down, 'Police in Wiltbury have confirmed that remains found yesterday are that of thirteen-year-old Ruby Morgan. A man is helping the police with their enquiries …'

Tip off from a member of the public indeed. Nell's childhood recurring nightmares and a lucky meeting with Max, who had used her newly blossoming psychic abilities to unravel the mystery, had resulted in the finding of Ruby. Emily could have had the same fate had it not been for Nell. A paedophile that had been getting away with it for decades was now behind bars and Nell could pick up her life again. Only she wasn't. The finding of Ruby and rescue of Emily should have brought Nell some peace at last, and it had at first, but now her latest worries filled her search engine; getting stuck on one of the five stages of grief; PTSD; and horror stories from people who had successfully tracked down an absent parent.

Nell tore the cuttings off her fridge, screwed them up in her fist and then dumped them into the bin, along with the remains of her supper.

The glass of the French windows was cold against her forehead as the tropical moment eased. Now all that was left was a strange smell of smoke that stung her nostrils. Probably bonfire smoke on her clothes and in her hair. But it brought back faint remnants of last night's dream. Something to do with fire. And had there been a baby crying? But she could remember no more than that. She filled the kettle and grabbed a mug; no point worrying, she would probably dream it again tonight.

As she stared at her reflection in the glass, she felt the misery descend. It was pathetic that the highlight of her week was popping along to the local bonfire display. The previous week, the news that they wouldn't be required to attend court due to the paedophile pleading guilty, had prompted an elegant meal in a fancy restaurant with Max and Austin.

'To the detective triad,' Max had toasted, causing shushing

from Nell and a flicker of amusement from Austin. Now, the sun was rising later every day while some days it was not seen at all. And the fact remained that her beloved grandmother was dead, and some days, like now, the pain hit her afresh.

Grief was a heavy burden to carry, making everyday life exhausting. Nell had read an article on how the Scandinavians coped with an extreme loss of daylight hours and had wondered if it would also work on sadness. So she now forced herself to take a walk every day. But that took effort and some days it took all her courage to leave the apartment to put out the rubbish.

Now bonfire night could be ticked off and, as the stranger had reminded them all, it was downhill all the way to Christmas. She grabbed her phone, selected a number, felt like a nuisance, and half-hoped the message service would pick up.

'Good evening, Miss Montague. How are you?'

It had become a habit that when she wobbled, she rang Austin.

'Ok, but today it occurred to me how truly pathetic my life is. My head is empty; empty of Gary's prattling rubbish and his bullying, I don't have to remember Nana's appointments or check she is coping, or worry about her dying. I don't even have Ruby, not the nightmares or the alter ego. I just have this shredded skin that I'm moving about in.'

She waited.

'I am listening,' Austin said.

'Before all this I knew how to keep myself brave, how to comfort myself, I had dreams and hopes. Now the phantom from my nightmares is in prison, Ruby is buried, Emily getting on with her life, and Gary probably drinking and smoking too much between some woman's legs.'

She paused, where had all that come from? This was the most she had spoken all week and her voice crackled with disuse.

'I don't know what to do, how to get up and motivate myself. There is no one to fight or to protect myself from. Sorry, God sorry, you don't want to hear all this. I shouldn't have called.'

'I am always pleased to hear from you.'

Nell plopped down on the sofa and pulled off her boots.

'Last week I was even thinking about going back to Wiltbury. Back to work. There is still a job for me. At least I would have some routine back, something to do and people I know to talk to while I try to grow back my personality, or create a new one. I mean it wouldn't be like before when I lived there. I've got Nana's money so I could buy a nice home, start renovations on Lark House, and return here for weekends if I want. I lived my life before for Nana, to keep myself safe from Gary, to keep going despite —or in spite—of everything. Now I feel so disconnected with the world.'

Silence filled her head for a few seconds, and then, as if satisfied that she had said her piece, Austin spoke.

'When we talked last week, you mentioned you might join a group or a class,' he prompted.

'Yes. I'm going to book some adult swimming lessons. Maybe I can ring them tomorrow.'

'Or, you could go to Barncroft Leisure Centre and book the lessons in person. Perhaps take a swim while you are there.'

'Yes. Yes, I could do that. I know how fortunate I am. I survived everything and Nana's money means I could escape in comfort. Escape to a penthouse and not end up homeless. I just don't want to waste this second chance but I don't know how.'

She heard a faint thud from his end and imagined Austin putting down a glass of something. Wine? No, he didn't seem the wine drinking sort somehow.

'If I may, I would like to share with you something I read once. It is somewhat trite but I offer it now in the hope you might find it insightful. "Nothing grows in a comfort zone."'

Nell let these words roll around her brain for a moment.

'Right. Ok. I'll do it tomorrow. Drive into Barncroft and book those lessons. Baby steps into making a positive change.'

'Excellent, and then perhaps we could meet for a coffee. I've a meeting in the next county so could easily drive over in the afternoon.'

Two things to do tomorrow. Nell felt a flutter of panic. But she needed this, she realised, she needed to plan something to do or she would do nothing again.

'That would be lovely, thank you.'

She could imagine the wry smile on his face. 'I am so glad you think so. So I'll see you tomorrow. Good night, Miss Montague.'

'Night. Thank you, Austin.'

He was gone but his voice hung in the apartment like the aroma of rich coffee. She hadn't realised how tightly she was coiled, but now, with a sigh, she let her shoulders relax.

One day at a time. And if that was too much then she just had to do one hour at a time.

2

'Oh, I'm so sorry. Are you ok?' The woman on stage tilted her head to one side and pulled a sad face.

Max shifted again on the lumpy seat, apologising to the family in front as she knocked her knee into their backs. *Bloody hell*, she grumbled; this place was built for height challenged people.

'Yes, yes, she is telling me that you recently changed the bedding and curtains and she thinks they look lovely,' the woman on stage continued. 'That is what she is telling me. That is what she is referencing to.'

Not exactly riveting, thought a thoroughly bored Max. Surely if the dead were visiting this pre-war theatre in the arse end of nowhere, they would have something more interesting to talk about than bedding. But then perhaps these were the little details that made the woman authentic. When Max had first walked in, a sign on the stage explained that the medium was tuning in to the spirit world. What she was actually doing was sitting on the stage wearing huge headphones. Her helper was sitting quietly, watching the room fill, occasionally speaking to her, and then her eyes would open and she would look at someone in the audience before closing them again. For just a few seconds they had locked on Max and something seemed to pass between them. *Or it probably hadn't*, reasoned Max. And what exactly was Max doing here, in this building that was desperately fundraising so they could mend the leaking roof? She was here objectively to see if this was something she could ever imagine herself doing. And for now it was a big, huge no chance. But it was certainly lucrative. By the time the witching hour arrived for the show to start only a few empty seats remained. Perhaps she shouldn't throw away the idea of becoming *Mystic Max* just yet.

Gradually the medium would be 'drawn' to certain people in the room and her assistant would bring them a chunky microphone.

'Don't come to me,' hissed Max with all the power of her mind. Obviously they couldn't speak to everyone, and there were offers of a private sitting for any of the audience, with a special price, as part of their attendance tonight. Really lucrative, then.

Max had nearly not turned up. Walking to the hospital car park after a busy shift, with the best fish, chips, and mushy peas in the whole of Barncroft nestled in her belly, the temptation to just go home had been overwhelming, especially as she was on an early tomorrow. But she had booked this ticket weeks ago and she really should follow her own advice about doing something other than work and rest. It was all too easy in the cold and dark of winter to just stay indoors with her feet up whenever she got the opportunity.

'Now the next person I have here is … yes, yes … she is getting very impatient with me.'

The audience had a little giggle at this. Max sighed and tried to adjust her long legs again without banging her knees.

'Yes, I can hear her clearly now. She has a message for a woman in the audience.'

Max raised an eyebrow sourly; nearly seventy percent of the audience were female so it was a safe bet.

'This woman has been feeling the loss of something, recently.'

They didn't just need to fix their roof, there were some sizeable draughts in this old place too.

The medium closed her eyes, nodded her head and looked over in Max's direction. Go away, thought Max.

'It's very urgent she gives this message, she has travelled a long way. It is for someone over in the far corner.'

The faithful assistant started to trudge up the slope to where Max sat.

Oh no. Please don't come to me.

'Oh, she is laughing now. She has a message for a young woman beginning with M. The lady is referencing to the caring profession, a doctor, perhaps, or a nurse.'

Shit. Suddenly the microphone was in front of her.

'Yes, yes. The message is for you, dear. Now you don't have to answer if you would rather not, but does the reference to the caring profession mean something to you?'

'Yes,' said Max grudgingly, standing and taking the microphone offered to her. She had assumed the woman was listening to the audience chatter before the show started, by way of hidden microphones or something similar. But Max was alone and had sat in silence so this was a little odd. She had also paid cash and given a false name when she booked.

'This lady says she is not related to you, no, not related.' Lately Max had been listening to some online mystic readings, and they often did this, she noticed, repeated themselves unnecessarily.

'She says that your talent has enabled you to help someone special recently, but now you fear it has left you. Does that mean something to you, dear?'

'Yes'

'Oh, she is laughing again. Laughing. Laughing.' Then suddenly the medium turned her back to the audience. Left holding the microphone Max turned to the assistant but he was scuttling back to the stage. A minute passed, then two. The audience as one turned to face Max who wiped her hands on her jeans to stop the microphone from slipping.

'I am so sorry, so sorry. I lost her for a second but she gave me your message. Something is approaching, a situation you will find yourself in. You can't help her this time, and you shouldn't try. You must be careful, very careful, not to get involved again. Your gift has left you temporarily so you are not tempted to use it.'

Deadly silence filled the auditorium and Max's face burned.

'Now, shall we have a short break and start again in fifteen minutes?'

The microphone was taken from her and Max sat back down.

What the hell was that all about?
And then another thought crashed into her head.
Nell.

3

6 November - Dawn

It had not started as a scary dream. Not at all. In fact it had been rather lovely. Nell had been apartment hunting in an old medieval city with narrow streets and gabled houses. All the streets were marked out in squares, or 'chequers' as she was told by someone unseen. She had to find the Church Bell chequer to view 'Gretel apartment', which was at the very top of the house. The moment the old door swung open, and she began twisting around the stone spiral staircase, she knew something was wrong, very wrong, and that she had visited this building in her dreams before. She also realised she was having one of her vivid dreams. Again.

Sure enough she recognised the room, but not the two dolls who sat on a miniature rocking chair in the corner of the room. Each had a cloth face and what looked like real hair braided neatly to one side. One with blonde hair and one with darker hair that looked like it would have curled if it had been allowed. Each was dressed in a thick beige material which might once have been white. Sitting on the chair, they leaned into each other, and their embroidered eyes gazed into the far corner of the room. Someone was talking; general chatter about the history of the building and its connection with a plague doctor from the seventeenth century. His hideous mask with its long beak and leather hood was proudly mounted on the wall above the dolls.

A creak ripped through the room and the rocking chair began to tip backwards, and then forwards. Of course, thought the sleeping Nell; rocking chairs always did that in horror films.

The dolls were flung forward and then backwards, their plaits lifted slightly as if caught in a draught, and then in a static charge of electricity, Nell felt her own hair rise. She shot to her feet; but then with a sharp cramp in her stomach she began to slowly float above the floor. Screaming filled the room like smoke, the chair rocked more violently, and the dolls were thrown to the floor. Floating towards the ceiling, Nell watched it all. And as she watched, she became aware of something watching her. The grotesque plague mask was suddenly inches from her face, and as her fingernails punctured her soft palms, she saw a movement from behind the eye socket as someone, or something, blinked.

She woke finally, her arms raised above her head, pressed against the headboard. Screaming filled her ears, but the moment she concentrated on it, it softened a little and changed until it sounded more like the frenzied laughter of an asylum.

Seagulls; she reasoned with herself. They were always screeching outside on her balcony. For a second she remembered the screaming baby doll from her dream the day after Nana's funeral. Did normal people dream like this, she wondered. Vivid dreams that were more like horror films, which left her exhausted the next day but were forgotten within minutes of waking. Probably just as well. No, she wouldn't let it get hold of her. There was no screaming, no maniac laughing, and there would be no more creepy dolls.

She lay quietly for a moment, letting her breathing calm and her hands unclasp. Waking up alone was still a delicious luxury. Her bed, in her apartment, drawbridge up and totally safe. Never again, she vowed, would she risk her safety and sanity for the sake of a relationship. Better to be alone. Alone, but not lonely. She now totally understood that expression but was still working hard to achieve it. You could be lonely amongst people, she realised, and although mostly fine on her own, she missed being part of someone's life. She could now look forward to a future she had never had before. But first she had to get through Christmas, the first Christmas without Nana, and before that there were swimming lessons to book.

The soft mattress was pulling her down again, but she feared falling back into the dream so dragged aside the duvet, pulled on her robe and shuffled into the kitchen. A half-full bottle of red stood on the countertop, but ignoring it she switched on the kettle instead. It was still dark outside and quiet except for the wind. A moment of unease washed over her and she struggled to understand why. Then it hit her. There was no chance she had heard seagulls when she woke up, so there was either a gibbering, screaming ghoul in the corner of the room which was now temporarily silenced or the sound effect had bled through from the dream. She poked her teabag with a spoon and inhaled the steam. Tomorrow she would attempt to get some routine back in her life and then maybe with real life to think about, the dreams would die down again.

As she sipped her tea and flicked blindly through a magazine, she couldn't get rid of the uncomfortable truth that she had been fully awake before the cackling laughter had ceased.

4

'Austin. How can I be of assistance?'

Mark took the hand that was offered and tried to work out if he was impressed or intimidated. There was certainly something rather unsettling about the smart middle-aged man who stood in front of him. Military veteran, thought Mark, and hoped that his gut had been right to hire this man.

'Thank you for meeting me here.' And then because he felt he needed to explain further, 'I want to keep this from my wife for as long as possible.'

With that he took the letters out of his briefcase. Austin pulled surgical gloves from his pocket and picked up the top letter to read.

From his eye movement Mark could see that he read it once, and then once more.

'May I?' Austin indicated his phone and when he was given permission, took a photo of the first letter then repeated the process for the letter underneath.

A man of few words didn't do him justice, thought Mark. He looked out of the window, not wanting to look at the letters any longer than necessary, but the words were burned into his memory.

'*She watches you and knows of your wicked plans. Stop now or she will unleash her fury,*' said the first one. And then a few weeks later:

'*You were warned. Now it is too late. The witch walks again.*'

'You mentioned a letter that threatened your child.'

'Oh, yes.' Startled, Mark pulled out the plastic A4 pocket

19

which held the last letter. He met raised eyebrows.

'Obviously it has dried now but I think it was written in blood.'

'Quite possibly,' Austin said, 'given the colour fluctuations of the ink.'

'I curse you on the blood of my slaughtered child. If you continue, I promise you an empty cradle at the Manor.'

Austin took another photo then fell silent.

'You contacted the police?'

'God no. I mean, I thought it was just the village dimwits being dramatic, or my spiteful ex-wife. And in a small place like this, everyone would have known my business by midday. But then when I got this, a direct threat to my daughter, I contacted you.'

'And still not the police?'

Now those piercing eyes were directly on him, Mark realised just how dry his mouth had become. He grabbed his wine glass, cursing as it spilt over his hand. Maybe this was a mistake; the man was a detective after all. Perhaps he could offer a small grain of honesty. A very small grain.

'My family … well let me just say that I don't entirely trust the police or have much faith in them. I found you on the internet.'

Austin's Slavic eyes assessed him for a moment, then he gave the smallest of nods. 'I will think on it and then let you know if I can be of any help. Expect my call this evening.'

Immediately afterwards Mark had felt relieved, the meeting had gone well. But much later the rumblings of disquiet began. If Austin accepted then he would investigate the threats to his daughter but what else might he learn? The man had a well-documented reputation for uncovering crime, and Mark had just given him free range to investigate his life. Much of Mark Corberley's history could be found on the internet, and was therefore available for anyone to read, but other matters had been kept private, secret, and now as he swung his Land Rover into North Chase Manor's driveway, he realised he might have just made a very risky mistake.

Each way he turned he could see danger; perhaps he should

heed the warnings, pack up and take his family away. He was beginning to wish they had never returned, but when his father had died the title and house had come to him, along with a mountain of debt. His father had already planned to sell the land at the edge of the estate, a move that would raise money and allow for some much-needed repairs and renovations to the house. But a fall whilst walking in the gardens had led to pneumonia from which he never recovered. Mark and his new wife had returned to the estate from their London home and picked up the pieces. For the first time in too long he felt he was in the right place at the right time. He had plans, was getting the various businesses under control, and if he was honest it was nice to be lord of a small town and not just another suit in the big city.

As he parked up he looked across to the garden path where his father had been found. It was difficult to estimate just how long he had lain there, the doctor had said that it was lucky his fall had happened on such a warm night. But the end had been the same. Still, he puzzled as to what his father had been doing in that part of the garden, and why he had been clutching a posy of rosemary in his hand. Some half-forgotten stories from his childhood raised their heads but Mark pushed them down again. *Damn them all*, he spat. It was his ancestral land and if he wanted to follow his father's wishes and sell a tiny pocket of ground to housing developers, he bloody well would.

The town was expanding and he was sure some nice smart family homes would be welcomed. It was just a few of the old families and their ridiculous superstitions about witches and curses that were causing him trouble. They had given his grandfather the same treatment when he had allowed a hospital to be built in a far corner of the estate. First it was used as a field hospital, but later catered for those suffering disorders of the mind. Post-traumatic stress disorder wasn't so well understood in those days but the local spring water and proximity to the lake had attracted physicians from across the country, including those recently arrived from Europe, and slowly the rehabilitation had changed from the body to include the mind. It had closed for several years but then Mark's father had supervised the rebuild and, again, patients had arrived, this time focussing purely on addiction. Then as purse strings tightened, a new source of income was needed and five years ago the Cedarwood Academy had opened its doors to help the offspring of the super wealthy who had gone off course. The glossy brochure sold a story of a privileged school, the opportunity to learn basic outdoor skills, and cutting-edge techniques in behavioural therapy. For a large figure, parents could dump their nuisance teen and get on with their lives in the belief that their little darling was receiving the best of care to kill their dangerous habits and make them acceptable for polite society again.

Then this summer, just after Lord Corberley had fallen in the herb garden, sixteen-year-old Hugo De Silva went missing. His social media account highlighted how the academy had made his depression worse by isolating him from everything and everyone that had been familiar. Surprisingly, only a few children had been hastily removed by their parents and when an inspection had declared the school not at fault, their places had been quickly taken. Statistics showed that over the last twelve months, the police and ambulance services had been called a total of nine times and Mark's father used to grumble that when sirens were heard heading towards the academy, the locals would raise their eyebrows and say, 'More trouble at Lordy's borstal.'

There was certainly a precedent for annoying the peasants from town. In an effort to appease them, Mark had contacted the paranormal investigation business 'Spooky Spots' and invited them to use some of the manor house for a ghost tour as part of the town's upcoming solstice festival. Apparently it was selling fast so perhaps not everyone hated him.

He looked up to the nursery and saw his wife's silhouette at the window. Daisy and Ava were the joy of his life. Daisy was his second wife, and thankfully very different from his first. He had been furious when he heard that Tilly was living in a cottage on the grounds. She had always smarmed up to his old dad, though, and had probably played the wronged woman card so he had felt sorry for her and let her return. Slippery and devious, she had shown her true colours soon after they had married and had nearly bankrupted him within a few years.

When he had been arrested, and she realised that her easy life was over, she had filed for divorce and he had been pleased to get rid of her. But now she was back.

Horrid for Daisy, of course, to have Tilly hanging about the place, and not for the first time he wondered if she was behind the threatening letters. She didn't care one jot if he sold the land, but the proposed site would be very close to the cottage she was squatting in and he had already hinted he wanted her out. But this didn't seem to be her style, somehow. At the back of his mind was also the worry of what she might have learned while she was here alone with his father. Sharp right up to the day he died, he would have been careful with the family secrets, and Mark had certainly never told her anything, but still, if she had decided to nose about at night, who knows what she might have found. It was a big house and his dad wouldn't have heard her.

He was being paranoid. The family secrets were locked away where no one would ever find them. And how would Tilly even know that there were family secrets to unearth? Mark smiled; his ancestors would have known how to deal with the likes of Tilly, and with the village idiots who were interfering in his business. Maybe it was time to remind everyone what it meant to be lord of North Chase.

The call was answered within three rings.

'Hello, Lord Corberley here. I'm ready to sign.'

Mark smiled; time to bring the bulldozers in.

Austin signalled for another coffee and opened his tablet. A few clicks and he had added the letters to the file he had already gathered on Lord Corberley. North Chase Manor was a handsome sandstone house built on the foundations of the original Tudor mansion. A fire had destroyed much of the original, with only the main house, east wing, cellars, and chapel remaining. Probably a similar story for most period properties, thought Austin. A local history group led by the honourable Matilda Corberley had produced the website several years ago and drawings from the regency period documented a picnic on the lawn with the imposing house as a backdrop. A few paintings of horses and dogs came next.

Austin sipped his coffee, scrolled through and waited for something to catch his eye. Sometimes there was just too much information in front of you and it was nearly impossible to spot that one thing you were looking for. Because you didn't always know what that one thing was. Something wrong, or out of place; something that didn't sound quite right or was slightly off key. It was always disguised in a mountain of information, words, or clutter, but he had learned a useful trick over the years: you hushed your brain, took a step back, and let your senses scan over it like a detector looking for illusive gold nuggets. Your senses often picked up the smallest signal, a warble, that it had seen or heard something that didn't belong. As he scrolled down pages of photos and speed-read the endless small details of the country house, he sensed it. A photo taken in the 1880s. A family group posed in the conservatory, mother, father and three children. A little faded and blurry but that was the way of old photographs which needed such a long exposure time. The youngest children were the blurriest, small children fidgeting in their smart, stiff clothes. A bland looking man with impressive facial hair stood behind his wife and it was the woman who initially caught Austin's eye. Hair scraped back, high-necked dress, blank expression on her pale face, like so many photos.

Look again, his mind whispered. And then he saw it. The oldest child, a boy of perhaps ten years old, was as clear as if his likeness had been taken with a digital camera. Perhaps he was just good at keeping still, but another thought crossed Austin's mind. He was seated and leaning against his mother, who had her arm protectively around him. Unusual affection for those days. His staring eyes seemed full of confusion and anger. The description below confirmed his suspicions. This family photo had been taken to commemorate the premature passing of Lord Corberley's heir.

Austin knew of the Victorian custom of taking photographs of the recently departed but he had not seen one of a child before. Morbid and rather distasteful, but then he supposed that in different cultures and in different times, different rules applied. He had once read that in certain remote communities, All Saints Day was celebrated by digging up the recently buried and bringing them home for the night as honoured guests. He glanced around the room, at the stuffed pheasant and fish proudly displayed in their dusty cases. Revolting in his opinion but then it was just that, his opinion.

He turned to another site now, one that was not available for the public. He needed a workaround to operate it but could still access much of what he needed by bypassing the usual entry point. He typed Lord Corberley's name into the search bar and waited. He did not have to wait long.

'How very interesting.' Austin sipped his coffee. *So this was why Mark Corberley distrusted the police.*

A cold draught from an opening door distracted him. A middle-aged man had just entered in what Austin could only describe as an apologetic manner. His chest was puffed out in a feeble effort to instil confidence, but there was something uncomfortable about the way he thanked the barperson who took his order and poured his pint. The stirring of recognition was already building in Austin's mind when the man, probably aware of his scrutiny, glanced in his direction.

Well, well, well. How very convenient. Austin didn't believe in coincidence but some would say that it undeniably was. Or fate, if they were feeling fanciful, which Austin was not. He believed in physics and probability. People often chose lottery numbers that were well scattered in a pseudo random manner, because they believed they were more likely to be lucky. In truth sequential numbers starting from one and ending in six had a similar chance of being drawn. Supposedly impossible odds but actually not at all. It was all down to your personality as to whether you were predisposed to seek connections or look for signposts that you were on the right path.

So, here he was in a small town with a very colourful past, wondering whether to take money from a lord, when who should walk in but another quarry he had been keeping tabs on. Very convenient.

When Austin finally slipped behind the wheel of his Mercedes, he had added a few photos to another file on his laptop. And this one went under the name of Montague.

5

1 December

Ric wiped the surfaces once more then tied down the rubbish bags.

'Leave them there, love. I'll take them out later.'

Ric sighed and thanked the manager. It had been a busy shift, but a good one. Everyone had been in high spirits, complimentary about the food and tipping heavily. It wasn't until the last plate had gone out and service was finished that the adrenaline which had kept her going all evening—all week actually—had run out and the ache in her shoulders and feet had started. And the best thing was that the manager's daughter had been out for the evening, on a jolly somewhere with all her entitled little friends, so Ric and the waiting staff had been able to relax and work as an efficient team.

'I'm taking the girls and guys home if you've changed your mind and want that lift?'

As usual Ric declined.

The sky was a winter filmset of cold twinkling stars, apart from one that appeared larger and smouldered like a distant sun. Rain-sodden leaves and wood smoke flavoured the crisp, cold air. Ric raised her hand as her boss drove by and then started on the short walk home. She turned to glance back at the restaurant. Dark windows reflected her own image, then, beyond the glass, something moved. Her phone was in her hand, her boss could be back in seconds, but doubt crowded her mind. The restaurant was strung with decorations so perhaps something had come loose. She quietly walked to the window and peered through. She scanned from left to right, but everything seemed to be in order. Chairs and tables were tidy, doors were closed, then one of the prints caught her eye. The walls were decorated with antique black and white prints of North Chase. Dull and depressing in Ric's view but tourists always liked them and Seb was fascinated by the ones of the manor house and grounds. One showed the now boarded up chapel that lay close to the house and as Ric stared at it she saw something she had never noticed before. There seemed to be a small figure by the crypt door.

Then a car sped by and for a second its headlights flooded the empty restaurant. Ric thrust her hands in her pockets and turned to walk home. The prints were gloomy and the figure had probably always been there, she had just not noticed it. But as she walked away she couldn't shake the feeling that lately she had been making too many excuses for too many weird occurrences. It couldn't all be just her imagination.

Then she turned a corner and there it was, the hanging tree in the middle of Church Field. She had walked past it so many times since that strange night a few weeks ago and felt nothing sinister, but then something else would happen and the unease would return. And this time it had struck closer to home, literally. Come to think of it, she had first heard the laughter and voices the same night as she had seen someone watching her by the tree, but had dismissed it, thinking it was nothing more than her imagination. But last night it had happened again. She had been able to think of nothing else since. And on top of it all Seb hadn't returned her calls for a few days.

She knew there was nothing wrong because he had been active on Facebook, so she didn't need to worry that he had gone missing. Like Finn. And as soon as she thought of Finn, she looked straight into his eyes. The poster attached to the lamppost was looking a little bloated and blurred now from where rain had slipped through the plastic sleeve. Actually, much of his face had disappeared, but his eyes still caught hers. She even remembered that photo being taken, just four months ago. It had been a spontaneous summer party, just the seven of them, all agreeing to get together on what turned out to be the hottest day of the year. The sun had soaked into the parched grass all day and by the time the moon rose, the air was still warm, sweet, and gentle on their skin. Damp from swimming in the lake, they had lit a small fire, drunk beer and talked about their futures. She had known them all since primary school, except for Seb. But now as she reminisced something new occurred to her. Finn was such a sweet, gentle soul, and Seb so genuine and funny, but as she remembered the day with some objectivity she realised that Seb and Finn hadn't got on. Although Finn had tried to talk to Seb he had been politely but firmly blocked each time. They had been like magnets that pushed each other away if they got too close.

Poor Finn: he had been reported missing a few weeks ago, and with his history of depression and recreational drug use she had a horrible feeling that the police weren't too worried about looking for him. There certainly hadn't been the fuss that the missing brat from Lordy's borstal had received. He had never resurfaced and as the days went by, the concern for Finn grew.

Finn's mother was convinced it was Seb's stepdad's fault, all because he was planning to sell off a few acres of his land and some of the older families were talking about a curse. She shivered, looked once more into Finn's eyes, and then hurried on.

What was up with her? She wasn't usually so jumpy. Was it the stories that were being retold again, like every year, as they approached Yuletide? Stories that were immediately forgotten about until the next midwinter loomed and usually made Ric roll her eyes and snort with disbelief. Tales of Mother Maundrell, the healer and wise woman who had been blamed for the deaths of so many children during the great plague of 1666, and who had been hanged at the very tree that now stood like a skeleton in the field. How fickle people were, thought Ric. When she had been able to use her herbs and potions to rid them of their various health problems, then she had no doubt been wonderful, respected and cherished by the town. But when nothing could stop the tide of plague victims piling up in the churchyards, fear had turned to anger and the church had taken their revenge on her. Maybe she had let the stories get to her, and there was a rational explanation as to what she had heard last night, coming from next door.

Ric had seen someone choke on a piece of meat once. The man had stood up, knocked over his glass, and clutched his throat, unable to answer the panicked enquiries from his wife as to what was wrong. Ric had rushed upstairs to get help. She had seen the Heimlich manoeuvre performed on training videos but worried that she would waste precious time if she tried herself. Especially when she knew the town's headmaster who led the St John's ambulance group was in the dining room upstairs. The man was saved but Ric, and probably everyone who witnessed it, had looked up the manoeuvre again online that night, and Ric had been sure to chew her food to mush before swallowing from then on.

And the reason her mind was churning over that particular episode as she walked past the hanging tree? Because lately she had tried to imagine what it had been like for Mother Maundrell, innocent and with her neighbours and family watching, to slowly choke to death as she kicked and struggled in vain against the rough noose. The panic the choking man felt must have been the same. Worse ways to die, for sure, but hanging from a tree was pretty horrific in Ric's view.

Her grisly imagination had got her past the field and outside her own house. There were no streetlights here and, as she squelched through what she hoped was just wet leaves and mud, she reached her gate.

There was still a light on in the kitchen. She pushed open the door and was greeted by the mouth-watering aroma of home cooking.

'Mum, I'm back.'

'Erica, is that you?'

'No, it's Mother Maundrell.'

Her mother's eyes sparkled in greeting and Ric knew it was pointless to tell her off for waiting up.

'I've got casserole bubbling in the slow cooker if you are hungry.'

'I reckon I could smell that near Church Field.'

Now she had made her mum smile. 'Well, I know how busy you are and I bet you didn't eat.'

'A quick mouthful during a lull. I'm starving. Thank you.'

'I'll leave you to it. Nighty night.'

'Night, Mum.'

The cottage was warm and cosy, and finally she felt her shoulders relax. Suddenly there was a sly knock at the kitchen window. The plate in her hand slipped and she just managed to rescue it when the door handle turned.

'Ric? Let me in, I'm freezing my bollocks off out here.'

Putting the plate down, Ric went to the door and turned the key. 'You knob, you made me jump, and keep your voice down or Mum with throw you out and lecture me again about the evil Corberleys.'

But Seb's bright smile, which brightened further when he smelt the food, made her stomach jump.

'So, I'm allowed in?'

'Of course, it's a nice surprise. I tried to ring you yesterday. Left you a message.'

Was it her imagination or did his big smile suddenly falter?

'Yeah, well as you said, I wanted to surprise you tonight. I went to the restaurant but must have just missed you.'

Ric grabbed her plate and then, seeing Seb's eyes widen further, got a second. Her one dream in life was to open her own restaurant, however small. If her dishes could bring delight to someone's face in the same way her mother's home cooking did then she would consider it a dream come true.

'I wanted to ask you something, Ric.'

And suddenly she felt sick.

'Have you still got 21st December off?'

Ok, so not what she had thought he was going to ask.

'I'll have broken up from college by then so I'll be working the lunch service. But they've promised me the evening off. Why?' Trying out all the different foods at the Solstice Festival was a tradition that Ric and her mum looked forward to, even though she knew her mother always carried her Bible in her bag to ward off any unchristian spirits.

'We're meeting up, aren't we?' continued Ric. 'If I can sneak off.'

Now he looked really uncomfortable.

'Actually I might have booked us a place on that ghost tour they're doing at the Manor.'

'Oh wow, that is a great idea. Thank you.'

'Seriously? Well, good. I thought you'd hate it. It doesn't start until late so you and your mum—'

'I thought you didn't believe in ghosts.'

'I don't, but nor do you. Thought it might be a laugh.'

He looked like a little boy now, pleased that his surprise had made her happy. Then his eyes rested on the crucifix on the wall.

'Your mum won't give you grief, will she? Ghosts, me, *and* the evil Corberley mansion?'

'What about your mum? She can't stand me either.' She was just about to add something lame about Romeo and Juliet but quickly changed her mind. They were friends, that was all. But he shrugged his shoulders and settled down to eat.

A ghost tour: should she tell him? She looked at the clock on the mantelpiece. There was another two hours at least before things kicked off, plenty of time to decide whether to risk it.

'Want to watch a film?'

'You are in a good mood tonight. Lady Alicia get a house dropped on her or something?'

'Lady Alicia was off tonight, skipping around town with her precious little friends, so we could all get on with a very busy service without her poking her oar in.'

'Nice. If I ever win the lottery I'll buy you that restaurant. You would be so good. And you could stick my photos on the wall to sell so I'd get my investment back.'

How cosy it was, she thought, curled up on the sofa with her best mate discussing their futures. She was exhausted but the last dregs of adrenaline were still running through her so they settled down to watch the new Christmas film on Netflix while she forked in her mother's delicious cooking.

Time ticked away and the room cooled down. With a jolt, Ric realised that this wasn't just the normal cold draught you'd expect in an old cottage. In panic, she turned to the wall clock but before she could the church bells announced that it was two in the morning.

'You need to go.'

'No, I think I need to stay.'

'Please. Now.'

'What's wrong, I thought we were having a nice time? You said to stay so I thought that meant you wanted me here.' He looked genuinely hurt, which upset Ric.

'I do but not now.'

'Why do you keep looking at the clock?'

'Please.' Ric's voice was so soft, she saw him frown and stare at her lips. But then something distracted him.

'Oh my god, your neighbours' kids are loud. They'll wake your mum up in a minute and she'll set the dog on me.'

'No, she sleeps at the other end of the house and we don't have a dog.' She attempted a smile, but then realised she wouldn't be able to joke herself out of what was happening. 'I'm not sure if she'd hear them, anyway.'

Heavy thuds pounded up and down the stairs next door. Then screaming laughter, 'Mama, Mama.'

'Wait a minute, didn't you say they moved out last week?'

'They did.'

'They did? Then you should tell your new neighbours that it is after midnight and their kids should be in bed.'

'They haven't moved in yet.'

'What? Then who the hell?'

Ric stared at the walls which were all that separated them from the noise next door. A layer of bricks that somehow did little to stop the cold which now crept from under the skirting board, across the floorboards and over her skin. Should she say? What she suspected? What she feared?

'Erica?'

'It started a few nights ago and I think it might be my fault, but ...'

'But what?'

'I don't think those kids are actually alive.'

He believed; she could see it flicker in his eyes. Just for a moment, he believed her.

'What? Oh funny. Really funny. Getting ready for the ghost hunt, right? Ok, I'll go. It is getting late.'

'Yeah.'

'See you tomorrow, well, maybe later today. Sleep well.'

'Ok.'

The kiss on her cheek was sweet. She saw him out and as

the door softly closed the noise started again. In her room, she put on her headphones and listened to white noise while the phantom children next door continued to scream with laughter and pound on the walls.

Then the low, tuneless humming started again.

6

The cold stung Seb's face as he cycled home from Ric's. The best route was along the main road and into North Chase Manor Estate through the west gate. But the quickest way was over the water meadows and through a section of boundary wall which had fallen into disrepair. Then it was a short ride through the woods to the cottage he shared with his mum.

According to the ordnance survey map for this area, the path across the water meadows, fields and woods was called Old Chase Path. However, to the inhabitants of North Chase it was called Broken Bridges, owing to the twenty-three rough bridges that straddled the two rivers that converged there and the various drainage ditches that fed off the water meadows. A sign at the beginning of Broken Bridges declared that it was managed by a local group of volunteers who would be carrying out essential repairs in the summer. Practically impassable during the spring floods, the rough planks and slabs of concrete that made up some of the bridges were muddy, but above the water. There was a third way to get home, a more secret way, but you needed two heavy keys and annoyingly his mum had recently found a new hiding place for them.

Seb loved the thrill of cycling at night, when there was no one to see him apart from the occasional fox or deer. Navigating the narrow bridges with only a head torch and bicycle light took some concentration in the dark, but once he was through the brick boundary wall the path widened and he could see the cottage lights in the distance. Just the swish of his bike wheels and the wind in his ears, he felt like a poacher or a member of some elite specialist force on a covert mission. As he bumped over the fallen bricks and entered North Chase grounds a light caught his attention; a light where there shouldn't have been one.

Before he could stop it, a warm flutter of excitement brought a smile to his cold face. But then he remembered and the smile was gone. Cursing his squealing brakes, he propped his bike against a tree and stepped into the woods to get a better look. Voices now; a shout followed by a ripple of nervous laughter. Every nerve in Seb's body told him to get back on his bike and get the hell out of there, but this was private property, his stepdad's land and whoever was here was trespassing.

The light came from a small fire with three figures huddled around it.

'Pass it here.'

Seb froze; he knew that voice, as one of the figures passed a bottle to the speaker. What the hell were Jordan, Brett, and the other dick they always hung out with doing here? Then a thought occurred to him; it was only a short walk through the woods to the edge of the borstal perimeter and it wouldn't be the first time they had been suspected of dealing. Three brainless teenage boys, but they still outnumbered Seb so he wouldn't stand a chance if it came to a fight. Climbing back on his bike, he stood on the pedals to accelerate and headed straight up to the main house to inform his stepdad.

Gravel flew as he hurtled up the kitchen pathway, the only door he had a key to. As he let himself in, he saw with relief that a light had been left on in the hallway; someone was still up then. Seconds later a door opened and closed nearby. He was just about to shout out when he heard a soft laugh, and then, 'Shush. You'd better go quickly before she hears us, but I'll see you tomorrow.' Mark's voice for sure. 'And don't forget that I'm here for you.'

Seb shrank back against the wall as a figure rushed past him and out through the door he had just entered. Above him the light was extinguished leaving Seb in total darkness, reeling from what he had just seen and heard.

'You utter bastard,' he whispered to the dark.

For a few seconds he listened to the old house creak around him, trying to decide what to do, and then sprang up to retrace his steps. Whatever Jordan, Brett and dickface were, or weren't, doing in the woods, they could get on and do it. Seb had other matters on his mind now. As he stepped away from the kitchen door, he scanned the moonlit scene in front of him. Yes, there was a figure at the end of the path, about to disappear into the woods. For the second time that night, Seb was certain whose voice he had heard with his stepdad, but he needed to make sure. Keeping to the grass verges to silence his tyres, Seb gave chase. Then a strange tingling at the back of his neck made him turn to face the manor, and sure enough a figure stood at a bright window, watching him. He was just trying to make out which room it was, and who it was, when the curtain was snatched across the window again and the house returned to darkness.

Heedless now of whether he was heard or not, Seb crashed through the trees. Unseen tree roots threatened to unsaddle him but he tightened his grip and kept his eyes ahead. As the pathway forked, he saw a figure ahead. It had come to an abrupt halt in a thin shaft of moonlight.

Something felt wrong. Was this the same person? The person who stood on the path before him, hunched over, seemed smaller somehow. And as Seb dropped his bike and approached he could see long tangled hair fanned over skinny shoulders. He'd chased after the wrong person. So who the hell was this—and finally he acknowledged—child who stood motionless before him? Deathly silence: he could hear his own ragged breathing but nothing else. As he looked around he realised he was at the edge of the Maundrell House ruins, which, although close to home, was a place he usually managed to avoid.

Just as he was considering his escape, a sound ripped through the silence. The child was sniggering. Seb was just heaving his bike around to flee when he noticed the figure in front was turning too. For one second he thought the scream had come from a fox but then felt his own chest heave. His brain froze and a single thought formed on his lips.

'Please not again.'

7

2 December

It had been a good swimming lesson, sort of. The intricacies of front crawl were beginning to make sense and Nell had even managed half a width without a polystyrene float. With five minutes to go before the end of the lesson, and her goggles fogging up, Nell backstroked to the pool side. Theirs was the last class of the day and the regular swimmers would soon appear, waiting their turn, so there was just enough time for something quick.

'Before you finish, why not try your surface dive again?' The instructor had clearly seen Nell dithering. Surface diving had seemed so scary at first but was teaching Nell that she could go underwater and not drown, and was therefore giving her more confidence with her front crawl.

'Now, remember to try humming when you go under to control that breath out.'

So as Nell bobbed up, then tucked herself under the water, she began a long, one note hum. The golden rule when swimming, she had learned, was to never hold your breath but to let the air out slowly until it was time to breathe again. Air hit her legs and she did what she hoped looked like a handstand in the water, but probably didn't. The bottom of the pool came into focus and she saw her outstretched arms reaching for it. Last week they had dived for plastic rings and Nell had had a moment of total joy when, for the first time, she had dived and swum under water, reached her ring and returned it jubilantly back to the surface. Enough, the hum was ending so she kicked up to the surface again. She needed air, but then her ears filled with humming. Not her one note, controlled hum, but a simple tune, flat and monotonous. She reached out, fingers tight together, frantically scooping the water above her, and although she knew she should have broken surface by now she still seemed too deep. Then her goggles fogged up, blinding her again.

'You ok there, Nell?'

Coughing and spluttering was a normal occurrence in the 'adult's improvement' class so no one took much notice as Nell stuck her thumb up to let the instructor know she was. Class was over and they went to change. As she stood under the shower, something bothered her. She had been the only one surface diving at the time, so who had been humming so close to her? And why had she felt a pressure around her ankles as she tried to surface, as if someone was pulling her down again?

Nell dumped her swim kit in her car and hastily rubbed her face. If she didn't tighten her goggles then water came in, but if she did tighten them she ended up with comical red marks around her eyes. Dotting on foundation, she peered into her rear-view mirror again, then realising the time, slammed her car into gear. Just a short time ago she might have enjoyed an autumn stroll from the leisure centre to the restaurant. Late summer sun would have dried her hair as she walked and left her feeling energised. Now, although the same time in the evening, the sun had set long ago and it felt like the middle of the night. The shorter distance from the town car park still involved walking through the marketplace which was usually deserted at this time, but now hosted the newly opened Christmas market.

As she stepped under the festive arch she walked straight into an aromatic bank of   mulled wine, cinnamon, and sweet sticky fudge. Her stomach growled but she managed to ignore it as she negotiated her way around the happy, dawdling shoppers.

'My bestie wants a Himalayan salt lamp,' trilled one annoying blonde who clearly felt the whole market needed to hear this fact. She was spinning round to talk to her impressed friend and blocking the walkway as she did so. Long false nails, eyelashes like a camel, and thick black eyebrows painted on a layer of orange makeup. Nell had the feeling that if this woman scraped off the façade she would look completely different. But it was all very jolly, very festive. People were happy, excited for Christmas. Well, apart from a stressed woman who, like Nell, was trying to make her way through the crowds. Multiple designer shopping bags hung from her elbows as she shouted into her mobile.

'No darling, that date doesn't work for me. Not at all.'

Had she fallen through to an alternative universe, mused Nell. Everyone but her seemed to be wound up and launching themselves into the holiday spirit. She felt like Ebenezer Scrooge; she wanted to stomp through the crowds suggesting where they could all shove their Christmas cheer. Perhaps Dickens had been a little mean to poor Scrooge. Maybe he was not nasty and miserable, maybe he was just suffering from the sadness of memories past, of times when Christmas had been magical and happy and then the year had come when everything changed, and despite playing that Christmas song that always reminded you of your childhood, or hanging the ornaments, or watching that special film, somehow nothing would light that Christmas magic in you. Nell vaguely remembered the first year that Christmas had lost its magic for her as a child. The first Christmas without her parents and the awful realisation that she was growing up. At secondary school, with the Christmas concert and play, she had recaptured some excitement again. Then Gary had made it a time of fear and false cheer. Well, this year she would bloody well celebrate it the way she wanted, which might be not at all.

With a sigh of relief she left the hustle of the market, but as she turned a corner found the streets were even worse. Not only was the Christmas market on, it was the first night of late-night shopping and the whole town seemed to be out. Vendors selling glow sticks and novelty headwear competed with doughnut sellers. As Nell picked her way through a particularly overexcited group of teenage girls, who shrieked and squawked like turkeys faced with an axe, she wondered again how she was going to face Christmas without Nana. Actually she did, sort of, have a plan, but according to her virtual guide on coping with bereavement it would probably fall into the category of 'avoidance' which was apparently a bad thing. Nell had spent most of her adult life trying to avoid certain situations and it had usually saved her from a beating. 'Avoidance' had been running away from Gary instead of suggesting they sit down and discuss their relationship. Avoidance worked for her.

But it would be the Christmas memories which would really destroy her. Even before Nana died, Christmas music had always reminded her of her childhood, good and bad, and the magical scent of a Christmas tree took her back to being five years old and helping her parents, both of them, decorate their tree with the addition of her own creations from school. Such happy times. She knew she was lucky to have such amazing, magical Christmas memories of her childhood. Even Nana had made it special, with mulled wine and eggnog. 'Oh, I think Eleanor is old enough to have a drop of snowball at Christmas.' Nell's first ever alcoholic drink had been at one of Nana's soirees with mulled wine, homemade mince pies and Nana's friends calling in with cards, presents and to sing a carol or two. After a few drinks the songs had become more up to date, the words forgotten and then swapped with rude ones. Despite herself, Nell felt her mouth twitch into a smile. That which could not be avoided must be endured, and like these busy, hysterical streets, the only way to get to where she wanted to be was to push through.

Austin did not say much, but he did listen and it felt like meeting with a parent. Not that Nell really knew what that felt like but as she was now totally lacking any other family she would take what she could get. And tonight she had something particular to ask him.

He was waiting outside the restaurant, a cashmere scarf in deep greens around his neck and black leather on his hands. He looked as terrifying as always, and Nell knew he could be dangerous and violent when the need arose. But on seeing Nell, his mouth lifted into a smile and Nell returned it.

'Miss Montague. Punctual as always.'

He held the restaurant door open as she left the dark street and entered the warmth.

Later, as she chased the last mouthful around her plate, she realised that however long the silences between them, they were never awkward and he never interrupted them. Perhaps, she pondered, living alone made them both respectful of each other's solitude and they felt no need to prattle.

'Austin. May I ask you something?'

He was swirling his single malt lazily in its glass.

'Your father, I presume?'

Austin was so sophisticated, and when Nell was with him she tried to be too but every now and then she blew it.

'Bloody hell. How do you do that? You always know what I'm thinking. Are you like Max?'

He shook his head dismissively. 'I merely guessed that we would be having this conversation at some point.'

Then there was no point stalling.

'Do you know where he is? Does he know where I am?' Had she planned to ask this last question out loud? Probably not because she now wished she could suck it back in.

Now the silence was awkward and through it she could hear the church bells ringing outside. It must be practice night, and they sounded like they either needed the practice or one of their pullers had dropped their rope.

Austin had made up his mind.

'Possibly, in answer to your first. And to your second ...'— he met her eyes—'I believe so.'

That was a kick to the gut. So her dad knew where she was and still couldn't be bothered.

'Oh ... well, I guess there is nothing more to say.'

'Would meeting him help you?'

'Um, I don't know really. I mean, he obviously isn't bothered or he would have made contact before now.'

What would she say to him? Quite a lot actually, and none of it very polite. One of the five stages of grief was anger and, right or wrong, she felt very angry towards him for leaving her without a word for so long and for letting her face Nana's funeral alone. 'I've got questions for him.'

'He might not answer. Or if he does, he might lie.'

'True, but at least I can tell him what I think of him for

running out on us. I don't even know what he looks like. Do you?'

Austin didn't answer this.

'But you could get in touch and tell him I want to meet him?'

'Probably.'

Nell listened to the bells again. This was one of those big decisions to be made; a crossroads. Stay in ignorance or start down a path that might cause new pain and open old wounds. She was already hurting so surely it was worth the risk, and at the back of her mind was still the hope she had kept safe, of finding someone who could fill that gap left by her mother and Nana's death. He had loved her once, even though he had left. Unless he had found himself a new family, surely he would want to meet up, even if it was just the once.

'Ok then. Would you do that for me? Obviously I'd pay for your time.'

He shook his head, and she knew him well enough to know that he was dismissing the offer of payment and not of helping her. So the conversation had been had and the decision made. Right or wrong, she wanted to talk to her dad.

A deep voice purred across the sound system and Bing declared he was hoping for snow this Christmas. A group at the table next to them began to sing along.

'Bloody hell, must they? It's only just December.'

Now the smile was warmer. 'I share the sentiment, Nell, but like it or not, there is no escaping the season. Or the 'C' word.'

'I know, but I want to. I want to go to ground until it all passes and we make it safely to January. I know that's not a healthy thought because Max has been nagging me about going out more.'

In fact, Max had become every inch the nurse when she had warmed on the subject.

'Nell, when did you last go outside?'

'It's cold outside.'

'Yes, I know, but you are becoming a hermit. All that Emily and Ruby stuff, you don't want that festering. I've seen it in nurses who do too many nights, particularly in winter. You end up working, sleeping and bingeing on boxsets and takeaways.'

Nell had considered an explanation, but then it had all felt too much effort, and she really didn't want to open more doors into the state of her fragile mental health, so instead had thrown back, 'Sounds fun.'

Max had scowled. 'For a limited time, yes, but do that for too long and you get lost in your own head. And knowing your head like we do, you shouldn't venture in too deep without a responsible adult. You need a healthy dose of reality. There is a reason some people go to the gym or the office when they could exercise or work at home. I'm writing you a prescription. Join a gym, take an exercise class, get a job, do something.'

'God, have you and Austin been comparing notes? I have started adult swimming lessons.'

'Perfect. But I thought you already knew how to swim.'

'Yeah, but only like a panicking dog trying to get to shore. I want to swim like I'm one with the water, all sleek and powerful, like a—'

'Dolphin?'

Now it was Nell's turn to scowl.

'I'll probably look more like a beached walrus but you know what I mean. I remember watching the Olympics once and when they did the underwater shots of the tumble turns—'

'Oh, listen to you with the swimming lingo.'

'—it just made me think that I want to be able to look that relaxed and elegant.'

Now Max was smiling again.

'Well, they all started somewhere. Someone once taught these Olympians how to swim and helped them when they struggled or got it wrong. So, good for you. Exactly what you need for the start of winter. A new project. Something to accomplish.'

Nell wondered if it had helped, as she glanced at the dessert menu. Perhaps; there was certainly something very satisfying about learning a new skill and seeing yourself slowly but steadily improving. Although it still did not stop the avalanche of Christmas that was heading in her direction.

Austin was watching calmly while the memories of her conversation with Max played out in her head. He must have realised that she had returned to the present because he continued.

'Have you considered a trip somewhere?'

'Is that what you do at Christmas?'

'I am fortunate to have friends who travel to warmer climates each year.'

'How lovely. And you go with them?'

The side of his mouth lifted slightly and he looked away. 'No. I make use of their ski equipment, empty house, and close proximity to the mountains. I like solitude.'

Nell felt her own mouth twitch in imitation.

'But you meet me for dinner each week.'

He regarded her for a moment before replying, 'I like your company. I find that you are a respecter of boundaries.'

Nell began to fold her napkin into a tight square. 'So, maybe I should go somewhere. I have something to do on 22nd December but after that I could fly off.'

'Has Miss Georgeham plans for Yuletide?'

'She's been too busy to answer many of my texts lately.' Austin's expression changed at this information. 'But she had said that if she gets the leave, she hopes to drive to her dad's in London. She invited me but …'

'Maybe the reason I find your company so cordial is that you too like your own space.'

She thought about this for a while.

'Yes, but Christmas … you know … we are all hardwired to see spending it on our own as the ultimate sign of being unloved and a failure.'

'Only if you listen to other people. May I ask what your plans are for the winter solstice?'

As Nell drove home the pieces slotted into place. She had to go to North Chase anyway, so why not stay for the week. Rent a cosy cottage, perhaps. And if she took her pad and pencils she might find her passion for art again. Was that sad? She shrugged; what was normal, anyway? Christmas with Gary had usually been a nightmare. Perhaps this way she could find some Christmas spirit of her own.

A real Christmas was a time for fire and snow, for spices

and good food, songs, and ghost stories. She could cosy down for the week in North Chase, do what she had to do there, and then play it by ear. If she felt lonely she could always take up Max's invitation and drive to London on Christmas Day, but somehow she knew that being part of someone else's family Christmas was not something she would be able to do this year. Unbidden, she imagined finding her dad in time for Christmas and spending it with him. A Christmas miracle; or a nightmare. She snuffed out the flicker of hope before she got too enthralled by it. Like the fireworks a few weeks ago, the hope was magical, but all too soon it would be gone and she would be left in darkness. A vision rose of Austin on the slopes, perhaps trudging through the snow in the evening to enjoy a meal in the shadow of towering mountains. It made her feel better. She could ring him on Christmas Eve, perhaps. Just to wish him a merry Christmas. Merry indeed. But it was a plan, she realised. She now had proper plans of her own and would avoid all the commercial loudness of Christmas that would just remind her of the things missing in her life. Yes, stick to a simple plan; she always felt safer with a plan.

She parked, locked up, and crunched her way to the front door. The idea of Christmas that the commercials sold was just that, an idea. Many people spent Christmas alone, or worked, or just ignored it. Or threw themselves enthusiastically into the whole thing and by Boxing Day were either having a nervous breakdown or planning a breakup. As Scrooge had so aptly said, she would keep Christmas in her own way this year, whatever way that was.

8

Max checked the ward roster as she crammed a mince pie into her mouth, quickly washed down with a swig of scolding coffee. Good. She still had the shifts she wanted. Normally she was happy to work Christmas Day, but this year the thought of spending a few days with her dad was so appealing it was almost a physical ache. Too many things had happened in the last few months and she was emotionally and physically exhausted. Her leave at the end of November had been cut short due to staff sickness and her advice to Nell about getting some daylight had been as much to herself. She needed sleep and proper food eaten at a relaxed pace, not just shoved down because she had to get going or had to get back on the ward. She also needed time to let her emotions settle. Her first exploration into her gift had unearthed—literally—the shrivelled up corpse of a young girl and although she knew her gift was genuine, she had not enjoyed the endless questioning of the police. By the end she had even sounded guilty to her own ears.

'Stick to the facts, don't add unnecessary details just to make it sound more authentic. Just the facts,' her dad had advised. At least there had been a result; a family had a body to bury, and an end of all that false hope. They had answers and could grieve properly at last. And they had a face to put to their demons. They knew who had raped their daughter, locked her up, then just left her to starve to death.

Max contemplated the open box of biscuits and shoved a piece of shortbread into her mouth. This package of goodies

46

had been delivered earlier by a beaming trio whose father had been cared for on the ward in September. Their arms were laden with similar Christmas bags filled with edible goodies for the emergency department, radiology and, by the looks of it, half the hospital. The general public were so good, she thought, and their gifts were always appreciated by the busy hospital staff. Proper festive cheer at a time when so many just thought about their own families.

Now she just had a few more weeks before she could trundle off to the big smoke. Blast, she had meant to pop down to the canteen to pick up her Amazon parcels from the lockers there. She was doing all her Christmas shopping online as she had no time to browse the shops. She had no time for anything now. Maybe that was why her gift seemed to have disappeared. She had just been getting used to the strange way the world sometimes went out of focus when there was a spirit close by. Now even *they* didn't want to speak to her. She was tired, that was all. Emotionally drained. She needed some fun. She tried to meet up with Austin, or one of her friends, once a fortnight and lately she had found she was jumping from one meeting to the other, as if they were stepping stones keeping her out of icy, winter waters.

Nell and Austin had been the one good thing to come out of the whole Ruby business. She enjoyed Austin's dry wit and long stories; he was the equivalent of a mini break in a foreign city. And Nell was just sweet; broken and fragile, and so innocent. Getting to know her was like adopting a younger sister. A lovely younger sister, who didn't whinge or complain but was always willing to take advice and was actively working to improve her life. Max hadn't realised how much she had missed not having a best friend until Austin and Nell came along. Sometimes she worried that Nell might get too clingy, and after that odd message from the medium the other week, she had been aware that she was pulling back a little. There had started to be too many texts, but lately Nell had eased off and seemed to be getting on with her life again, so Max was planning to get back in touch.

And talking of Nell, she had the most wonderful present for her. Well, Max thought it was wonderful, and it was something she would enjoy herself so it was actually a present for Max too. That was the problem with not having a significant other, children or lots of family; the yearly haul of presents was rather limited. Which was why she wanted to see her dad; she wanted to go to the ballet or a concert, to listen to the Salvation Army band play while sipping hot chocolate, to wander through Covent Garden, but most of all she wanted to cook him a huge Christmas Day meal, watch some old films and be a daughter again.

She had five minutes. Brushing the crumbs off her uniform, she headed for the doors of the ward and out onto the main corridor. Blocking her way was an elderly man in tracksuit bottoms, a hospital blanket, and one slipper. Hospital was a disorientating place for anyone, but particularly hard for those who were already a little disorientated.

Smiling, she went over to reassure him, showed him the picture on the toilet door and then got him safely back to his bay. Here she was thinking about her own hardships when all around her everyone was facing their own problems, and that most wonderful time of the year could be extra painful for so many. Christmas on a ward, or the emergency department, could be quite festive. Always busy, but there was sometimes a little time for some festivities. One Christmas Eve, in a lull between the drunks and punch injuries, one of the doctors had suggested they tell true ghost stories. She had been a junior at one of the older London hospitals and over the years there had been plenty of unexplained footsteps, figures and voices, but this one always stayed with her.

'One Christmas Eve we were dealing with a road traffic collision. It got to us all because they were just a young family on the way to parents for Christmas. We did what we could but the mother passed away in resus as the little boy was transferred to ICU. Later, I asked how his brother was doing, but no one seemed to know what I was talking about, even when I described the boy I'd seen standing by his bedside in majors. When I worked with the same shift a few days later, I was told the father had said that they had lost his older brother the previous Christmas at the same hospital. He was only a young father and he had now just one member of his family

48

left. I like to think that the boy I saw was this little fellow's older brother keeping him company, to make sure he wasn't alone at Christmas. Or maybe he had come to guide his mother.'

It had broken Max's heart at the time. Yes, Christmas could be very difficult, which is why she had wanted to give Nell something different to think about while she faced her first one without her grandmother, and Austin had recently given her a very useful bit of information which fitted in with Max's idea perfectly.

With any luck it might just help her out of her psychic block, or whatever was stopping her ability. Uncomfortable as it had sometimes been, she did miss it. It had been something new, something exciting, and even a little scary, and she could do with a little of that at the moment.

That was why she had gone to see that fake in the old theatre. She thought it might give her gift a little jump start. Some might say the woman was genuine because she had got Max's initial and profession right. She had even given her a message. Max frowned. She still wasn't sure if she believed it. She had half believed at the time, and then dismissed it again when she got home. But as she had tried to fall asleep later, one thought kept her awake. The medium had seemed so unnerved by this phantom woman with a message for Max that they had gone to a premature break. She realised she was being a hypocrite. When her gift was working, there was no doubting it, but the very reason she wasn't open about it was that she thought people wouldn't believe her. So she just did sittings for friends, informally, like she had for Nell. And now she was casting doubt on this poor woman who had the guts to stand in front of an audience and open herself up to any spirits who came calling. There was still something slightly off about her. Maybe it had been the crocheted shawl, velvet Alice band, and shocking pink tights.

This was all a problem for another day. The gift had come to her gradually and might just come back again when it was ready. Or when it was safe.

It was still dark when Max finished her shift. She changed

49

quickly, said a hasty goodbye to her colleagues and darted for the door before she could get called back. An aroma of fresh toast contrasted with the floral scent of floor cleaner, making her stomach growl as she bolted down the main corridor. They would be cooking up a sumptuous breakfast in the canteen below, and for a moment she nearly turned off at the stairs, but she needed to get home. Outside the main entrance, patient transport and taxis were already queuing to drop off for the morning clinics and tucked away was Max's favourite van. 'Dangerous, Delicate, Difficult' it announced on its side. It was the daily transport of isotope for the nuclear medicine unit, and a radioactive warning sign was still in place. It always made Max think of herself, Austin, and Nell. No prizes for guessing which one she was, she thought.

She should ring Nell, check she was doing ok, but somehow she just didn't have the energy. The nurse in her found it so difficult to be objective, and although she wanted to support Nell, she sometimes found that her energy was being slowly drained.

You can't help her this time, and you shouldn't try.

With a groan Max acknowledged that her last ounce of self-preservation had just washed away in the memory of the psychic's words. She'd text her later, but first she needed food and sleep.

9

There was something about the smell of an old church that always made Tilly feel nostalgic. As a child she had often hidden between the pews of her local church when she was in trouble. Her parents were long gone and she sometimes wondered what they would have thought to see her now. Perhaps not quite where she would like to be. Divorcing Mark when he was making such a mess of his life had been a good move. As had moving back to North Chase. But now the old lord was dead and Mark had waltzed back with his new wife and baby, totally ruining her careful plans. Lady Daisy Corberley indeed; that should have been *her* title, but who could have predicted the old lord dying like that? He should have had years left. It had all happened too soon. Before Tilly was ready.

Now she was up to her elbows in green foliage and flowers, preparing the church floral displays. Unpaid work was so good for her soul and for once she was being truthful when she said she enjoyed it. The selection of each stem, trimming and placing, to create something so special which would be seen and admired by the congregation. 'Oh, that's Tilly Corberley's handiwork you are admiring,' the reverend would say, and everyone would compliment her. Though, of course, she would make a point of mentioning she was just one of many who selflessly gave up their time for the church. She had also encouraged the reverend to resurrect an old Christmas tradition: the St Stephen's Pie competition. There were vague references to it throughout the history of the small town. It had

51

no doubt started as a way of giving alms to the poor, and enthusiasm for it had waxed and waned over the centuries. Well, Tilly was determined to have it back this year and had whispered in all the right ears. She couldn't run it herself though, because she was determined to win.

Voices outside interrupted her pleasant daydream. She was alone; it was how she preferred to work, liking the solitude and peace. So who was that making a row? She put down her secateurs, hesitated, and then, picking them up again, crept to the doorway. The heavy door creaked slightly as she pulled it open a crack to peer out.

A snarl spoiled her immaculate makeup; it was that brat from town and his half-witted friends. She watched as Brett continued to hold court while perched on the churchyard wall. Then, with a bellow, he fell backwards, spilling his beer over himself. Tilly smiled; that was true karma, ignorant little hoodlum. But he was on his feet now and one of the graves had caught his attention.

'Martha Maundrell. Want a drink Martha?'

To Tilly's horror, he unzipped and urinated against the stone angel. She should stop him, shout at him, but they were drunk, and a strong sense of self-preservation warned her off. Instead, she slowly closed the thick wooden door and lowered the latch.

Tears of rage burned her eyes. How could they? Tilly had been behind the fundraising for that angel. It had been her first community project when she moved back here, to ensure that the remains of Mother Maundrell had a fitting monument. There was still some doubt as to whether historical records had accurately recorded the resting place of Martha—and no one was going to dig her up to check—but Tilly liked to think that even if she didn't rest there, and was instead lying in an unmarked grave somewhere, or under the hanging tree as others believed, that *she* would know that the town's people still thought of her and wanted to do something nice for her. And now this horrible little boy had defiled it. She wished she had the power to do something. Something real. Not just set up a women's group—she had done that too—but to really empower the women of North Chase. If *she* were Lady

Corberley she would have that power. But instead she was the unwanted ex-wife who was in the way. Well, she wouldn't stay where she wasn't wanted but she'd be damned before they drove her out of town. When she was married to Mark they had lived in his London apartment, only visiting North Chase for holidays or family occasions. But the old lord had welcomed her back and she had grown fond of the place. He had even encouraged her to research the family history, although perhaps she had found more than he intended and there had been some very interesting facts to unearth in the church records.

She had finally found herself and Sebastian a home. She had never been one for village life but she could see the benefits of a smaller place, of living in a community where she could make a difference, have a positive influence. An accountant by trade, she found that in this modern age it really didn't matter where she was based and for the first time in her life she was comfortable; financially and spiritually. But comfortable was not enough. Comfortable could turn to struggling so quickly and then what would happen to them? How would they live?

Later, when the flower displays were finished, and after checking the coast was clear, she locked up and headed to her car. A stain lay across the angel's face and shoulder. *Bastards.* She'd make them pay for that, and if she didn't then she was sure that Mother Maundrell would. As if receiving a message from the wise woman herself, she remembered the children's rhyme,

> 'Mother Maundrell listens still,
> And she'll gladly do your will,
> Just knock three times on the old yew tree,
> Then make your wish, so mote it be.'

The last bit always irked Tilly, it didn't sound quite right, but then it was supposed to have been said by the town's children for centuries and maybe 'mote' was a word they used. She glanced at the urine stain again and then with reckless abandon, trotted over to the nearest yew tree and knocked three times on the trunk. She paused, and then remembered to make her wish. Mark had never been interested in his own family history, or that of the town, but Tilly had found it fascinating. A little extra research of her own had uncovered some truly powerful knowledge. Powerful and dangerous. Perhaps, this Christmas, it was time to resurrect one of the oldest and most secret Corberley traditions. A tradition that even Mark wasn't aware of. Two teenage boys had gone missing in the last six months; maybe there was room for one more.

Giggling at her silliness, but feeling comforted and back in control, she headed for the car park and then stopped in embarrassment. She didn't recognise the woman pushing the old pram but there could be no doubt that she would have seen Tilly's childish behaviour. She shrugged. Let the woman think what she liked, Tilly could honestly say that for once she really didn't care.

Tilly pulled up by the garden wall and glanced up at Sebastian's window. The light was off so he was either out or asleep already. Inside there were chores for her to do; she unloaded the dishwasher and put the contents away, then, pouring herself a brandy, took it into the living room where the wood burner still faintly glowed. Sebastian had only just gone to bed then, he would never have gone out and left even an ember still alive. Tilly added another log and then settled down with her laptop to answer work emails.

This was her favourite time of the day. All the other jobs done, her house in order and her child safely in his bed. She flicked through a few emails, marking them in the diary to be answered fully tomorrow. Business was steady, perhaps they should consider moving to their own home. Part of her loved being a fly in Mark's ointment but it wasn't healthy, she knew, for her to be stuck in the past like this. Time to find herself a new home. And better for Sebastian too; she always worried about him cycling these country lanes. He had been talking about getting a motorcycle recently and this filled her with total dread. There was a plaque on the stone wall, just down from the train station, to commemorate the untimely death of a young cyclist ten years ago. He had been hit by a van going too fast around the corner on such a steep hill. Yes, cycling was dangerous, but not as dangerous as a motorcycle. Perhaps she could stretch to buying him a little car, or better still get Mark to reach in his pocket for one. Although not his father by blood, he had always considered Sebastian his own, and that had been the one good thing about Mark moving back to the manor; that he and Sebastian could see each other more often. Fate had dealt her this hand, and she would try to see the good things it brought and ignore the bad. Or, make sure she hustled it into a more agreeable outcome for her and Sebastian.

Emails dealt with, she closed her laptop and sipped her brandy. Her mobile pinged and she smiled at the message, then hastily deleted it; just in case. The fire crackled and the house around her creaked. Then a soft voice drifted into her ear, followed by a gentle laugh. Not asleep then, and there was something in Sebastian's voice that brought her to her feet and to the living room door. He was clearly trying to whisper but his laughter rumbled through the floorboards and walls.

'I do, you know I do, but it's not always that easy. I promise to try but I'm still pissed off with you for the other night. I thought I was special.'

Tilly's mother alarm was now trilling loudly in her head. There was something in those words, in the tone of his voice that didn't sound right. Her Sebastian was so open and relaxed, but this sounded like something he had been hiding from her. If it was that little weirdo Erica, well, Tilly knew about that. It was a mother's job to know about those potentially harmful friendships. And they were just friends, she was sure of that. Whenever they argued, and they often argued about Erica, he had made it clear that they were just friends. And Tilly knew that had it been anything more he would have been delighted to have told her. To rub her nose in it. So who was he talking to? Sebastian's voice reached her again, louder now.

'Why can't you tell me? I'm good at secrets, you know I am.'

No, this was something else and for the first time since they had moved back, Tilly felt an icy shiver in her heart.

10

Whilst her hot chocolate cooled, Nell continued to flick through the internet. North Chase; Nana had rarely spoken of it, instead calling it the 'village where I grew up.' It might have been a village in Nana's day but it seemed to have grown to the size of a small town now. Silver and arsenic mining in the nineteenth century had dwindled out after a few decades but was apparently why North Chase benefitted from a railway line and station. There were four churches but she easily found St Edmund's, the church she would need to follow out Nana's wishes. As she took a sip of chocolate, a headline caught her eye.

'Mysteries of North Chase'

Oh, no. No more mysteries for her. She walked over to her window and studied the rain racing down the glass and her own reflection watching it. She could easily become a hermit. It was cosy and comfortable here. Safe. And she had spent too many years feeling in danger in her own home. This was nice. Like a bear in its den, she could cosy down for the winter and lick her wounds.

She had gotten into the habit of lying in each morning. Not too long, it was still barely light when she surfaced, but after years of being up and dressed by seven, even at the weekend, it was such a luxury to wake up naturally around eight o'clock and slowly bring herself round to consciousness without alarms and shouting and the sound of Gary's razor. But that also meant that she had turned into a night owl, reading, or listening to music until well past midnight.

Up in her eyrie she listened to the wind tear around the eaves, and sometimes she could hear the roar of surf on the rocks below. Seagulls were a constant soundtrack and when the couple downstairs were staying for the weekend, she could sometimes hear their voices or their television drifting up. She could also hear any door slam, particularly the main heavy front door. But tonight all she could hear as she crawled under her duvet and settled her head on the pillows was the wind moaning.

Ribbons of memories floated past her eyes, and then scraps of past dreams. She was aware that she had fallen asleep as she suddenly found herself trying to make her way through a market only to discover it was a maze and the walls were getting higher and higher. Then she was walking down a dimly lit street. Snow fell in large down-like flakes and children weaved in and out of the shoppers, squealing in delight. Around a corner and Nell found herself in a quieter street, with cobbled stones and gas lit lamps. An old-fashioned toy shop had caught the children's attention, and they pushed and jostled to see through the tiny frosted window panes.

In the dream Nell drifted forward. In the window stood a doll's pram with delicate wheels, a gleaming carriage, and an ornate curved handle to push it. As Nell watched, the hood slowly retracted to reveal the pram was filled with dolls. A jumble of white arms, legs, and bald heads, all piled together, like a macabre burial pit for toys. They began to shift as a larger doll surfaced, dressed in flowing pink satin and its glossy ringlets were tied back with a velvet ribbon. Slowly, it turned to face the window where the children were crowded and, as Nell continued to stare, the doll's eyes clicked open and its painted mouth split to emit a deep, hoarse laugh. Nell gasped, and the children heard her. One by one, they began to turn around.

She woke, curled in a tight ball, eyes wide. The sound of throaty laugher still filled her head. All the children's faces had been blurred, like a photo altered to protect a celebrity's child, and the last scene she remembered as she properly woke up was faceless children walking towards her. And at the back, climbing out of the pram, was the porcelain doll.

11

This close to Christmas the Angel Inn at North Chase was full. A continuous din of voices, cutlery and overzealous laughter competed with The Pogues and Nat King Cole. A proper Christmas hostelry, concluded Austin, as he edged his way to the bar.

'Single malt please, no ice.'

A couple of locals eyed him with hostility as his drink arrived. Austin glanced at the array of fine single malts behind the bar with approval while letting his peripheral vision scan the men around him. He was in here somewhere; his car in the car park confirmed that. Using the mirror behind the bar to full effect, he checked out the far wall. And there he was, seated alone at a table for four which he was now offering to two young women who had just returned from the bar. Friendly eyes, making a small joke for the young ladies. His thinning hair was ruffled with gel and his shirt showed good taste, though was perhaps a trifle young for him. One song finished and just before the other began, Austin caught a little of the conversation.

'I thought I recognised your face from the papers. Wow, what you are doing is so incredible. Wow.'

Oh dear, thought Austin, *perhaps you might be trying a little too hard.*

Montague now had the face of an overexcited schoolboy as the young women hoovered up his flattery. A ripple of disappointment hit Austin; he wanted someone better for Nell. She deserved more than this sad excuse of a middle-aged man sniffing around young blood.

The door opened and icy air wrapped around his legs. Two men spotted the women and they made their way as a four to the restaurant. That had wiped the smile off Montague's face. Time to make his acquaintance.

'If I might offer my opinion, I feel they were a little on the young side?'

Confusion then annoyance, 'I beg your pardon?'

'Surely they were more your daughter's age.' Austin had seen this look before on his prey's face. He liked to think of it as fight or flight. Arrogance usually meant a fight, verbal if nothing else, but Montague was clearly considering the latter. Fear, or common sense, usually made them consider escape but he could see arrogance was winning through.

'Do I know you?'

'May I sit down?'

'Do I have a choice?'

The whisky was good and the fact that the barman had automatically offered him the best had pleased Austin. He took a sip now as he pulled a chair out.

'I am acquainted with your daughter.'

There. The first flicker of fear, then confusion. Montague sensibly said nothing, waiting for Austin to continue.

'Some might call your recent activities stalking.'

'Who the hell do you think you are?'

Austin sighed. 'You haven't exactly covered your tracks.'

Finally he saw defeat implode the man's foolish ego. 'Does she know?'

'*I* know. But what I don't know is *why*. What do you intend to do next, I wonder?'

Confusion and anger chased each other across Montague's face as he squirmed in his chair.

'I don't know who you are or what this has to do with you. So …'

'Miss Montague is a dear friend. Perhaps you should think of me as her guardian angel.'

Austin couldn't stop the smirk creeping out as Montague erupted, 'She is my daughter and I have every right to make sure she is ok, especially since—'

'Yes, well, it was quite an eventful birthday for our Nell, wasn't it? Now to business; what are you doing here?'

Montague gulped his beer and stared at the table.

'Family business. I've been here for a while now and wondered if my daughter might turn up.'

So, there it was. He had considered reaching out. Austin closed his mouth again and pondered over this information. It was what Nell thought she wanted, to reconnect with her father. Perhaps he should just let events unfold and, again, he questioned the fierce protectiveness he felt towards her.

'My mother was born here,' Montague continued, 'and she once told me my grandmother's ashes had been scattered at the churchyard up the road. I guessed that my mother might ask Eleanor to do something similar either at the winter or summer solstice.'

Such honesty was not what Austin had expected and, looking at the man who had made such a mess of his life so early on, he felt a stirring of pity. What wouldn't he give to have his own stepdaughter back? Was this why he found himself pulled to Nell so strongly, was it nothing more than the remains of fatherly protection for a young woman who clearly needed it? Attachment to anyone, or indeed anything, was a dangerous complication he circumvented at all costs. He had friends for when he wished for company, and indeed he found Max most pleasant and amusing, but with Nell he found a peace he had not felt for too long. Although fiercely protective of his privacy and always seeking solitude, a result of years on the force when not one minute of his day or night had truly been his own, he was grateful to the million small steps that had led him to this current status. The sharp scent of aftershave brought him back to the present and the apologetic man seated opposite him.

'She has been through a great deal,' Austin reminded Montague.

'I know. The papers didn't say much but it must have been horrible finding a body like that.'

'Ruby Morgan's body.'

'Yes.'

'Your pupil, I believe.'

'Yes'.

That was odd. For a moment he had seen a flicker of guilt in Montague's eyes. Now why would that be? But he was weary, and trying to prevent the inevitable would just mean he lost control of it so, with Nell's face in mind, he made his decision.

'Nell plans to spend the winter solstice here and will probably stay for Christmas. Let me speak to her first and then we can perhaps arrange a meeting.'

The hope that flowered in Montague's eyes was nauseating but he was agreeing and handing over his contact number. Which was a sign of good faith, thought Austin, who had had the number for some weeks now. As he returned to his car, he decided that although this meeting was not something he wanted, at least he had established full control again. He would ring Nell and give her the news. But not quite yet.

In the penthouse, high above the crashing surf, Nell awoke with a start. She had been watching TV and must have dropped off. What had woken her? She listened. Voices downstairs perhaps, or the front door closing? Apart from the whine of the wind in the eaves and the roar of the waves at high tide, there was nothing specific. She felt a little queasy, and breathless as if something was pressing down on her chest. Was it a panic attack? She had never had one before but there was always a first time. With Max's warning ringing in her ears, she grabbed her laptop and Googled it. As she read the description and realised it was nothing like she was feeling, a small itch of worry made her stomach lurch. She'd been having one of her horrible dreams, she knew she had, and it must have been exceptionally bad to wake her up with such a shock. But whatever it had involved was wiped blank from her memory. Not the faintest strand lingered apart from the greatest sense of impending danger she had ever felt.

Somewhere, somehow, something had been set in motion, and like the avalanche of Christmas she was dreading, there was nothing to stop it or Nell crashing into each other.

12

Nell seemed to have developed a routine for leaving the penthouse which suggested the word *ritual*. Or maybe *neurotic* was more appropriate. But as she lived alone she had to be extra careful, she reassured herself, then double-checked all the sockets were switched off and the fridge and freezer doors were closed securely. She had already checked the windows and the taps were all turned off. Two suitcases were packed and her wallet, phone and keys were safely in her backpack. Now her keys were back in her hand, just to make sure they didn't somehow fall out of her bag before she closed the front door.

Right. She was all set and ready to leave. The lift seemed to always be on her floor these days and with so much luggage she would throw caution to the wind and use it. A bitterly cold day greeted her as she trudged across to her car and began to load up the back seat. The website said there was ample parking at the Rectory in North Chase and yesterday she had checked her tyres and filled up with petrol. Seat belt on, doors locked, she put the key in the ignition and turned it. Silence. She turned the key again. This time there was a small cough, but the car quickly recovered and was silent again.

'Oh for …' swore Nell, then went through her options. She could ring the breakdown service, but then remembered she hadn't renewed. A local garage? Hire a car? She got out her phone to search and then remembered North Chase had a train station. Pulling her cases out of the car again, she dragged them back to her front door and heaved them inside. Plans up in

62

smoke and new ones to forge, she might as well make a coffee and do it in comfort.

Resilience. That was what it was called, she remembered. Being able to face challenges with positive action, rather than throwing a temper tantrum and start wailing, which was exactly what she wanted to do. Instead, she poked her laptop into life, switched on the kettle, and made a mental list of things to check. Taxi to Launton train station; check out train times. It was Christmas so maybe there wouldn't be any seats, but then looking at the map, she saw that the journey was barely over an hour so she could stand if necessary. As if her bad luck was being flushed out by positive action everything now seemed to work out. There was a train to North Chase in one hour, she managed to book a seat, and the taxi company she rang said they would be with her in the next twenty minutes.

Well ok then, she thought. What was Christmas anyway without some last-minute travel drama? Just as she was about to close her laptop, a new email alert sounded. The Salvation Army. Exactly one year ago that very day, Nell and Nana had been listening to the Salvation Army band play Christmas carols in the market square. Nana had always given generously to charity at Christmas, and Nell supported the Wiltbury Hospital, so before she left for her Christmas break she sent one more present. However messed up her life was, she had a roof over her head and money in the bank; two things that many didn't have, and as the rain began to pelt against her window, she shuddered to think of how desperate it must be to be out in this weather, trying to find shelter. The email of gratitude came back immediately, and it was as if Nana was giving her approval.

The train platform was packed. Excitement and anticipation spiced the air and Christmas jumpers, Santa hats, and sparkly scarves brightened the dark day. The rain had stopped, but now an icy fog began to creep across the platform and, shivering, Nell could easily imagine what it would have looked like in the days of steam trains. A suited woman marched past just as the train arrived, absent-mindedly humming 'Jingle Bells' and leaving an aroma of gingerbread latte in her wake.

Nell hesitated as the carriages flew by and people began to group together, anticipating where the doors would stop and where there might be room. The train stopped and there was a moment of tension before the doors finally opened, people spilled out and passengers from Launton were gratefully sucked into the warmth. Impatiently, a man pushed past Nell, towing his wife behind and barking orders that he wanted a table. You are on a day trip, not gathering the troops for invasion, thought Nell while she waited for him to get out of her way. Finally, she heaved her cases onto the train and headed in the opposite direction. The long-distance train had the luxury of a first-class compartment and it was here that Nell had treated herself to a window seat. A single seat positioned on its own, just for her. Travelling in style. Austin would certainly approve.

The train window gave her an amazing view of everyone's Christmas lights. Trees sparkled in living room windows and huge displays brightened hotels and public houses. The gloomy afternoon leached light and cheer but the sparkling lights flashing and chasing on buildings and trees brought warmth to the most remote parts of the countryside.

Then the lights got scarcer and soon, all that Nell could see through the grimy train window was her own reflection. Large eyes like moonlit rock pools shone from her pale face. It was quiet apart from the rattle and grind of the train, and getting greyer and greyer by the minute. Melancholy drifted over Nell like snow; heavy and cold. Last Christmas had been hectic; playing taxi for Gary and his various meals or drinks with friends, and for Nana and her hospital appointments. But Christmas day itself had managed to produce some old-fashioned magic; Gary had been on his best behaviour for once, and she had spent some lovely hours with Nana at the home which had produced full throttle Christmas charm. Carers sported antlers and flashing jumpers, music was playing, the chefs had created Christmas magic in the kitchens and Nana had been in excellent spirits. The matron's west highland terrier trotted around to show everyone his Christmas jumper, and the home's cat played with and then chewed some tinsel he had pulled from a tree. Everyone tried to catch him and retrieve it from his mouth before his Christmas involved a visit to the vet. Nell and Nana had joined in with the singing around the piano and Nell was told about an unexpected visit the day before.

'There was a knock to my door and when I opened it, there he was, the little sweetheart.'

'What, they brought a donkey upstairs? How the hell did they get him up to your floor?'

'The same way we all do, my darling girl. In the lift.'

'They put the donkey in the lift?'

'Well of course, Eleanor, you can't expect the poor thing to climb the stairs.'

Nell had just laughed and shaken her head in amazement.

Nana had also been taken to the city's pantomime on Boxing Day. Her last Christmas had been full of fun and everything Nell would have wanted for her. Had it not been for Gary, she would have invited Nana to stay. Gary had even suggested she join them for Christmas Day, but Nell used Nana's cancer as an excuse; Gary was too unpredictable, Nana too precious, and the home was bursting with boisterous fun and Christmas spirit.

And now Nell was alone at Christmas. Tears stung her nose but she shook them off. Nana was out of pain and Gary out of her life, unable to bully her anymore. Yes, this Christmas would be different but that didn't mean bad. Alone didn't have to mean lonely, Austin didn't seem to mind, nor Max when she stopped to think about it. But then Max had her job at the hospital, she had work mates, or 'work family' as she often referred to them. Nell had spoken to her supervisor back in Wiltbury a few days ago and was amazed to hear that nothing had changed since she left there. There were staff shortages, so always an opening if Nell changed her mind, but otherwise it seemed to have frozen in time.

So she wasn't without friends, Nell reminded herself. Or options. The finding of Ruby and Emily had forged a strange friendship between herself, Max, and Austin. Three introverts, who, she suspected, found making close friends a long process. Max dropped into conversation the names of work colleagues, but apart from occasional outings, Nell did not get the impression that she socialised out of work with them much, and there had been no mention of any interesting women lately so Nell deduced Max wasn't dating. For a moment she thought about Austin. He had certainly never mentioned a significant other and somehow Nell couldn't imagine it. Another thought jolted her; she didn't even know his first name. The solicitor had mentioned it, she was sure, but in the confusion of statements, police, and the agony of retelling the events that had led to the closure of a very painful time of her life, she simply couldn't remember it.

What was it about Christmas that made everything so bittersweet? But then would the lights sparkling brightly on a lonely tree look so special if it were not for the extreme dark, the remoteness around it? A lone candle flickering, made more powerful because of the blackness surrounding it? And who would enjoy warming their hands against a roaring fire, if they were not already so bitterly cold? So, she must not give in to feelings of sadness; she was on an adventure, after all, and she had two people to ring on Christmas Day, so she was luckier than most.

Looking around the train compartment, she wondered about the lives of the other people sitting there. Across the aisle from her sat an elderly man tapping at his laptop. His overcoat and shoes literally shouted money as he yawned and popped his feet up on the seat opposite. He had the whole table of four to himself so why not, thought Nell, though she hoped his expensive shoes were clean. Further down, a young man dozed in a crumpled suit, surrounded by bags filled with brightly wrapped Christmas presents. A little girl suddenly cantered through the carriage and up to the snoring man.

'Daddy, daddy. I found it and didn't touch anything. See, I used my sleeve like this.'

The man smiled indulgently, rubbing his eyes with the back of his hand, and heaved himself into a sitting position.

'You did? Well, aren't you clever.'

No more than about eight years old, the little girl sparkled with excitement. She was now bouncing across the seat to peer out of the window. Wiping it with her sleeve, she pressed her nose against the glass and then turned again.

'Are we nearly there?'

'Nearly.'

What was their story, pondered Nell. Father and daughter going to visit grandparents, perhaps? The vision of a cosy homecoming filled Nell's imagination, of hugs and kisses and doors opening to release the enticing smell of good home cooking. It chased away the shards of ice that had settled in her lungs.

'How long are we staying?'

An innocent question surely, but the man shifted in his seat and sighed.

'We are staying for Christmas, remember? I've got to work for a few days but I will be back on Christmas Eve, I promise.'

Nell winced. *Don't promise that. Don't say you'll be back, and plant all that hope in the little girl's heart only to disappoint her.* But then, some fathers kept their promises and returned home when they said they would. Not like hers, who had kissed her goodbye in the morning and was never seen again. She looked at the father and daughter for a moment more; the girl was pretending to take presents out of the bag. There was squealing and laughter. The ice was back in her lungs. She had to remember that for most people Christmas was a joyful time. The daydream of spending Christmas with her father wriggled out from under her heart and, for a moment, she let it warm her, but only for a moment. With a firm hand, she pushed it back in its place before she could get too attached to it.

Suddenly, a burning sensation poured over her skin. The train was slowing and as she looked out at the surrounding woodland, she spotted flames. Flames that danced and flickered between the trees and bushes. As she craned her neck to see, she realised that it was coming from a bonfire deep within the woods. With a creak and squeak of metal, the train picked up speed and the flames were gone, but the burning sensation lingered on her hands as if she had warmed them too close to the fire.

Further down the carriage, out of view but reflected in the train window, sat a woman in a black coat with either dark hair or perhaps a headscarf. As if aware she was being watched, she turned to face the window and although her hair and coat could be seen clearly, no features were reflected. No eyes, nose, or mouth, just a blur of pale skin. Fragments of a recent dream drifted by but were gone before Nell could really remember it. Then the guard announced the next station and Nell eagerly looked out of the window as more Christmas lights and a long line of traffic came into view. The woman in black must have got out at the station because when Nell remembered her and looked again, she was gone. A young woman got in and sat at the same table. She frantically waved at someone left on the platform, and as they pulled out and away from the lights, her heavily made-up face was reflected in the window. Again, Nell experienced the slightest feeling of unease. A bruise from the business with Ruby and Emily, no doubt, but still, Nell felt it like a cold draught or a bead of sweat down her neck. Something not quite right, and possibly things would never be quite right again.

13

Although only mid-afternoon, the light was already fading as if it had given up on the day. Resigned that he would not get much more done, Will switched off his saw and prepared to pack up.

'William?'

He hastily removed his hardhat and ruffled his hair.

'Wait, I'll come out to you.' He had not been looking for a relationship again, or whatever he and Tilly were, but he now knew he had missed having an intelligent and beautiful woman in his life. She was fussing, commenting on the progress he had made since she had last visited the site, complimenting, and offering suggestions.

'We are still meeting up later, aren't we?' The relationship was new and bringing all his insecurities out.

'Of course, I have new research to show you, though how I'll have time to write a book when I have so many other jobs to do, I really don't know.'

They had met when he had enquired about viewing the church records. They soon discovered they were both researching North Chase history and had formed an alliance. Will's knowledge of medieval history and Tilly's access to historic documents had been the perfect opportunity for them both. And they were both single.

'I have an early Christmas present for you.' He loved how she giggled like a young girl.

'Well, I am very sorry but you will have to wait for yours, it is not quite ready yet.'

He passed over the package and enjoyed watching her elegant fingers and manicured nails open it. The small cry of delight, the joy in her eyes, as she unfolded the scarf, spread a soft warmth through his body. What was it that increased the value of something in a person's eye and heart, he wondered. Perhaps because it was intended to be theirs and only theirs. They alone were in the giver's mind when it was chosen and wrapped, so the emotional attachment was already formed. Tilly was holding the scarf, which had been printed on eighty-year-old parachute silk, against her powdered cheek. The giving and receiving of a gift was a powerful piece of magic indeed, thought Will.

She knew nothing about him really, and he liked it that way. They spent hours discussing the lives of people who had been here hundreds of years before them, but never spoke of their own pasts. Bringing the house back to life currently resembled an autopsy. Uncovering, discovering, discarding, and creating. He had not put down many roots in the past few years but his mother's passing had given him a new chance. Tilly was chirping happily over the scarf and again, he felt contentment wash over him. This could be the best Christmas ever.

'I hear it is all going to get busy on the estate after Christmas.'

He was making small talk but Tilly stopped fiddling with the scarf and shot him a look.

'Your ex, he's given the go ahead for that building work.' Her mouth opened but she was mute. 'That will stir up the Pagans again.'

As her 4x4 disappeared up the road, Will went over what he had said. He had expected her to moan about her ex again and then hoped to steer the conversation around to a discussion on her moving into town. Perhaps moving in with him. For a moment, he imagined Tilly, Seb, and himself laughing over the breakfast table. Seb was a good lad and perhaps Tilly's fears were unfounded. She had insisted on secrecy and Will admitted he had enjoyed the spice it added to their relationship. And as he tidied the site, he added one more person to his daydream of domestic bliss; his daughter.

The road from the train station was nearly vertical and in the fading light, Nell glanced around for a taxi. But she had not been the only one to alight and those left behind were not waiting for the taxis to return but were flowing downhill purposefully. Not wishing to stand alone in the freezing dank afternoon, Nell began to follow. A pathway veered off from the road and appeared to continue through a park, clearly a shortcut to the town. So she trudged down the slippery pavement in the gloom, pulling her two unbalanced suitcases behind her.

The park was flooded. Where grass should be were huge pools of water reflecting the clouds above. Where once had been a path was now a torrent of water, weaving through the bank side trees. A couple of swans preened in the water meadow, more water than meadow now, and two women were gazing around in frustration, debating loudly. As Nell got closer she realised they were attempting to adjust the route for the Christmas Day park run. Perhaps that was something she could do. She was bound not to be the only single there and it would be fun and festive. She stored it away as a possible plan.

Despite the flooding and arctic temperature, the park was busy. Dog walkers politely acknowledged each other as their dogs barked, raced into the puddles, and sniffed each other's tail ends.

'Megan, come here. Oh, I do apologise,' said an elderly gentleman with an over-excited spaniel who had just bounced up to Nell, ears flapping, and splashed her with mud.

'No problem.' Nell smiled as she watched Megan bounce off again.

'Here for the Solstice Festival?' he enquired, spotting her suitcases.

'Absolutely.' It seemed the appropriate answer.

'Smashing. They were going to cancel it altogether because of that poor young man but his mother said no.'

Poor young man. What had she arrived to this time?

Incredibly, despite the late hour and sharp wind, the playground was hosting four toddlers as their parents chatted together and checked their phones.

'Nanny,' shouted one little cherub with white curls spilling from her knitted hat.

'Nanny is at home,' corrected her mother.

'No, Nanny,' insisted the cherub, pointing past Nell who found herself turning around to look. There, disappearing behind a grove of yew trees, was a dark figure pushing an antique perambulator. A sudden gust brought strands of humming as she rounded a bend and was swallowed up by the trees.

The temperature was dropping alarmingly so Nell headed past the skate park and into the main town. Resting her shoulders for a moment, she saw an old red telephone box on a corner of the road. They always brought back memories for Nell of the smell of greasy plastic, stale urine, and graffiti, scratched or written on the inside walls. A cold draught would creep in through a broken window as she had searched for more coins before the beeps went.

'Mail, text and phone' was displayed on the roof but a homemade sign had been added to say 'books, books, books'. Peering inside the miniature library, one caught her eye: *Myths and Legends of North Chase*. If she finished the collection of Christmas short stories she was reading tonight she could drop it off tomorrow in exchange. Cramming it into her backpack, she grabbed her case handles again and carried on down the road.

The solstice fair was setting up in the main square. Wooden chalets like those in Barncroft were strung with lights, selling crystals and dreamcatchers, brightly patterned knitted gloves and hats, and the local artists had set up their stands to display mystical looking prints. Incense spiced the air, and cinnamon and orange drifted from a stall selling gluten free 'solstice muffins'. Despite herself, a smile formed on Nell's cold face and she was just contemplating what pine needle tea might taste like when a logo caught her eye. 'Spooky Spots' were just putting up their stall and were swearing over the contrary banner they were trying to fix. Seeing Nell stop they turned with a smile.

'Here, take a leaflet so you know what's going on with the festival. And here's one of ours, but we are sold out tomorrow night,' said the stallholder helpfully.

'Thank you. Looks fascinating,' seemed the correct response.

Now they were all smiles and the other man who was still wrestling with the banner dumped it on the ground and came over.

'We do sometimes get last minute cancellations at this time of year so if you are interested maybe give us a ring tomorrow morning.'

Nell chatted with them and then, stuffing the leaflet in her pocket, picked up her suitcase handles again and wheeled her way to the church. A beautiful Christmas tree stood by the lych gate and Nell was just admiring it when a couple stopped in front to pose for a selfie. They kissed and then took another shot. The woman gazed up at her boyfriend, grabbed his hand, and together they sauntered up the road. A towering tsunami of loneliness hit Nell. It was Christmas and she had literally no one to be with and nowhere to go, so she had turned a ten-minute task into a seven-day break. Perhaps the rectory would be as cosy as the advert had suggested and Austin would find her dad in time. Looking at the sparkling tree and inhaling the nostalgic scent of pine, she sent her Christmas wish up to the stars again. It could happen; she might be part of a family again for Christmas.

A drum and penny whistle started a cheerful tune as a group of people rounded the corner and headed her way with burning torches and some very fancy costumes. Spotting the rectory on her left, Nell ducked into the porch, twisted the iron handle, and pushed open the heavy wooden door. A gloomy hallway stood before her with large dark furniture and dusty tapestries. It felt like a museum that had closed decades ago. A radiator stood against the back wall but if it was on it was doing little to add cheer to the room. Something moved and Nell saw that what she had taken to be a cushion was a black cat curled up on a saggy armchair. It opened its eyes and gave her a sly glance then, with a bored yawn that revealed some scarily sharp teeth, put its head back down again. An envelope, with her name misspelt on it, was propped against a dresser. Inside was a brief note of welcome, a warning of what time the front door would be locked each day, and two keys. The keys felt good in

Nell's hand, as if she had control.

The shallow wooden steps leading upstairs, seemed to be tilting slightly making Nell off balance as she walked up to a wide landing. Standing by the window was a beautiful rocking horse and Nell couldn't resist giving the smooth wood a stroke. Another flight with even wonkier steps and she had reached her apartment. Strange how she never seemed to be on the ground floor, she thought, but then almost every other place she tried had been fully booked.

Nell inserted the key, it turned, but for a moment the door handle would not move. Outside she could still hear music and the beat of drums, but a softer sound seemed to be coming from nearby. From within the apartment. Then the handle turned and she was in. Quite a strange introduction to North Chase; all the bustle outside contrasting with the low mood of the rectory. Somehow North Chase's solstice festivities did not annoy her or bring on painful memories like the Christmas market at Barnscroft had, and she decided to spend as little time as possible in the apartment until she could cheer it up a bit.

Heaving the curtains aside, she watched as the burning torches continued to wind their way around the streets. One by one she gave her aching shoulders a rub; she could now relax. But something kept tugging at her mind like an annoying tune she couldn't get out of her head. Something had been wrong about what she had seen today. Not here, but earlier when she left the train. Or perhaps on the train. The woman whose reflection had no face? The child pointing to the old-fashioned nanny? She gave herself a mental shake; she had an overactive imagination and really had to stop looking for spooky goings on. No more ghosts. Not this time. It was Christmas, or solstice, or Yule, whatever, and the only ghosts she wanted to know about would be from *A Christmas Carol*. A sudden vision slapped in front of her eyes of Butlers Yard and the hidden doorway in the cellar where they had found Ruby. No, not today. She would unpack and then go out to join the festival.

As she opened the first case, she caught herself humming the simple tune again that she had heard in the park and tried to work out where she had heard it before. Was it a carol or a nursery rhyme? Shaking her head slightly, she gave up and concentrated instead on the cheerful sounds coming through the single glazed windows.

'Stop it, Nell. Your days of being haunted are over.' She grabbed her coat and bag and headed for the door. She needed to be amongst living, breathing people so that her ghosts stayed away.

14

20 December – Evening

Somehow, Nell had thought that a solstice festival would be a little like a Christmas market but with more tarot cards and fewer Christmas jumpers. But if anything, it felt more Christmassy, as if it had floated from the pages of a Dickens story. The festival logo seemed to be a tree, bedecked with ribbons and stars. It was everywhere; on the leaflets, on posters, and on brightly coloured flags that draped across the stalls. The strong aroma of cinnamon and ginger blended with incense and spicy food. Frozen-looking stallholders watched street entertainers spin flaming torches, and the town hall steps were being used as a stage.

A peel of laughter and shouting caught her attention, so Nell ambled in that direction. A medieval jester was cavorting and tumbling for a delighted but wary crowd. His hat jingled with small bells, as did his felt shoes. Nell froze and began to back away; the jester and his bells reminded her too much of Diablo, the monster from her childhood nightmares, so she quickly turned to head in the opposite direction.

A group of teenage boys poured from a side street, like a flash flood. She quickly jumped out of their way but not before receiving a knock to her shoulder.

'Sorry,' she said automatically, and then shook her head. Why did she always apologise when some idiot knocked into her? But they had spotted the jester and headed in his direction to make a nuisance of themselves.

Closing ranks, the fire dancers came down from their steps and joined him.

'Give it here. My turn,' spluttered one of the lads who now had a flaming torch in his sights. Swelled by numbers, the jester began to make fun of the boys and their drunken staggering. A part of Nell cringed, remembering school yard bullying sessions and fearing that this was not the way to deal with it. But incredibly the audience began to laugh. The lad realised that he was being made fun of and attempted to defend himself.

'What did you say, you fucker?'

But the jester was drawing on the energy of the crowd and gave him another volley of abuse.

'Mate, leave it,' suggested his slightly more sober friend, tugging on his arm.

'I'll remember your face.' He tried one more attempt at saving face and then let his friends pull him away. The crowd jeered and parted to let them out, but one little girl was not quick enough and the lad crashed into her. She began to cry, the crowd shouted abuse, and Nell turned away, almost colliding with a church group who had stacked Bibles on their tables.

'Would you like one?'

But before she could answer, her pocket began to vibrate. Pulling off her gloves, she extracted her phone and peered at the caller ID. Max.

'Hello?'

'Now, don't get angry.'

'Why?'

'Well, I've planned a little surprise.'

It wasn't the word *surprise* that made Nell sigh, but that Max assumed it would make her angry.

'Go on then.'

'Oh good. Well, when I heard that you were spending Christmas at North Chase, I did some digging and there is a brilliant ghost hunt happening tomorrow night. It's part of their yearly solstice festival apparently.'

'And?'

'So succinct; you've been spending too much time with Austin. *And*, I've booked you a place. My Christmas present to you. Well, to me too because I'm coming with you. North

Chase is sort of on my way so I'll drive to Dad's after.'

Oh great, thought Nell, just what she needed; another ghost hunt. Then she remembered the friendly men at the Spooky Spots stall had said they were fully booked up. It felt too unlikely, like she was being corralled by fate somehow. She certainly felt like she was being slightly manipulated by Max.

'Are you excited?'

Silence.

'Nell? Did you hear me? Are you smiling?'

Actually, if they had been FaceTiming, Max would have seen that Nell had ducked into a quieter street, was shaking her head slowly, and hissing through her teeth.

'Yay. Ghost hunt. Honestly, Nell it will be fun. And really Christmassy.' Max must have sensed the raised eyebrows. 'You know, there is always a ghost story at Christmas and you are staying at a place that celebrates the winter solstice, for heaven's sake.'

Despite herself, Nell felt a prickle of excitement. Typical Max.

'We can have an early supper and then maybe get to the place early and have a poke about the grounds ourselves.'

'Why? What time does it start?'

'Um, late. Well, no, not too late. Eight o'clock. And it finishes around one.'

'Right. Ghost hunting at night, outside, in the cold. Thank you, it is a kind thought but—'

'Now is *that* excitement I hear? Happy Christmas, Nell, or should I say, "bright blessings"'.

'Didn't feel like getting me a voucher for Christmas, or something? No? A book or a pair of gloves? No, instead we are ghost hunting again, this time in the cold and dark, and probably wet.'

'I think we are losing signal, Nell. Shall I come to your rented crypt? No scrap that idea, I'll book us a table somewhere so we can eat before we go. Oh, and I hope you packed something warm. Perhaps buy some wellies. And bring a torch.'

Great, thought Nell as she trudged on, all enthusiasm for the festival now gone. How could Max possibly think she wanted to go hunting ghosts again? Then a thought occurred to her. Company. She wouldn't be totally alone. Even if it was just for one evening. In her hunt to find a way through her grief and the shock of starting her life over, she had come across a site which mentioned gratitude and how you could change your life by just changing the way you saw things. Her initial reaction to Max and the ghost hunt had been that she was being pushed into something she didn't want to do. Different for Max perhaps, being a psychic, but their last bit of dabbling into the occult had shone a bright light into the nightmares of Nell's childhood. It had also found her in the cellar of the spooky house, also from her nightmares, and there in a hidden room, they had uncovered little Ruby Morgan. At least the nightmares had stopped, about Ruby anyway, and she had stopped seeing Emily in every reflective surface once they had found her in another cellar. Emily was hopefully living a normal life once more. She danced apparently, and Nell hoped that once she recovered, mentally and physically, she could find some comfort in dance again. Gratitude and mindset. Maybe she should see the gift from Max for what it was; a gift. It might be cold, wet, and tiring, but it might also be fun. And the fact that Max was coming too meant that she wouldn't be alone.

It was beginning to rain so Nell bought some vegan food from a nearby vendor, took a leaflet on forest bathing, and headed back.

'Hello, can I help you?'

Nell was just twisting the door handle when a woman touched her arm.

'Door is a bit heavy. Reckon it must be ancient.'

'They will be pleased to see you made it home at last,' the woman continued. '*She* will be pleased. No, I want to go in here. I want to see the others.' A second woman had reached them and was trying to coax her away.

'Sorry about this.'

'It's fine,' answered Nell as she saw the mental health lanyard around the second woman's neck. 'Nice to meet you both.'

'And nice to meet you both, too. No, don't pull me.'

'No one is pulling you. It's getting cold, shall we get some hot chocolate?'

'Yes, but she's back. And they have waited so long.'

As Nell gave them both a cheerful wave goodbye and slipped through the door, her heart panged for the poor woman. She had grown used to Nana's dementia; she'd had no choice. But in it she had met a new person, a different side of Nana was unveiled, and although it was deeply sad, she could also be sweet and funny. At times angry and frustrated, but at others like a mischievous child, and Nell had learned to respond to whichever version of Nana she met on the day.

But that chapter in her life had finished. For a moment she wondered about Nana as a child and tried to imagine her in this town. Had she walked through the park, played on the swings? Did the places we visited in our lifetime leave trails invisible to the eye that could be felt many years later like psychic footprints? This town may have been Nana's family home but she had never visited it again, or taken Nell. Was that by choice or had her life just moved in a new direction? In a box back at the penthouse, Nell had rescued one of Nana's old photo albums. She remembered others as a child but they had vanished long ago. Nell had gone through the album yesterday, looking for a link to Nana's childhood. One picture, tiny and blurred, showed Nana as a teenager, picnicking under a tree. A tree like millions of others, which might or might not have been here. Which might or might not have been Nana, actually. But it was all Nell had. Again she felt the vast emptiness of her life echo around her. So many questions, so many secrets, and no one left to answer them for her. Except for her father.

15

Crypt: that was what Max had called the rectory apartment, and as Nell fiddled with the heating, she began to acknowledge it was a good description. It was spacious and clean, but somehow the lighting just didn't seem bright enough, and despite some enthusiastic clanging, the radiators had not managed to get much above warm. She was used to her penthouse, bright and warm despite the relentless sea breeze outside. But the rectory did have some charm and in a strange, slightly damp smelling way, it reminded her of Nana's home, Lark House, where she had spent most of her childhood growing up. It needed more light, and thankfully in Nell's second case she had all the battery-operated fairy lights that she needed.

Solstice festival: Nell still wasn't sure she entirely understood the difference between what she had just seen and a Christmas market. Was it all just a difference in religious belief? Between Pagans and Christians? Or was there something else happening? The market stalls were still selling products, and people were still shopping. The church stall handing out Bibles; were they there to support the festival in these days of equality or to save the corrupt heathens? Everyone seemed to be planning for the holiday to come, and Nell was aware that she was still faking it, just so she wasn't left out. Perhaps the book she had picked up in the phone box would explain things, so she went into the bedroom to grab it. As she picked it up something fell out from between the pages.

A satin ribbon in dark green lay where it had fallen, and as Nell held it between her fingers the faintest scent of lavender rose from it. It must have been between the pages all along, marking a page for the last owner. For some reason, Nell suddenly wanted to know *which* page and as she fanned them, she sniffed. But it just smelt of damp. She kept the ribbon and settled on the lumpy sofa. *Myths and Legends of North Chase*; this should tell her more about the place. She was just flicking through when angry voices erupted outside.

'You are making a mockery of everything. The balance has already been tipped.'

Cursing her nosiness, Nell got to her feet again; there certainly seemed to be a lot of angry people in this little town, she mused. A woman was shouting and pleading with people who just walked by, pretending not to hear or see her. Above her head was a board with the blurred face of a young man on it. The word 'missing' was written above in large letters.

'The count stands at two and there will be more, I promise you, unless her ground is respected.'

An older woman and a girl in black with tattoos framing her face rushed up to her.

'Come on now, love. This isn't the way,' pleaded the woman as she tried to take the placard from her.

'He was your friend,' the now tearful woman said to the girl.

'Finn *is* my friend. He *will* turn up, I'm sure he will.'

Together they led her away.

Nell closed the curtains and went back to the book; although she felt the mother's pain and desperation, she had had enough of missing kids to last her a lifetime. *The count stands at two and there will be more.* But she closed her mind to it and settled down again. Time to find out more about North Chase. She knew Nana had been brought up here but nothing else, and it would be good to be a little more clued up than Max on the tour tomorrow night.

Instantly, a woodprint caught her attention. A figure was hanging from an old tree, surrounded by what could only be devils. Mother Maundrell apparently, who was hanged in 1666 for witchcraft. Nell skimmed through the paragraphs dedicated to the various methods they used to extract a confession from her, until they had finally resorted to threatening to kill her baby son. Once they had the confession, he had been killed anyway. More paragraphs about the various men of influence in the area who had brought her to trial and how she had cursed Lord and Lady Corberley that their children would never thrive, as they dragged her to her death. Her body had been buried at the crossroads but then the next day, there were reports that nothing lay in the ground but a gaping hole. The town had taken her to their hearts ever since, the woman who had tried to save a town decimated by plague but been killed by men of power who had felt threatened.

A charming tale to read before bedtime. And *Corberley*, why did that sound familiar? Nell looked at the leaflet she had picked up from Spooky Spots and realised where she had heard that name before. The ghost hunt was taking place at North Chase Manor, at the invitation of Lord and Lady Corberley. Now she was excited. North Chase had quite a gory past. Why had Nana never told her the story of her ancestral town? Perhaps many towns had similar stories but North Chase had had the sense to turn them into profit.

Quite the day she had had. From the car not starting this morning, to the lovely train ride, to the festival tonight. Shame the rectory wasn't living up to its description of a 'cosy, historical base to explore the charming mining town of North Chase'. North Chase did have some charm, and the rectory *was* historic—the heating had to be decades old—but the word 'cosy' was a total lie.

She opened the second of her cases and looked at the decorations inside. She could put them up tomorrow, but it wouldn't do any harm to put up a few now to add some cheer to the place. So she strung a few strings of fairy lights and draped tinsel over a broken grandfather clock whose hands had been set to midnight. Or midday. Twice a day it would be telling the correct time. The walls were hung with dark black and white prints of the town and did nothing to cheer the room. One smaller print showed two children disappearing into a dark wood. Their little hands were joined and their feet bare. Something about the print made Nell shiver, so she slung some bright tinsel over it. Memories of her childhood crept out as she sniffed the tinsel. The sooty smell from Nana's old coal fires took her straight back to those Christmases of long ago. For a moment, she stood in the middle of the room, the tinsel under her nose, and let her mind drift back. With eyes closed, she saw the blazing fireplace from Nana's living room, crackling, and spitting as she balanced on a ladder to fix paperchains onto the picture rail. An icy draught sent a shiver down Nell's back and reluctantly she opened her eyes again. Unshed tears blurred the room around her and her last drop of courage made a bolt for the door. Nell took a steadying breath, grabbed a string of lights and wound them round the coat stand. She wouldn't let herself give in to the misery for fear she would never climb back out again. The room looked a little more cheerful so, grabbing a tasselled throw from a nearby chair, she wrapped herself up and settled down to her book again.

Unfamiliar sounds kept her company; the knocking of the radiator, the bang of the front door downstairs followed by voices and footsteps, and Christmas music which drifted from the apartment next to hers. Nell jumped as the church outside chimed eleven times. She should get some sleep, and as soon as her brain thought of how tired she was, a massive yawn overtook her, making her jaw click. Slowly, she located the batteries in all her lights and turned them off, then checked that her door was locked. The floorboard creaked from the landing outside. She stopped; another creak, and another, as if someone was creeping past her door.

'Stop it, Nell,' she whispered under her breath. It was as if she was determined to scare herself. As she crossed the room to head for the bedroom, a movement caught her eye. She span round, her heart racing, and inspected the scene before her. A string of tinsel suddenly slid off the print of the two children in the woods, obviously caught in a draught. Nell grabbed it and slung it back over the picture until most of it was covered. 'Stay put,' she instructed, and then headed for bed.

16

Brett stumbled in the direction of home. Lame fuckers with their tarot cards and hippy clothes. Nothing but a bunch of rich bastards cashing in on old folktales. When he was a little boy his gran would threaten him that unless he behaved 'the witch will take you into the woods and leave you there, all on your own, and no one will ever find you again'. And he would shout back, 'Good. I'll get away from all of you.'

Kids had probably been threatened in the same way since they had first strung the hag up. Now here he was at the bloody church and another pile of superstitious bollocks. At primary school they had been shown the Spicer family crypt besides which, apparently, the body of the witch had been secretly placed after the church refused her a Christian burial. Brett never understood this; she was a witch, of course they wouldn't let her lie in the graveyard of a church. Hallowed ground, and all that. He'd seen enough horror movies to know that. The Spicer crypt was now totally covered in a thick blanket of ivy so unless you knew it was there, it would just be mistaken for a fenced off area of shrubs. And there was the stupid angel that the town do-gooders had bought for her. What a waste of money. Half the families on his street would be relying on the food bank to provide their Christmas dinner and a load of snobs had wasted money on an ugly stone angel.

As he stumbled through the graveyard, tripping on the uneven ground, his bladder gave a lurch. One too many cans, obviously. He'd be home in five minutes, but there was something about this place which made him want to piss all over it, and he often did. An owl hooted as the steady stream of urine hissed over the bed of yew needles, and then a flash of white swept over the field which lay just beyond the graveyard.

Brett was still irritated by the events of the evening. Stupid fuckers daring to make fun of him in front of those rich bastards; most of them weren't North Chasers anyway. They moved into the area and then suddenly adopted the town history as if it was their own. Solstice festival for fuck's sake. What did they know about it? His dad said that no one seemed to give a shit that the new lord of the manor was bulldozing the very site where the witch's cottage had once stood. His parents could tell those new age knobs something about solstice and motherfucking Maundrell. And what they feared would happen was probably already happening, now her home was being disturbed. None of his street cared about that borstal brat who had gone missing, but they knew Finn, liked Finn, and his own parents had asked him to be careful so he wasn't the next to go missing. Not that Brett was worried; he could handle himself just as his family had for centuries. His dad reckoned their family tree would take them right back to the plague days, if they'd had the money to get it researched, and his prized possessions were faded photographs of his great-grandfather in front of one of the mining chimneys. They still filled the nearby hills, and when he'd been a kid he'd loved to see the mist coming out of the old mining shafts.

You had to be careful at night in those woods, wouldn't want to go falling down one of those shafts or passageways. And now the rich folk were trying to claim the woods as well, with their survival training and mountain bike trails.

Suddenly from behind the yew tree, a shadow moved.

'Jordan, you knobhead. Stop pissing about.'

But apart from the owl there was no sound. The shadow darkened and began to grow, but still there was no sound of footsteps, or breathing.

What the fuck? He stumbled backwards, urine splashing his boots. Then the anger spilled over. Fucking superstitious bollocks. Now he was seeing stuff. But just in case, he zipped up and turned to leave.

An hour later, the first snowflakes began to fall. Each flake blotted out and finally covered the scuff marks that started at the yew tree and ended at the vestry door. By dawn the ground lay innocent and unsullied by the events of the previous night.

17

Seconds after leaving the rectory Nell considered turning back. The warm sun which had flooded through her window was clearly a trap. It was cold, nasty cold, and already the wind was finding its way through her gloves and sneaking under her scarf.

But she was out now, and the fresh air chased away the remnants of the nightmare that had left her breathing carefully over the toilet bowl that morning. Her stomach contents had remained in place but were still bubbling on a low simmer, so she held her breath as she walked past a café. It was good to be outside; the rectory apartment had started to pull her into the walls, down to the floorboards, until leaving felt like she would have to cut or unstick herself. Safer and nicer to stay in, away from people. This dangerous, insidious feeling was one she recognised; when there was always a good reason to stay in her cocoon, step off the world and hide within her own thoughts. Max had once kindly pointed out, 'in years to come, they will find your mummified remains on the couch, still clutching the remote.' Sometimes you had to do the things that scared you; yesterday she had left her penthouse and headed to North Chase, and today she was leaving the rectory.

So much about her life these days was out of her comfort zone, but as Austin had said, if she wanted to move on she had to leave the safe, the easy, and the familiar. She was so lucky to have friends offering advice and she shivered to think where she might be mentally if it were not for them. She spent too long looking back, living in the past. Leaving Wiltbury was supposed to have been a fresh start, but so far all she had done was mope and lick her wounds. She glanced at the leaflet on forest bathing and the local trails it suggested. It had seemed like a good idea this morning, something new to try, but as her fingers began to stiffen, she promised herself fifteen minutes and if she was still too cold she could turn around and run back.

As she rounded a corner, tall metal fencing appeared protecting a terrace of mining cottages being renovated behind. New brickwork supported old and the new slate roofs glistened where the frost had melted. The windows still displayed their manufacturer's coverings and a neat brick pathway surrounded the cottages like a moat. Nell tried to imagine them in their hay day, with washing hanging at the back and children sitting on the steps, waiting for their fathers to come home from the mines. Now they would house new families. Nell thought about Lark House which was waiting for planning approval before it underwent its own rejuvenation. There was something charming about making old properties new again.

This thought soon evaporated as she continued to the next street. More building work going on, but this house stood out like a rotten tooth in the otherwise picturesque street. Advertising signage for the electrician was displayed in the garden alongside a battered skip, a pallet of reclaimed bricks, and a green plastic portable toilet.

Nell felt for the house, once handsome, but now shabby and abandoned, humiliated and exposed to everyone passing. A rustle of wings and two pigeons erupted from under the eaves where the tarpaulin flapped in the wind. Two elderly ladies approached in their best coats, talking animatedly about the annual Christmas pie competition they were entering. Nell saw one of them glance at the cottage and then, falling silent, look the other way. Something in the determined position of her head seemed too deliberate and sure enough, when they had passed they continued chatting. Poor house, thought Nell, shamed in the street like a child being cleaned up in front of its nursery friends after a toilet accident.

A man came out of the house then and removed his hard

hat.

'You should have seen it before I started renovating.' Nell turned around and smiled politely at the weak joke, and then something awkward seemed to pass between them. The man's smile faltered and he seemed to be on the point of saying something else, but Nell turned back around and continued walking.

A bike swung in front of her, the rider barked, 'Move!' and then turning in his saddle, 'Stupid bitch.' Nell froze. Where had he come from and why was she being shouted at for being on the pavement? She thought of a retort, but as a couple of thousand pounds worth of bike and cycle equipment disappeared around the bend, the moment was gone. Perhaps he would meet a wall, she thought unkindly, and went into a puzzled self-analysis of what she had done to deserve being shouted at. Then it dawned on her; he was an idiot to be cycling so fast and then swerving in front of her on a pavement. Obviously some sort of attention deficit, like the stupid kids who walked purposefully in front of cars so they had a moment of attention, of being noticed, albeit by being sworn and beeped at. They could then scream back abuse at the driver who had just saved their life, but in their minds this probably counted as meaningful social engagement.

Twisted and weird. Now she did want to go back, but her mobile humming stopped her. Hunkering out of the wind beside a fragile-looking brick wall, Nell pulled off her gloves and found her phone. Why did no one ever ring her when she was indoors?

'Hello, Austin. How are you?' She smiled.

'Very well, thank you, Nell. I have news.'

That could only mean one thing, and as Nell stared at the moody sky above she suddenly felt uncertain.

'I have been in contact with your father.'

'Ok.' She could hear fear in those two syllables.

'Do you have a family connection with North Chase?'

That surprised her. 'Yes, Nana's family came from here originally.' For some reason she felt the need to explain further. 'She asked me to scatter her ashes here, tomorrow actually, so I thought I might as well stay for Christmas.'

'Well, it would seem that your father also currently resides in North Chase. Your grandmother left him a house in her will.'

A crow landed on the wall opposite and cawed at her insistently. Large and black, he almost sounded like he was mocking her, and as the adrenaline chased around her body he began to look a little blurry around the edges.

'Wow. I wasn't expecting that. So he's here?'

'He is.'

'Right. Ok then. Will he meet me?'

Now the words were out she wished she had thought about it some more. But then, wasn't that why she had asked Austin to track him down? Wasn't that the Christmas wish, that she would see her dad?

'He will. He has suggested a time and place if that is agreeable to you?'

'Right.'

'Tomorrow, at the Full Moon public house, at 2p.m.'

So soon. She remembered seeing the Full Moon last night, and 2p.m. was a good time actually, not lunch and not dinner. Just a drink to see how they got on. Suddenly she desperately wanted Austin to come with her but knew that was overstepping the boundary of their friendship.

'As luck would have it, I have a free diary tomorrow. If you want I can come with you?'

'Yes, yes please.' But then she imagined the very real possibility of making a fool of herself in front of Austin. 'Actually, perhaps I had better do this by myself. I've put you out enough.'

'Not at all.'

'But can I ring you afterwards and let you know how I get on.'

'I would like that, Nell.'

For a very deep voice, Austin always sounded so mellow. A slight accent which she had never worked out and would never ask. He didn't shout or raise his voice, even when he was breaking down doors and running after paedophiles.

'Thank you, Austin. Seeing as I'm being all sociable perhaps I can take you out for a meal sometime to say thank you. When do you fly?'

'Christmas Eve morning.'

'Good, well we will try to sort something out. Unfortunately I can't do tonight because I am ghost hunting in some old manor house.'

'Ah, the lovely Maxine, I presume.'

'Yes, my Christmas present, apparently. I think it will be fun.'

'Knowing Miss Georgcham, I am sure it will be.' There was a pause and then he added, 'An old manor house you say? Might I ask which one?'

'North Chase, owned by Lord and Lady Corberley, somewhere just out of town.'

'I see. How very interesting.'

The call was over and Nell contemplated the next 24 hours. This is what she wanted, to see her dad. But she had expected to be taking a long train ride to London or another big city. The fact that he was here, in this small town, had floored her. But then, she was only here because it was Nana's wish and didn't Austin say something about a house? Just how many houses had Nana owned? So many secrets. She remembered Nana's solicitor's answer when she had asked about her father.

'That is a separate matter.'

So *he* had known. And Nana had known. Everyone knew that her father was still alive except for her. Why was she feeling so nervous? He was the one who should be feeling nervous, he had a lot of explaining to do. A tricky day tomorrow, then, but at least she had the ghost tour tonight and Max to keep her brooding mind occupied. Now she really did want to return to the rectory, but knowing that she would only start fretting, she decided to carry on with her walk. Before she could stop it her nerves fluttered away in the cold breeze and excitement began to grow. Her Christmas wish was going to come true. The smile that bloomed on her face was so wide it made her eyes water. Tomorrow, she was going to see her father.

18

21 December – Evening

'Now I know one shouldn't do too much research before an investigation, but …'

'You did anyway,' said Nell with a smile.

Max's grin spread across her face as she grabbed a notebook from her bag and produced it with an enthusiastic flourish.

'Oh my, you are prepared.'

'Hush now and listen.'

Nell had felt the excitement, and anxiety, build in cycles all afternoon. Strange, but now she was sitting opposite Max in the Angel public house, she felt the friendship was as strong as ever and was ashamed of how brusque she had been on the phone last night. Confident and loud, Max was her polar opposite and a little of her did go a long way. And maybe, because she dragged Nell out of her comfort zone, she could be considered as good for her, albeit in carefully measured doses. Like medicine. Perhaps it was sensible to have friends like Max, that you didn't see all the time but when you did you could expect a fun time.

Max was practically bouncing in her seat, waiting for their order to be taken and excited for the night to come. With another theatrical flourish, she opened her notebook and began.

'So the story goes a witch was hanged in 1666 and with her last breath she cursed the village of North Chase, so they burned her house to the ground. The ruins are apparently on the estate we are going to tonight. But it gets creepier. A priest and some local nuns were asked to bless the ground the next day. They sprinkled holy water and said some prayers and all that stuff, but as they prepared to return to the convent, one of the nuns noticed a box sticking out of the charred remains. And in that box was the perfect body of a new-born baby boy. Dead, obviously, but otherwise unblemished. They buried the baby in their own graveyard, and then rumours began that the nun who had found the baby had become pregnant herself. They walled her up alive in the convent and left her to die.'

'A bit gruesome, Max.'

'I know. People avoided the area where the witch's house was burned, but over the years medicine advanced, people realised that she was just a midwife who had some knowledge of herbs, and that all she had been trying to do was help the villagers gripped by plague. It is really sad actually, when you think of how many poor women were hanged or burned when all they were trying to do was help. But people continued to die and someone had to be blamed. At extreme times like this people see things very simply; it is either God or the devil, one of them must take the blame.'

'What sort of box was the baby in?' asked Nell.

'What sort of box? What the bloody hell has that got to do with anything, Nell?'

'I was just thinking about how a body might survive in a house fire. Perhaps if it was lead lined or—'

'But it didn't, did it? It was either put there after the fire, once they knew priests and nuns were about to descend, or it is all utter nonsense and someone added it to make the story more interesting.'

'But the story must be based on some truth. I have also been doing some research, oh yes, you can raise your eyebrows, but I found this book and it talks about the witch as Mother Maundrell who is supposed to haunt the whole town and has been blamed for the disappearance of children over the centuries.'

For the first time in their short friendship, Nell realised that she had managed to impress Max. Well, she assumed that was what the expression on Max's face implied.

'I must congratulate you, Nell, you really have found a wonderful place to spend the festive season. And isn't this story so appropriate for present times? I mean, first she was a valuable healer, then became an evil witch who steals children, and now people see her as a saint, a martyr. The town has made quite an industry for themselves. Did you see all those new age shops? The whole town is so hipster.'

'What?'

'*Hipster.* Maybe I'm using the wrong word. Oh, never mind. Honestly, history is totally unreliable. Talk to two people after a football match, they will both know the score but their opinion on everything else will cloud their judgement, and you will hear something else when they tell you, so if you repeat it the story will be changed again.'

Something was tugging at Nell's memory.

'Max, last night I saw this woman with a placard. She said her son was missing and it was because 'her land had been violated' or something like that. Finn, I remember they said his name was Finn.'

'Like I said, someone has to be blamed.' Max was busy tapping keys on her mobile phone and then held it up in triumph. 'I can't find anything for your boy Finn, but it says here that another boy went missing recently. Hugo De Silva. Two young men from the same small town. Quite the coincidence. I think you and I have done quite well with the research. It will be interesting to hear what Spooky Spots have to add.'

The waiter came to take their food order.

'Please may I have the steak, and could it be cooked rare?' said Max.

'I'll have the lentil curry, please,' and to Max's raised eyebrows, Nell added, 'What?'

'Lentil? This place having an effect on you?'

'No, I've just gone off meat … lately,' Nell finished lamely. Then, glancing at Max, she acknowledged that this was the one person with whom she could be completely honest.

'Ok then … I had a weird dream last night.'

'One of your 'Nell' dreams or just a *normal* weird dream?'

A wisp of memory caught in the back of Nell's throat and

for a moment, she thought she might throw up.

'Oh yeah, definitely a *Nell* dream.'

'I thought you said the dreams had stopped.'

'They had. And then, one night, they came back.'

'They? Plural? Do you remember when?'

Unease began to flutter in Nell's belly; it was so easy just to ignore them, but Max would want each one displayed on the table for analysis.

'Oh, I remember them. There has been quite a number now. The first one I really took notice of came on 5th November, but there was one on the 1st.'

'The 1st November?'

'Yes, that night.'

'That's exact.'

'Yeah, well, I was half expecting something nasty on Halloween night, you know because of Ruby, but the dream came the next night. Can't really remember it, but it had something to do with a fire. Oh, and a baby that kept crying. And then, on the 5th—'

'All Saints Day? 1st November? When martyrs are remembered.' Max was reacting exactly how Nell had expected, but already she felt the burden begin to lift. Her dreams never appeared in a cluster unless there was a very good reason and Max could always see any patterns objectively.

'Right, if you say so. Anyway, on the 5th I was looking at this bonfire, a real one, and then had a funny turn, and then later that night I dreamed—'

'Define 'funny turn'.'

Nell sighed in mock exasperation at Max's habit of interrupting when she was excited by something.

'It's a bit difficult, but it was like I was being dragged *into* the bonfire, just for a second but—'

'Burning up?'

'Yeah, but literally just for a moment, and then I had the first really weird dream that night. And then the eating one was last night. I was there. I could smell it, I could … taste it. But then I had just eaten a solstice pasty, so it was probably indigestion induced.'

Max's eyes glinted as she leaned forward. 'Now you just

heard me order steak, *rare*, so although I am dying to hear more, I have to ask the question.'

'Go on.'

'Is there anything in what you are about to tell me, about this dream, that will put me off my meal?'

'Possibly.' And despite her flippancy, Nell felt her stomach lunge. Time to tell all.

19

Tilly sighed in frustration.

'No, I didn't mean that, darling.'

'Yes you did. You hate her,' retorted Seb.

'No, listen. All I am saying is—'

'Get nicer friends.'

'Well, alright then, if you must be so difficult. I do think there are more suitable people for you to be friends with. And if you went back to university then you wouldn't be so starved of company, you'd have other people to hang out with, rather than Ric,' she said.

'Don't say her name like that. Like she is shit on your shoes. And don't wince. I said shit, not piss.'

'I don't know why you have to upset me like this when all I want is the best for you.'

'And *you* shouldn't listen in on my private calls.'

That hit a nerve. 'If you didn't talk so loudly and in such a vulgar tone, I would not hear you at all. Trust me, after all the thousands we spent on your education I really don't enjoy hearing you speak in some sort of street accent. Using slang and swear words, it's not how—'

'You brought me up to behave? Yes, I know. Anyway, it was Dad's money, not yours.'

Now the wince was genuine and Seb felt a stab of guilt.

'Don't call him that.'

'Why not? You were married to him and he is the only dad I've ever known. You may have divorced him, but I didn't.'

Somewhere at the back of his mind he remembered a

phrase he had been taught: *pick your battles*. He could argue with her all day about his stepdad and the fact that he still enjoyed being part of his life, and that of his new wife and baby. But that was not the battle today; it was about Seb spending time with Ric.

At the thought of her, his features softened and a small smile brushed his lips, but it was soon chased away by a crashing wave of guilt.

'Just admit it, you hate her.'

'Yes, well, alright then, I admit I think you could do better,' Tilly spat back.

'Ric is really sweet and a talented chef.'

'Oh, I seriously doubt that, darling. She works part-time in a pub.'

'Kitchen assistant in a restaurant—'

'And that mother of hers, well, I'm not surprised they sacked her. The academy has strict policies about confidentiality, and everyone knows she sold those stories to the press.'

'She had nothing to do with the leak and you know it. It's just small town mentality that made the locals go all pitch forky—'

'Oh, and you know that for sure, do you? No, I didn't think so.'

This was not what Seb wanted tonight, but he couldn't always avoid an argument. 'Ric works really hard and is doing great at college. Everyone must start somewhere. Look at some of those celebrity chefs you follow, they all had to start at the bottom. God, you are such a snob.'

'I wish we had never moved back to this cursed town. If I had only known that your ... that Mark was going to get himself in all that bother ... and then get trapped by a teenage gold digger, then I would never have agreed to come back here to look after his father.'

She was starting on a familiar rant and Seb had heard it enough. 'Yes, and why did you drag us here, mother? You jumped at the chance to move to the estate because you knew you could get busy snuffling for money around Granddad, like a pig looking for truffles.'

Tilly's mouth opened in indignation; it closed again, and then she began to laugh.

'No, don't look at me like that when I am so cross with you. You are a very naughty boy to be so cruel to your mother.'

Now he was laughing too. Fight over, for the moment. God, they were so alike. Always bickering and snarling, but then one of them would say something funny and the anger would defuse. He did feel for her, he truly did. She had had everything, been the honourable Matilda Corberley. How had she landed such a prize, people asked, but Tilly had been well connected before she met Mark, and even as she slid towards fifty, she still turned heads. Ric said she had true beauty, the sort that just got better as you aged. Like wine, she had joked. But it was true. How hard for her, then, to be replaced by a younger model. She had stood by Mark when he had run off to have a midlife crisis, and then Granddad had suggested they both move back to the family estate and wait for Mark's recovery; it had all made perfect sense. But recovery turned to needing time out, time to re-evaluate his life, and although Seb did not know the full story, within six months his mum and Mark were talking divorce. Well, screaming divorce down the phone. A few months after the decree absolute, there was a new woman appearing on Mark's Facebook timeline. That shock had settled and it hadn't been so bad when Dad had lived away with Daisy; Granddad had mentioned them, of course, but Seb was back in touch with his dad and Tilly would just smile that tight smile of hers. And Granddad had been so proud when Mark had announced they were expecting.

'A new baby Corberley for us, Sebastian,' he had enthused, his sharp eyes sparkling. He had made Seb feel special and still treated Tilly like family, so there was no mention of her moving out. Of course, Tilly was happy to pop over to see Lord Corberley with a casserole, to put up some shelves for him, run him to the city for his hospital appointments, to play the dutiful daughter-in-law. Perhaps in the hope that Mark's crisis would pass and he would come to his senses. It had all been really lovely. And then just after they found out Mark had married Daisy, Granddad unexpectedly died, and Mark and Daisy became Lord and Lady Corberley.

'Over my dead body are they moving back here,' his mother had hissed, but of course, someone had to take over the estate. And all the debts. It was lovely for Seb to have Dad back. Daisy was really sweet and Ava, a cherub.

Mark and Daisy had tried with Tilly. And to a casual outsider, so had Tilly. She had been polite and charming, but when they were alone, she would rant and rage. She seemed particularly angry about Ava, for some reason that Seb couldn't work out. Perhaps she was jealous that her baby days were over. Anyway, she never stayed angry at Seb for long. He had wanted her to be nicer to Ric, thinking that if he won that battle then she might be weakened for another, much more difficult discussion he needed to have with her. But that battle would wait for another day.

'Mum. Why don't we move into town or further; get away from this old place. If you don't see them all the time, then you won't get so annoyed.'

'Yes, but I live here practically rent free. Mark hasn't said anything, has he?'

'No. He likes me living here. But I could get a job, help with the new rent.'

'We have money, darling. No, we're staying on the estate, and someone must keep an eye on the place for old Lordy, God rest his soul. He wouldn't be pleased to know that land is being sold off like that, upsetting everyone.'

Seb kept quiet. Granddad had confided in him just before he died that the debts were getting out of hand.

'First the bloody roof, then the electrics. I don't know, Sebastian my boy, the old manor is haemorrhaging money everywhere I look.'

His words had been 'get shot of the witch's ground and save the old homestead. Sod the bloody curse.' But Seb hadn't had time to find out any more because a week later he had found him collapsed on the old herb garden path. Building work would start soon and a close friend had mentioned that he'd spotted Tilly hanging around the ruins, as if she was mourning its passing or something.

'You are not still going to that stupid ghost hunt, are you?'

Seb froze. Please don't let this be round two.

'Paranormal investigation, and yes, I am. Should be good fun.'

His mother's contemptuous grunt was as good as he could hope for, so he didn't mention that Mark was planning to pop by. Seb didn't believe in ghosts, not for a minute, but he did like history and it was his way of showing support for Mark. People may criticise him for selling off land, but if they knew that he was trying to save the various businesses from bankruptcy, and to stop people losing their jobs, then perhaps they would be more understanding. The academy always seemed to need extra money too, which Seb had never understood. If it was full of filthy rich pupils then how was it not making money? Grandad had never fully explained it to Seb, and he didn't like to ask Mark.

The investigation would be something different to do and Ric had been keen. Sometimes, when he went round to her house, Ric would talk about the history of North Chase. Her mum was one of the main people opposed to the building site, which confused Seb because she was a firm churchgoer and hated the growth of the Pagan movement in North Chase. Seb tried to keep neutral, but it all seemed really stupid to him. If they didn't sell the land and settle the debts then the whole place would have to be sold anyway, and then it would be more than a small housing estate being built.

'You will need to take a nourishing snack with you if you are determined to mess about in the cold tonight,' warned Tilly. 'Take some mince pies with you.'

'I don't like mince pies.'

'Don't be ridiculous; of course you do. Everyone does and this is my own special, *medieval* recipe.' So that decided it then, thought Seb ruefully. Best to humour her.

A whine and a splutter outside announced that Ric and her mum's 50cc were weaving their way along the estate's main road.

'Take some of my medieval mince pies for Erica too.'

The peace offering surprised Seb.

'She's vegetarian. She says that if you don't take responsibility for the kill then you shouldn't eat the meat. Or something like that.'

The look his mum gave him was one he had never seen before. For a second, a stranger stood before him. And then with a blink his mum was back.

'They happened to be vegetarian, my own recipe. And gluten free.' The last detail was lost on Seb, but eager to leave, he took the peace offering and went outside into the biting cold.

A headlight flickered through the trees as she came nearer and for a moment, he thought he saw a figure illuminated. A figure that was walking fast towards the manor house. But it must just be a trick of the light. It stirred memories of a few weeks ago, memories he had all but forgotten, but none of it had really happened so he ignored the fact that his heart was beating faster and concentrated on Ric.

Helmet removed, Ric took off her hat and shook out her hair.

'Makes my head itch,' she explained.

Her eyes glistened; either from the cold ride, or she was excited.

'You got everything you need?' he asked.

She patted her backpack.

'Think so.' Then something caught her eye. 'Whose car is that?'

'Mum's. It's new, why?'

'She should clean it.'

'No, she shouldn't. It would only get muddy again and covered in mud is the country look.'

'But it's illegal to have your license plate covered over like that. Friend of Mum's got done by the police once.'

'She's home actually. Do you want to go in and tell her to clean her car? No? I didn't think so.' The look of terror at the suggestion amused him no end. 'Since when were you bothered about stuff like that?'

Ric shrugged, but as they walked past the car, she glanced at it again.

'What's up with you tonight?' But she just shook her head so he decided to let it go. There was already enough tension between Ric and his mum, and he didn't want to add any more fuel to it. He didn't want to know; that was the truth.

20

21 December - Evening

Max thought for a moment and then laughed. 'Oh what the hell, I am starving and could eat a scabby dog so go ahead. What did I say? You didn't dream about eating dogs, did you? Because I might have to change my mind.'

Nell looked around the crowded restaurant. This really wasn't the place for such a discussion, but Max would be gone in the morning. It was literally now or never.

'Oh, no. No dogs. The flesh of choice in my dream last night was that of a young child.' As Nell said this out loud, she looked around again to check if anyone else had heard her. But no one was staring at her in disgust and horror. Apart from Max.

'No?' For a moment she looked genuinely revolted, and then the wide, joker smile was back. 'Do go on.'

'Everyone else dreams about work or family or something ordinary. But I suppose because I don't have these things, I found myself laced into some sort of bodice, with heavy skirts that dragged me down, and a very sick child.'

'And you ate the child?'

'No. Let me tell you from the beginning, and no interrupting or I shan't say another word.'

'Ok, sorry.'

'It was really dark everywhere, but the person whose eyes I was seeing through didn't seem to notice. She went up and down the stairs with a candle thing in her hand.'

'Candelabra?'

'Probably. Anyway, she had no problem with the lack of

light. She was anxious and so very tired. Her son lay in a large bed surrounded by curtains.'

'Four poster bed with canopy?'

'Yes, alright, Miss Antiques Roadshow. Anyway, as I was saying, she approached the boy—he must have been about seven—and saw that he hadn't eaten his supper. It looked like a bowl of something beige with bread in it and I don't entirely blame him. Then it was as if a decision was made. She fled down a long corridor and ended up in a dark cellar.' Nell could not suppress the shiver that ripped through her as the dream replayed in her memory.

'What is it with you and light?'

'Nothing, it was just so weird that the woman had no problem with how dark it was, but I wouldn't have been able to see without the light switched on or a torch in my hand. Anyway, this bit gets nasty. No, don't look so excited, Max. It was horrible. There was a sack, and when she opened it the body of a small child fell out. A little girl, about three years old.'

Max attempted a grimace, but her gleaming eyes betrayed her.

'The woman then grabbed a big knife, and thankfully I woke up at that point. But when I fell back to sleep she was spooning some stew to the little boy.'

'Did he eat it?'

'He did, and I could feel her happiness. And something else. Hope. Like she realised that feeding her little boy with human flesh would revive him or something.'

'God, Nell. You have some horrible dreams.'

'Which is why I am having lentil curry tonight. I've had very little to eat since the dream.'

'There is nothing wrong with a vegetarian, or even vegan, diet. You just need to make sure you get enough protein and nutrients from other sources.'

Nell listened to the normal conversations lapping their table. Glasses clinked, cutlery scraped, but in her head she could still hear footsteps on a wooden staircase and the swish of heavy skirts.

'It's not normal, is it, to dream such horrible things?' But Max was clearly taking this as rhetoric.

'Nell, quick question. Would you recognise the house from your dream again?'

'I doubt it. It was night, and I wasn't really taking much notice of portraits on the walls. Why?'

'Probably nothing, but I am beginning to get an odd feeling about our ghost hunt tonight.

'Odd as in *Maxine* odd?'

'Fortunately, yes. Since I arrived this afternoon, my psychic antennae has been having a low buzz to itself. It is probably all this witch-solstice stuff going on. But it started when I drove in, and got louder when I began my research.'

'I quite like this place, but that dead tree in the middle of the field gives me the creeps. It is where this Mother Maundrell was hung.'

'Hanged.'

'What?'

'*Hanged*. Curtains are *hung* but a person is *hanged*.'

'Right. Thanks for the grammar lesson,' said Nell shaking her head, but it was lost on Max who had lit up in excitement.

'I wonder how far from the manor her burned out house is. It might be on the tour tonight. If not, perhaps we could have a poke around ourselves.'

It was true, thought Nell as she ate her delicious curry and kept her eyes from Max's bleeding steak, it really did help to talk about it. To say the words out loud, release them into the air and see them reflected in someone else's eyes and mind. She had always had vivid dreams; finding Ruby and Emily hadn't brought them to a halt after all. Maybe that was a good thing. Perhaps she should follow Max's example and explore this gift of hers. Although, surely her dream had just come from reading the history of North Chase late at night and her overactive imagination had conjured up something grisly. Would a mother really kill an innocent child so her own child could be saved? But of course a mother would. There were examples across the animal kingdom of mothers killing another's offspring to give their own a better chance of survival. To save her own flesh and blood; what mother wouldn't do that? And history books told of besieged people resorting to cannibalism. Right up to the Second World War, and probably since. Perhaps she'd read about starving peasants turning on their neighbours while doing her research. She remembered poor Ruby in her sealed room, and shivered.

'Nell, my lovely. Don't let it make a home in your head.' Max's concerned eyes locked on her, then she gave a deafening squeal.

'Austin. What the bloody hell are you doing here?'

And there he stood, a light dusting of snow on his wool coat. He removed his hat and, with a wry smile, made his way to their table. Yet again, Nell watched in amazement as the crowds just parted, as if they feared getting too close, leaving Austin to sail through.

'Miss Montague, Miss Georgeham. I thought I might find you here.'

The scent of pine and wood smoke settled around their table as he took his seat.

'I have a little job for you both tonight at North Chase Manor.'

'How did you know we were going to be in here?' said Max. Then she looked across at Nell and laughed. 'Stupid question. What do you want us to do?'

Amazingly, a waiter appeared with a glass of amber liquid for Austin before removing their plates.

'You will be at the home of Lord and Lady Corberley tonight. I doubt you will be given access to their family rooms, but you will be told the history of the house, and perhaps something that is not widely known. If it is not brought up, I would like one of you to ask about secret passages, false walls, priest holes, anything of that ilk.'

'We can do that,' agreed Nell.

'May I ask why?' asked Max.

'I am here on business.' He glanced at Nell. 'Incredibly, two jobs have brought me to North Chase. One has to do with Lord Corberley, but we will keep that amongst ourselves, if you don't mind.'

'Oh, how exciting. No problem. Leave it with us,' enthused Max.

'I would be grateful. Now, are we having dessert?'

How comfortable it was, thought Nell. After all the anxiety

of the last few weeks, she now sat at a table enjoying spiced apple crumble with the two people in the world whom she felt most relaxed with. When Austin was around, Max was less excitable, on her best behaviour, and everything just felt safer and under control when Austin was breathing the same air as her. She couldn't help wondering how long he had been in North Chase. Two jobs in one small place; obviously, the first was finding her dad, but the coincidence puzzled her. What did that have to do, if anything, with Lord Corberley? The moment she thought about her dad she found her eyes straying to the happy people around her. Strangers, except for the people at her table, but since she had arrived yesterday she had felt a slight feeling of being watched. No, that was too strong a word for the sensation. A feeling that her presence was noticed and acknowledged. Now Austin was near she itched to ask about her dad, but that was for tomorrow. For now, she would just relax in the atmosphere.

Christmas music began to play, and although Austin exchanged a wry look with Nell, Max began to chirp along to it and soon Nell joined in. Then other tables began to sing and Nell's eyes prickled at the spontaneous gush of Christmas cheer sweeping over the pub and restaurant. When the song finished, a cheer went up before people returned to their conversations. But underneath it all, the chatter, laughter, the noises of cutlery and glasses, Nell heard a faint murmur, as the same few notes she had been hearing for weeks now grabbed her attention.

'What's happening?'

Max was turning her head, her eyes round.

'You can hear it, Max?'

'Humming. Really creepy humming, but it is in my head, not my ears, if you know what I mean.'

'Well, at least it's not just my imagination. I've been hearing it for weeks.'

'Something is going on here. Or rather, something has started. I think this could be an extremely interesting night. Austin, do you hear it?' But the humming had stopped.

'I am afraid not, but then I don't have your sensitivity. What time does the investigation start?' asked Austin.

Max glanced at her watch. 'Let me settle the bill—don't argue Nell, it is part of your Christmas present—and then we'll make tracks.'

And like a knife sliding through the throng, Max slipped up to the bar.

'It is good to see you, Nell.' Austin smiled. 'I had not planned to drop by this evening, but sometimes detection needs more subtle methods.'

'It's good to see you too. May I ask you a question? Is he here now, in the pub?'

'He is not. Are you nervous about tomorrow?'

'Yes.'

'Try not to get your hopes up.'

'You don't think he'll turn up. But you said—'

'He will be there, but I fear you might have created a personality for him based on what you remember, and what you need. Just be a little wary so that you are not disappointed.'

It was good advice, but Nell did not need it.

'I loved him when I was seven and then he just walked out and left me without a word. Thank you for the warning, but I have a low threshold of respect for him based on our history. I think, one way or another, I just need some closure.'

'Have fun with Max tonight, then get some sleep. I'll meet you both tomorrow at some point. You can tell me about your ghost hunting adventures, and then later I'll speak to you privately.'

'Ok.'

'Yes? Good. Ah, here is Max now. Enjoy yourselves and try not to scare the ghosts.'

Austin disappeared into the night and Nell resisted the urge to confide in Max. She had only just got her own head around meeting her dad, and Max could be quite clumsy with other people's feelings sometimes. She could not get the feeling out of her head that she might have already seen her dad and not realised. But that was for tomorrow.

'Right, let's make those tracks. My car or yours?'

Nell had to explain why it would have to be Max's.

'Good, you can navigate; I'm rubbish and my satnav keeps trying to dump me in fields. On the way here I went wrong, and my nice main road sprouted grass in the middle and ended at a huge brick wall.'

The temperature contrast from the stuffy pub to the car park was drastic.

'Do you have enough layers?' asked Max as she rummaged in the back of her 4x4 and emerged in waterproof boots and a waxed jacket.

'Good lord, did you bring your gun too?' asked Nell

'Don't be so rude. This is what they wear in the country, don't you know.'

Nell smiled. 'I am going to look like your poor relation. My gloves don't even match my hat.'

'But at least you have a hat. And so do I.' With a flourish, Max slapped on a waxed cotton hat with a wide brim and a feather. 'Too much?'

'Ridiculous,' laughed Nell. 'Come on, then, Lady of the Manor. Oh, and here is a little Christmas present for you to open … not now … on Christmas Day.'

Max held up the small package, gave it a sniff and a shake, and then stuck back down the corner she had begun to lift.

'But don't you want to see me open it?'

'Christmas Day, Max, not a day before.'

'My mum always let us open one present on Christmas Eve,' Max bargained. 'And you're getting your gift early.'

'Christmas Eve, then. Now, let's get this hunt started.'

21

This was the second investigation that week, and Nelson was beginning to wish he had let one of the other teams do it.

'Stop yawning,' came the order from his side. 'I should have made you drive, might have woken you up a bit.'

They were pulling off the road now, and through the gateless posts of North Chase Manor, the location for tonight. 7.15p.m. Loads of time. As they pulled up to the elegant mansion, three cars were already parked up. Nelson groaned, no chance of a quick nap then. Stan, behind the steering wheel, had other ideas.

'Great,' he said as he spotted the tall blonde and waif-like brunette. 'I think we already have two eager punters.'

'It's too early.'

'Exactly, they can help us unload.'

'Here they are now.' Nell turned at Max's words and saw the black transit van crawling up the driveway.

'Showtime, Nell.'

Whatever Nell had expected, it was not this. Maybe she had imagined Rory the ghost hunter from Launton, but on a larger scale. As the aluminium cases were unloaded along with a large plastic crate of crisps and biscuits, she began to feel her interest roused. When Max had said they were tech savvy she had no idea that their unloading would resemble technicians from a theatre company or rock band.

More cars were arriving now, and when the last name was ticked off they were led into an entrance hall that reached up to the roof. Although the lights were lit, a cold gloom still penetrated, and Nell barely contained the violent shiver that rippled through her body as the family portraits glared down at her.

As if on a director's cue, a tall figure in black appeared at the top of the stairs. He paused, perhaps aware of the striking figure he made, and then began his descent.

'Ladies and gentlemen, may I present our kind host for the evening, Lord Corberley.'

He had a smiley face, thought Nell, and when he smiled, as he was doing now, his eyes nearly disappeared into his face. Mid-forties perhaps, his hair was already streaked with silver, but he moved with the ease of a much younger man. Then he stopped, as if hearing a distant call, and his eyes shot to Nell. Not so smiley now, he looked positively hungry, like a cobra about to strike. Just as quickly, he diverted his gaze. Nell turned to see if Max had noticed his strange behaviour, but she was just gazing around with a huge smile on her face.

'Welcome to Corberley Manor, folks,' said Lord Corberley in a voice that filled the vast hallway but at the same time was barely above a whisper. The spell was broken and everyone was suddenly chatting, all except for Nell. Never the most sociable person, she had become so hermit-like lately she had forgotten the few social graces that she had once possessed. Max, of course, was having no such problem and was soon chatting to the group as if she had known them forever. Lord Corberley was in deep discussion with the investigators, and Nell was just thinking that she had imagined the unease when she felt his eyes scratch over her again. She shot him a look, but he had turned his back and was pointing at a large family painting at the top of the stairs.

'Alright, Nell?'

Max was by her side, her smile quickly flipping to concern. 'My God. What's wrong? Do you recognise the house from your dream?'

Nell shook her head with a smile. 'A little nervous.'

'If it gets too much, let me know and we'll make our excuses, but I think you're going to have a great time. Honestly.'

Fifteen minutes into the location tour, Nell was grateful she had read the pre-investigation email Max had forwarded which had mentioned wearing comfortable, non-slip shoes. There were five main locations they would investigate: the ballroom, the library, the attics, the kitchen and cellars, and the abandoned church.

'Just a quick reminder that the manor is now a family home, so please keep to the areas we've pointed out. We don't want to disturb Lady Corberley and her daughter. Take an ESP meter and let us know if you see any amber or red lights.' The ESP reader reminded Nell of a remote control. It was showing a green light but apparently would change to amber or red if a potential paranormal source was nearby. 'Just keep them away from your mobile phones or you will get a false reading,' they were warned.

There was so much other kit to try out: folding tables for glass moving, a Ouija board, video cameras, and something called SLS which would be revealed later.

'What are these for?' asked a young woman with tattoos on her face and hands who was pointing at some round balls on the table.

'Cat toys, seriously, let me demonstrate.' As he lightly touched one, it erupted into coloured lights. 'When we place these in a room, we stamp in front of them, just to show you that they will only operate if touched. And I have a special surprise to reveal for later.'

Half of Nell hoped that this would be the last time she saw them light up, but then one look at the excited faces around her told her she was the only one.

'Right, we all know where we will be investigating, and most importantly where the coffee, snacks and toilets are. Let's put you into groups. Who has been on an investigation of this type before and is happy to use the Ouija board?'

Most hands went up, Max's amongst them. As Nell looked around, she realised that she wasn't the only one with her hand down, and she was placed in the group with a couple of teenagers.

'Nell? Would you rather stay with your friend and go up to the attics?'

Nell shook her head. She had watched too many films involving these objects, and although this was a proper, organised group, she still felt scared of them. Also, what if Nana or Ruby came through, or something pretending to be them?

Max was trying to catch her eye, and then mouthed, 'Does it look familiar?' Nell shook her head. The staircase was too grand, and it was a dream after all, not real.

The tattooed girl smiled over to her, and her friend bounded up to make Nell's acquaintance.

'I think we are in the sensible, non-Ouija board group with you. I'm Sebastian. This is Erica.'

'Or call us Seb and Ric.' The girl smiled.

He was a likeable young chap who looked on the verge of erupting into laughter. He reminded Nell of a golden retriever, the way he practically bounced up the staircase. The rest of the group were made up of some giggling late-teen girls and their loud mothers, who took one look at Ric and her piercings and then made it very clear that they would not be mixing.

'Actually, we are quite a big group so perhaps I'll split you again.' And with that, Nell, Seb and Ric were sent off to the library with a table and glass.

'This used to be part of the old nurseries, but the present owners wanted their daughter closer so turned it into a library instead.' The Spooky Spots investigator showed them how to place their fingers on the glass and how to create energy before they started.

'This side of the table represents yes, and the other side is obviously no.'

'What do we do?' whispered Ric.

'Perhaps see if there is anyone here who wants to talk to you. Remember to just ask one question at a time and make sure the answer is either yes or no. If someone makes contact, perhaps go through the alphabet slowly to see if they will spell their name. But don't forget that at the time this house was built, a lot of people were unable to read or write. Same with ages, not everyone will know how old they were when they died.'

Nell shuddered. Seb caught her eye and grimaced.

'Now I'm going to see how the other group is getting on, back in a minute, but don't forget the golden rule: don't ask a question if you don't want to hear the answer.'

He closed the door softly and left them. It was dark except for one desk lamp, and the shadows added to the tension.

'What did he say happened here again?' asked Nell, remembering that she was supposed to be investigating for Austin too.

Ric's voice was soft and low as she recited the tale of the children who had died of plague in the room.

'They were three and five, the heir and spare of the then Lord and Lady Corberley. I think they were still using the chapel on the estate at the time, so they are probably buried in the graveyard outside.'

'Well, let's give this a go,' said Seb impatiently.

They each placed a finger on the glass as they had been shown and began to move it round in large circles to build the energy. The glass scratching across the small table was the only sound until, as one, they stopped and returned it to the middle.

'Is there anyone here who would like to make contact?'

Nell stifled a giggle at the solemn voice Seb had adopted.

'Stop, take this seriously, Seb,' said a frightened Ric.

'Sorry.' Smirking, he repeated his question.

Ric gasped and, looking down, Nell realised that the glass had moved slightly towards *yes*.

'I didn't make it move, before you accuse me,' said Seb.

Nell's right index finger was resting so lightly on the glass that she could hardly feel it.

'Thank you for answering us,' continued Seb, looking at the others for approval. 'Are you a man or woman?'

'No, that won't work,' interrupted Ric. 'Say 'are you a man?''

Before Seb could open his mouth, the glass moved again, but this time towards the other end of the table.

'No. So you are a woman, or girl?'

With a slow scratch, the glass moved again to *yes*.

'Nell, do you want to ask something?'

This couldn't be real though, could it, Nell reasoned. They must be making the glass move subconsciously. Then Ric squealed and pointed to the ESP she had left on the table. It was dancing with red and amber lights. Somewhere close by she could hear one of the women in the other group laughing.

'They're not taking it seriously, then,' said Ric. 'Come on, Nell, ask something.'

'Are you a child?'

As soon as the words were out she wished she could suck them back in as a wave of something icy blossomed across her chest.

YES

After that the questions flew from them.

'Did you live in this house?'

YES

'Is there someone else here with you?'

YES

'Are you both happy for us to be here?'

NO

Nell's shoulder blade began to itch and, again, disbelief stole over her. She felt like an actor on stage waiting for her line to come up. Suddenly, a waft of vinegar stung her nose; someone had opened the crisps, then. She could hear Nelson returning and turned to the door, but then realised the sound was coming from behind her, from the next room. She jumped as a cold draught brushed her hand. Again, she turned to the door expecting to see it had opened.

Her eyes drifted to the wall and a wave of rejection hit her in the gut. She was not wanted here. She did not belong. The silence was solid around her, and she looked from the wall to see Ric and Seb staring at her.

'You ok, Nell?'

She nodded, and then remembered that they had been in the middle of a conversation with the so-called spirit.

'Is the other person, the person who isn't happy we are here, a child?' she asked, and was shocked to hear her voice shake.

NO

Why did that seem so much worse, thought Nell as she suppressed a shiver. They all jumped as the door opened and Nelson walked back in.

'How's it going?'

Nell let Ric and Seb tell him, but Nelson had noticed her silence. And he seemed to have noticed something else. Quietly, he began to film the three of them, making sure he got the wall behind Nell in the shot.

'Remember, only ask a question if you don't mind hearing the answer.'

But Nell couldn't help herself.

'Did someone just touch my hand?'

That got everyone's attention but the glass refused to move.

'The adult in the room, is it your mother?'

NO

'Your father?'

NO

'Do they want us to leave?

It was at this point that the glass slid right past *yes* and off the table.

Nell gasped. Scary. Or was it? The thought that there had been an unseen adult in the room who did not want them there was a little unsettling.

'When we get a break, we will have a look at our footage and see if we've caught something,' enthused Nelson. 'We won't give the other groups too much detail, it will be interesting to see if anyone pays them a visit.'

'Sounds like they were having fun, anyway,' said Seb 'We could hear them laughing.'

'They are in the grounds,' said Nelson. 'But I left a recorder on the stairs, so we'll see if that picked up any of the laughter you heard.'

The tang of vinegar still dented the air and, with Nell's stomach raising its head, hopeful of more food, they moved out of the cold room and on to the next location. The ballroom had been painted recently, but there was still the faint smell of damp. Here, they sat in the near total darkness and kept their eyes glued on the cat toy and their ESP readers.

Nothing happened apart from some stomach rumbles, until suddenly the cat toy began to flash.

'Would someone like to communicate with us?' asked

Nelson.

There were no more lights until the ESP next to Nell turned to amber, and then red. This was the most exciting thing that happened in the ballroom. Somehow that fact wiped away the last doubts Nell had, that this was real and not rigged. If it was fake then surely something would happen in every room and to every group.

It was break time, so they adjourned to the foyer downstairs which was to be used as headquarters for the evening. As they padded down the carpeted stairs, movement caught Nell's eye and she saw the family nanny quickly slip through one of the side doors and out of sight. There was something familiar about her, but then Nell recognised the old-fashioned nanny from the park.

Downstairs, Max's group were already drinking coffee and snacking.

'So, any excitements?' asked Max. Her eyes were literally glowing, clearly having the time of her life.

'The glass moved, but I'm not sure if it was spirits,' whispered Nell. 'I felt a draught on my hand, but it could have been my imagination.'

Nelson came over then to show them the video footage. A small white light seemed to be buzzing around Nell's head.

'Is that a moth?' asked Nell.

'That, my investigating friend, is an orb.'

Everyone was very excited by this, except Nell and Ric who weren't sure what an orb was.

'An orb is the manifestation of energy, and it is thought by some to be the first indication of a visitor from the spirit world. However, it could also be a particle of dust or, as you said, even a moth.'

The three women with the teenage daughters continued to chatter amongst themselves while he was explaining this, and Nell thought she caught a dismissive look from one of them. One of the rules was they mustn't make anything up or pretend. It was supposed to be fun, but Spooky Spots were very scientific about the whole thing and were only interested in genuine happenings. Even if they suspected someone of pretending, no one was to accuse them of it. Max's group explained how two of the men seemed to be particularly targeted.

'I didn't feel anything, and I was standing next to him,' said a middle-aged woman who seemed decidedly put out. The burley bloke next to her looked embarrassed at the attention; so no prizes for guessing who was targeted, thought Nell.

'The fact that Lord Corberley was also targeted adds an interesting dimension to what we experienced in the attic.'

Now everyone was looking at the poor man who seemed quite shaken.

'Well, I might leave you now,' he said with a quick smile. 'But good luck everyone, and please let me know how you all get on.' He headed back up the stairs. As Nell watched, he stopped, and once again he turned to look at her.

'Oh hello,' whispered Max. 'Is our lord checking you out, Nell?'

But there was something almost accusing in his angry stare that Max had clearly missed.

Max was trying to catch her eye so Nell headed towards one of the towering portraits, and sure enough, Max followed.

'So? You enjoying yourself?'

'Actually, I am,' said Nell. 'And I like my little group. It was a good present, Max, thank you. What do you think about those overexcited women?'

'Oh my God, what a row. Really drama queens. All we could hear from the attics was them shrieking and laughing. One of those stupid girls is a real screamer.'

'I think they were outside.'

'Really, I could have sworn they were on the floor below us? Must have come through an open window somewhere. Oh, and I managed to drop in casually about secret entrances and priest holes, and got a very strange look from our young lord.'

'Austin will be pleased.'

'Well, he said he'd not heard of any, but his face said something else entirely, if you know what I mean.'

'He didn't say where?'

'No, but I'll ask the investigation guys what they think.'

Then a thought struck Nell. 'What happened in the attics?'

Max's eyes were glowing in the memory. 'Whoever was

coming through on the Ouija board was female and kept repeating that *she* was back, and there was *danger*. When we asked *who* was in danger it didn't answer, but our lord got a little agitated. I think the other guy was just claustrophobic, it did feel really tight up there.'

Again, Nell was grateful that she hadn't joined her. But Max clearly had something else on her mind. 'What do you think of that young girl you are with?'

'Ric? Yeah, sweet.'

'Hmm, well I picked up something weird from her when we all first met.'

'Weird how?'

'Don't know. Just a strange buzz like I told you I'd felt earlier when I first drove into town. I'm going to come with you next to find out if it happens again. Oh, and the boy with you is Mark's ex-stepson.'

'Who's Mark?'

'Our Lord Corberley who nearly vomited in the attics and keeps checking you out.'

'Ex … stepson. Wow, that sounds complicated.'

'Yeah, he's quite the gossip when he's a bit nervous, and after his funny turn in the attics he was trying to laugh it off, saying that Sebastian would find it very amusing to know his ex-stepdad nearly fainted.'

'Mothers and daughters, fathers and sons,' mused Nell.

'What do you mean?'

Nell wasn't sure. 'Just that there are three sets of mothers and daughters on this tour. Then we have Mark and Seb. We supposedly got a little girl in the nursery, but a woman was also in there who wasn't her mother and she wasn't at all happy for us to be there.'

'Now that's interesting.'

Stan from Spooky Spots was heading in their direction.

'How are you finding it, ladies?'

They made enthusiastic noises and assured him they were having a great time. And they were, thought Nell.

'We are going to try the SLS camera in the kitchens next, and Max, I think you should lead on asking any questions when we are down there. With your experience, you might get more of a reaction.'

Interesting use of words, thought Nell as they made their way down to the kitchens, leaving the mothers and daughters to visit the old nursery.

'Now, a little bit of history about these kitchens. These are the oldest parts of the house, believed to be built in the 17th century. Stories include doors being found open in the morning after being closed the night before, footsteps heard on the stone steps, and the sound of something being dragged. The servant bells are also down here, and although they were disconnected years ago, there are reports of them being heard to ring at odd times in the day and night.

'Lord Corberley mentioned that he heard them as a small boy, and he also heard the most consistent report of haunting down here; that of faint crying, possibly of a very small child.'

Nell's body shuddered before she realised what was happening. Why did it always seem so much worse when it involved a child, a distressed child at that? Involuntarily she thought of the child from her dream, but the kitchen didn't look familiar. What about the little girl in the nursery? Could it be the same one? Stan must have seen the thought cross her mind.

'So far we have had a presence in the attics, a small child and woman in the nursery, and the Spicer family thought that someone in their family was trying to reach out to them in the stables. Let's see what happens here.'

He opened his laptop and explained the electronics that were set up in the room. 'This is SLS, it will work in the dark or light and will let us know if any spirits are with us. On the screen you will see a real person as a series of dots joined up by lines. And if we are lucky we might see another series of dots and lines appear alongside. Now, we are trying something new tonight; everyone say hello to Effie, our detection doll. We'll just set her up over by the fireplace and see if anyone comes forward to play with her.'

Nell stared as the small doll, in a pink satin dress and ringlets, was placed carefully on the floor. Another dream bobbed to the surface and her breathing quickened.

'I will also set up a white noise detector, so let me know if you see, hear, or experience anything. Max? Would you like to start the questions while Ric stands in front of the camera?'

Ric looked like this was the last thing she wanted to do, but encouraged by the group, she went over to the fireplace where indicated.

'Hello. We mean you no harm.' With those words, the temperature seemed to drop. A device in the corner began to alarm and flash, and Stan indicated that the sudden cold wasn't their imagination.

'Is there anyone with us who would like to make contact?'

Ric's slight body appeared on the screen as a combination of red lines like a stick person.

'Are you happy that we are down here with you?'

Now Nell understood the need for warm clothing; the cold was biting in the old kitchens. Partially underground, she guessed, but then they would not have had freezers or refrigerators in the old days, so they probably needed it cold to keep the food from spoiling. An image of a small naked body tumbling out of a sack flashed in front of her again, but she pushed it firmly aside. There was also a nasty damp feeling down here, and the choking smell of soot that came from the gaping mouth of the chimney became stronger the more she focussed on it.

Max carried on asking questions, and the white noise transmitter began to whine. Just for a second, everyone got excited, and then it went to static again.

Ric's turn was over and the burly bloke was up next. More questions, more silences. Nell began to realise just how tired she was and began to shuffle about a little. Then it was her turn. Standing in the near pitch dark, the smell of soot stronger than ever, but then she was practically in the fireplace.

'Cold down here,' observed one of the group.

Seb suggested they light a fire and suddenly Nell could smell roasting meat. It was just her imagination sparked by the suggestion of lighting a fire in the very place where cooking pots would have hung and meat would have been turned. Questions were asked; did anyone want to talk to them? Were they happy that they were there or did they want to be left alone? Stood on the spot, Nell felt herself beginning to sway a little. She glanced towards the chimney and a flash of recognition hit her. To the side of the fireplace was a square hole which would have been the oven, and the large cooking pot would have hung from the hook above the fire itself. Marks in the brick still showed where the spit would have been positioned, and she realised that unless all kitchen fireplaces looked the same, she had stood in this very place and stirred a pot before. Impossible, it had been a dream, probably brought on by eating too much before bedtime which had conjured up a scene from a horror film she had forgotten. But there had been too many details. Her stomach lurched and she suddenly felt sick. The lights from the doll began to dance in a medley of rainbow colours, and a low humming came from the transmitter. She felt she was falling asleep, and then the other dream came back to her of the dolls in the rocking chair and how she had floated off the ground. Activity erupted all around her, people moving, gasping, excited. Max grabbed her arm.

'Oh my God, you *are* frozen. Wow, that was something.'

Nell looked at their faces in bewilderment.

'What?'

She was being helped to a chair.

How embarrassing. Now *she* had nearly fainted. Stan was excited.

'Three near faints on one investigation, a galaxy of orbs and a definite figure standing in front of you.'

Nell winced, and the burly bloke met her eye and pulled a face which earned him a hard slap from his wife.

Her, thought Nell. Why did it have to be her? Why not Max, who was the psychic after all?

'So, what happened, I seem to have missed it?' she admitted.

Apparently a blue stickman had appeared on the screen next to her. A small shape like that of a child. Two small shaky arms had seemed to raise as if it was asking Nell to pick it up. Then the static white noise had changed to a faint humming just before her whole body had disappeared when a large blue stickman had rushed onto the screen. No one seemed to have noticed the doll, Nell thought, but then she supposed they had had more interesting and exciting things to look at.

'Humming, what sort of humming. Did you recognise the tune?' she asked.

Max was nodding, her green eyes glowing like a cat's. When several of them started telling her and imitating the slow, simple tune, the same slow, simple tune she had been hearing for weeks, she began to feel lightheaded again. Chocolate and coffee was the answer, apparently, which sounded good to Nell. Then everyone agreed that they needed chocolate and coffee, and the atmosphere began to be quite animated again.

The final location for their group was outside. Now this should be scary, thought Nell. They were in the dark, in the cold, and after three of them had 'gone off' as Max had laughingly called it, surely she should be ready to call it a night. But somehow it was still fun, still didn't feel quite real, but she was with some really nice people, stomping about looking for ghosts. Then it hit her, apart from Max these were strangers, but they were all getting on, and they were having a laugh. After months of being so alone, it was reassuring that she could still operate successfully in a social situation. Swimming lessons didn't really count, but then the other women and herself always had a good natter while they changed. They congratulated each other on their progress, or encouraged and commiserated when someone had had a bad class. Somehow, one of them always did have a lesson when nothing went in but a mouth, nose, or lung full of water, which caused much spluttering and coughing. Nell had even had problems with burping loudly and been told that this was due to the water she had swallowed. Disconcerting to know, especially since the class before theirs was the over-seventies water Zumba class and comments were made concerning continence. Or the lack of it. It had been her autumn challenge, to learn to swim properly, and she was achieving it. Big tick for Nell. And here she was again, facing her fears and achieving, and having fun while she did it. And tomorrow she would see her dad, which might not be so successful, but at least it would be another fear faced. Her comfort zone was a distant blur, she thought contentedly.

Maybe because the ghosts tonight weren't connected to her personally, she could feel more detached. Anyone would have got a little dizzy, standing in the dark in a cold underground room at close to midnight, she reassured herself.

As they crunched in torchlight across the long, frosted grass to the abandoned chapel, she wished she had not been so smug. A sign was nailed to the boarding which blocked the church entrance. *Danger. No entry.* Stan explained they would just be in the graveyard, so nothing to worry about. The tombstones had fallen, and it was as if the ivy and grass were trying to suck them into the ground. It would make a great film set, thought Nell as she hobbled over the uneven ground. The stained-glass windows were mostly covered by ivy, but tiny sections had escaped and twinkled in the light from Nell's torch. Something else caught her eye; bushes crowding around wide stone steps which led down to a heavy wooden door. Stan saw Nell's torchlight on it and smiled.

'The Corberley family crypt. It's not been used for centuries but Lord Corberley told me that he remembers his father and grandfather putting a wreath on the door each Christmas. Apparently the tradition died out with his generation.'

The door stood before Nell like a gateway to hell, and she reluctantly acknowledged the faint stirrings of recognition.

'The crypt that Nell is illuminating has an interesting history. It was certainly in use when the church was first built, but if we cross over to this tomb, it is believed that family members who died during the plague are buried here. The writing is worn away, but records tell us that in 1666, or possibly 1668, John Corberley was laid to rest here. Two of his children were also buried here, aged three and five. Historical records tell us that they all succumbed to the plague, despite asking for help from Martha Maundrell who was the local midwife and healer.'

Max and Nell exchanged a glance.

'Interestingly, at the time yew trees would be planted over plague pits. They felt it would protect and purify the dead. Makes you think every time you see a yew tree, doesn't it, makes you wonder who might be buried at its roots?'

Nell shuddered, it was a graveyard after all, and her left boot felt like it was slowly sinking into the ground. Into the ground where there were coffins and skeletons.

'The chapel here has not been used for many centuries, and the story goes that one Christmas Day, the bell crashed down and killed a young boy below, who just happened to be the lord's eldest son. Many people believe that the Lady of Chase, who is supposed to be seen all over the town and at the manor house, is Martha, coming after the descendants who hanged her for witchcraft. A figure of a woman is also reported to have been seen at the rectory near St Edmund's church.'

Nell's head whipped round so fast her earring got caught in her scarf and tugged painfully.

'The rectory?'

Stan saw the glint in her eye and mistook it for fascination.

'They say that just before the Lady of Chase is seen you can hear her ...'

At this point Ric tripped over a stone slab and fell heavily to her knee.

'Ric? You ok?'

'Stop laughing, Seb. It hurt.'

'It's normally me who falls over.'

'Quite true.'

'At least you didn't half faint,' said Nell as they both helped Ric up.

'So, she was hung from the oak tree in Church Field? That's what we are all told, but is that fact?' asked Ric.

'Well, the records don't tell us how she was killed, but hanging was more common than burning. Though many women, and men, died during prolonged torture. Various methods were used—'

Whose bloody idea had it been to do this ghost tour, thought Nell, feeling queasy again. Max. And what was Max doing? Trying to look horrified and mournful while her broad smile betrayed just how much she was enjoying every gruesome detail. And here was Nell, stumbling about in the frozen grass, being told that the place where she was staying was haunted. Of course it was. It was impossible for her to be anywhere without a whole pack of ghosts and ghouls coming out of the walls and up from the floors to keep her company.

'As I was saying, the Lady of Chase is supposed to be heard before she is seen. A low humming. Some say a nursery rhyme, others a hymn. Which is why I was so interested to hear what seemed to be a tune coming from the static white noise of the transmitter in the kitchen. But there are other reports of people hearing cackling or low laughter.'

So, there it was. She was being haunted again, but this time it was the wretched Lady of Chase. Oh, Max was having her best night ever, thought Nell mutinously.

'Let's see if we can get someone to make contact,' said an enthusiastic Stan, and again he invited Max to do the call out to any spirits listening. This time there were no replies.

As they trudged back onto the path, Nell glanced again at the battered wooden door to the mausoleum and again her memory flickered. Taking a deep breath to settle her stomach, she saw Ric tug at Seb's arm. He rolled his eyes and laughed, but Ric didn't seem so amused. She saw Nell looking and explained.

'He doesn't believe me, but I think I've heard that laughing, the other day when I was walking home. He says it was the wind in the branches, but I know what I heard and it sounded like that laughing we heard when we were in the library.'

Ric looked so afraid that Nell immediately said, 'I'm staying in the rectory for Christmas, so after what I've just learned, I'll be questioning every bump and thud.'

Now she had everyone's attention. Should she admit that she had heard the humming before? Sharing her fears about Ruby and Emily with Max had helped, and somehow she knew that this group would believe her without question. Max had heard it at the restaurant, so whatever was making that noise was real and, yet again, she had managed to find herself targeted by something paranormal. *Merry bloody Christmas, Nell.*

Then a thought hit her. 'But you both live in North Chase, don't you? Haven't you heard this humming or laughing before?'

'Never, but there has been talk about weird stuff happening for the last few weeks. Some of it is probably just hype to big up the festival, but people are saying that Lord Corberley has woken the witch—Mother Maundrell—because he's sold some of the land here, where her house used to be. She's upset, so the curse is happening all over again.'

Stan had been busy talking to Max, but this got his attention.

'Yes, one story says that small children started going missing days after Mother Maundrell was killed, and that a woman in black was seen leading them to the lake in these grounds. In the spring, when the lake thawed out, they found the bodies of the children who had drowned there.'

'That was one of the tests for being a witch, wasn't it?' added Max.

'Yes, if you drowned you were innocent; float and you were guilty. A bit of a lose-lose situation.'

A picture drew itself in Nell's head of tiny bodies held under the dark ice and the shiver made her shoulders ache.

'I really have found myself a cheerful place to spend Christmas, haven't I?'

They all laughed as she had hoped, but it did little to warm the icy grip which she now felt at the back of her neck.

The hoot of an owl made them all jump, and then laugh again, and finally the warmth returned to Nell's blood. Perhaps this was the Christmas she had been looking for: dark and light, fear and cheer. What had she said just weeks ago; Christmas was a time for ghost stories, of being chilled to the bone so that you could then enjoy warming yourself by a fire. Stumbling about in the cold and dark, hearing that the place she was spending Christmas was haunted, and beginning to get seriously nervous about meeting her dad tomorrow, was perhaps very nearly the Christmas she had wished for. The only way to get through this was to keep going; she had passed the point of no return a long time ago.

22

'Should we ring 111? Take her to the emergency department or something?' Daisy frantically sought for an answer in Mark's dark eyes, but he was gazing out of the window at the departing Spooky Spots guests.

'She's a baby, and babies cry.'

'That's not crying, Mark. That's screaming.'

'What does it say on the NHS website again?'

'Oh, there is a whole list of things to check, but I've already checked them. And I'm rocking her, she normally likes that. *Mark.*'

With an exaggerated sigh, he closed the curtains, frowned at Ava, then at Daisy, and then at Ava again.

'Put her in the pram, maybe. Wheel her about.'

'It's all the noise from the ghost hunters,' Daisy muttered.

'Paranormal investigators, and they were nowhere near her. Look, I know you weren't happy about it, but I think it will help public relations. It was quite good fun actually, and interesting. They'd certainly done their homework. Strange how much I learned about my own ancestral home tonight, *and* I kept them well away from this wing.'

'I heard footsteps upstairs again.'

'You can't have.'

'There were strangers in the house, thundering about, and now they're slamming car doors.'

'Don't exaggerate, Daisy.' Something caught his eye. 'There's a print missing from here.' In answer to Daisy's raised eyebrows, he added, 'Over there, the little children in the

129

woods.'

Daisy looked back at her daughter.

'You moved it, didn't you? Why would you do that?' Mark asked.

Daisy glanced at the empty wall. 'It was creepy, sinister.' She was on the verge of telling him the real reason when the look in his eye stopped her, so she finished lamely, 'Ava hates it.'

'Don't be ridiculous.'

Daisy turned her back on him again. 'Baby girl,' she crooned into Ava's furious face. 'What's the matter?'

'Maybe she's hungry. You hungry, Ava?' Then, under his breath, 'Actually I'm hungry too. Do you want—'

'She's not hungry, Mark, she's distressed.' Rocking always worked, and Daisy had tried everything else. Then she had a sudden thought; there was one thing she had not tried yet. 'Look, it's rag dolly, Ava. You like rag dolly.'

'Don't shove that hideous thing in her face, no wonder she's screaming.'

Stung, Daisy placed the small cloth doll back on the dresser. 'I had one just like it when I was little and I loved it.'

'God, I'm sorry, love, I'm being a beast. It's just been a long night and I hate seeing her, and you, so distressed. Come here.' Mark pulled her into his arms.

'Mummy made it for me out of an old dress she loved to wear, like I made this one for Ava out of my—' The next words were drowned out by the increase in pitch.

'Bloody hell, Mark. I'm going to ring 111.'

Ava looked at her mother for a moment, and then merciful silence swelled around them.

'Oh, thank goodness.'

'Phew. You are really putting your mummy and daddy through it, aren't you poppet.'

Ava spotted something, and that something was slowly peeping out from behind her mother's back.

'Oh no, I thought she'd stopped. Maybe she's cold. Does it feel cold in here to you? I can feel a draught on my arm.'

Each scream seemed to rip off small pieces of Daisy's brain and ground them into her eyeballs.

The little girl kicked the cot again.

'Did you hear that? A bang. Is that stupid cat up here again?'

Job done, the girl faded back behind the wall. But not empty handed.

23

Headlights caught Austin's attention. He drove on, but once out of sight, executed a handbrake turn and retraced his steps. Taillights disappeared around the corner, and to his left he saw the side road that he had missed before. There were no signposts to inform you that this led to the exclusive Cedarwood Academy. No advertising board or notices either, although, thought Austin, confidentiality and privacy would be essential to their success. No sign of security cameras at this point, which didn't mean there weren't any there. For a moment he considered killing his headlights, but then decided that perhaps a different approach would be more fruitful. A narrow single track, bordered by trimmed grass verges, disappeared into thick woodland. Hardly welcoming, perhaps that was the point; let the troubled teenagers know that this was their last chance to regain their life.

Would it have helped Lily? His stepdaughter had been lured into a life of drugs and prostitution, and although he had rescued her, the self-destructive path she had started along had attached itself so tightly that he could now see that nothing could have altered the ending. It had been like watching his wife die of cancer all over again; the small steps of progress which were futile against the insidious growth, that once set on its path of destruction, could not be halted.

And now, finally, here was the huge brick wall he had been expecting. No doubt part of the original estate wall, and although pots showed where flowers would bloom in the summer, it still looked like what it was: a secure mental health facility, or prison. Planting a smile on his face, he lowered his window and greeted the fast-approaching security guard who had appeared from nowhere.

'Hello there.'

'May I help you, sir?'

'I do hope so. I am trying to find North Chase Manor and I keep getting lost.'

As he was given unrequired directions, he continued the pretence.

'That is so kind, thank you very much.' He even attempted an embarrassed shake of his head. As he returned the way he had come, he saw the guard raise his radio to presumably report their unexpected visitor's registration plate. Well guarded and professionally run. Interesting; this backed up his research and confirmed that whoever had leaked the details of Hugo de Silva's disappearance had most likely been on the inside. One of the catering staff had apparently been questioned, and although she had fiercely denied involvement, had later resigned. Or been sacked. Perhaps she would have grounds to threatened Lord Corberley, who was head of business here, but most vexingly, not one of Austin's associates had managed to breach the academy's IT system. Someone had leaked the disappearance to the press, but whether to discredit the academy or for some other reason, Austin still wasn't sure. Someone else had thrown a lot of money at it to ensure the story died. Still, Hugo remained missing so someone was mourning his absence this Christmas. For a small place there certainly did seem to be an unusually high percentage of missing children, and Austin had gone back through the archives four decades. And now young Ava Corberley had been threatened. As Austin headed back to the main road, one thought kept him company: this time there was a warning shot, a threat, but there was no record of there being any such thing for the other children, they had simply been spirited away in the night.

Lights flickering from the woods warned him that a vehicle was approaching from a side road, and then his own headlights illuminated the sign for North Chase Manor. Hastily, he pulled into a convenient layby and killed his lights. A black transit van hesitated and then pulled out onto the road. Glancing at his timepiece, Austin frowned; who would be leaving at this time of the night? As he switched his lights back on and turned into the side road, he remembered Nell and Max's investigation. A small smile twitched; he was looking forward to hearing all about it later today, and of any information they might have for him.

Driving with only side lights, he crawled along the rutted driveway. No doubt it had once been smart and inviting, but what was left of the tarmac now bulged with tree roots. As the lights of the manor house came into view, he killed his own lights again and pulled over. Closing his door as silently as he could manage, he listened for a moment, and then walked towards the house. The entrance foyer was still lit, as were several rooms on the upper floors. Movement to the side of the house caught his attention and he dropped behind a garden wall. A tall figure had emerged from the house and was running swiftly across the lawns. Within seconds, it had disappeared into the woods.

A flick of curtain from an upstairs window revealed that he hadn't been the only person to see the figure. Confident that his presence was safely concealed, he withdrew his binoculars and aimed them at the window. Sure enough, a figure stood there and in a gap in the curtains he saw a light that was clearly from a mobile phone. Several thoughts crossed Austin's mind as he waited for more movement. If the late visitor was connected with the investigation or a member of staff then why run across the lawn in such a sly way? And why was Mark Corberley watching them?

The figure had shot off to the east of the property, from the direction Austin had just come from. High walls may keep prying eyes at the entrance from seeing Cedarwood, but they wouldn't extend all around the building. Austin remembered from their website that there was a lake close to the modern building, and in the background, over the treetops, could be seen the tall chimneys of North Chase Manor. No doubt security kept the students—inmates—from wandering off by themselves, but there was always a flaw. Strange that with a group of frustrated, rebellious teens in their grounds, Lord

Corberley had not thought to suspect the threats had come from one of them. Austin waited until the curtain was replaced and the figure withdrew before he walked back to his car. Innocent people did not usually act in a guilty manner. Then he remembered the security guard. Perhaps he had informed someone else of Austin's presence. If Mark was head of business, a title which in Austin's experience covered a multitude of roles—not all of them legal—he might know more than he was divulging.

There was something about Mark that annoyed Austin. Rich, titled, with a beautiful young wife and baby daughter. Such things came with restrictions. They dictated how your life should be. Being a husband, a father, meant you stopped thinking for yourself and carried out direction from your family's script. Mark was whining about some letters while he still allowed his ex-wife to live on his grounds. Why would that be? Austin considered then that perhaps he was feeling a tinge of jealousy; Mark was starting again, progressing, while Austin seemed to have stalled. He had freedom, money, friends, but that freedom came at a price and lately he had begun to wonder if the price was too high. This job was not exactly taxing, but it was convenient given that he could help Nell at the same time. He just wished they were not connected.

It was getting late, and there was little more to learn here. Just before he turned the ignition, he sent a quick text.

'Hope you both had fun. Sweet dreams and we will talk later.'

24

At first Nell thought she was still awake, but then cobbles underfoot abused her bare feet. Cold, wet, and slippery, she hobbled along, her hand reached out to the stone wall beside her. Twilight: the sky was inky blue and the new moon a silver sickle. She jumped when the voice spoke.

'Is someone there? Please?'

Nell awoke in the dream at those words. This was new, but was obviously a connotation on that morning years ago when she had heard Ruby calling for help. When she had ignored her and left her to die. She walked on. She could wake herself up, but her curiosity was roused. The huge stone slabs that flanked her reached up high, and she could now see it was the wall of a towering castle.

'I can hear your footsteps, please answer me.'

So close. Nell spun round, but she was alone on the path. Now it was changing, smoothing out, becoming a wooden floor, and as she looked up the stone wall, its cold face turned to those of portraits, some small, some towering above her. All of them contained stern, menacing figures who stared down at her in rage.

'I can see you.'

Now the voice was threatening. Nell stared at the portraits again to see if one of them was moving.

'Where are you?' she asked. Lying safely in her bed, Nell knew this was a mistake but her dream self was being rash.

'Here.'

From behind a portrait of a woman in a stiff looking black

136

dress, a hand reached out. Only a hand, the hole was too small for more, but as Nell peered, she saw a face.

'I don't understand.'

'They left me in here to die. I am so hungry, so thirsty.' *Just like poor Ruby.* 'Help me.'

The voice had changed again. It was no longer pleading, it was angry.

'I have been trapped here for over three hundred years.'

There was a sudden roar and distant screaming. Like a huge wind was ripping through a hidden part of the city; birds tore across the sky, trying to outrun whatever was coming.

'Quickly, take my hand,' demanded the thing encased behind the wall.

Nell had heard this roaring sound before, in another dream, and as panic rose in her, she frantically tried to remember what it was.

'*Quickly.*'

Without realising, she had been backing away from the sound and was now against the wall. Sharp fingernails grabbed at her neck and pulled her to face it.

'Your turn.'

The bricks dissolved and in the narrow cavity stood a horror with matted hair and black rags. With a scream of laughter, the hag tightened her grip and pulled Nell in. The monstrous laughter matched her own screams of panic, and then a new sound came, a sharp scrape and slap of mortar as invisible hands rebuilt the wall. The air grew rank with the breath from her scream as she thrust her hands into the disappearing gap. Just before the last brick was placed, blocking out all light and air, she saw a huge wave crest the walls opposite and flood the passageway she had just walked.

Time to wake up, but as the rectory ceiling finally came into view, the stench of damp bricks still filled her nostrils and her head rang with the fiendish laughter.

Her tsunami dream was one she had very rarely, but walled up alive? Where on earth had that come from? Was it some obscene variation of poor Ruby's last hours when she had been locked in a room and forgotten about? Left to die. She heard the slap of bricks being laid and remembered Max's story of walled up nuns. Nell let her eyes scan the rectory's walls surrounding her. All old houses had thick walls, so anything could be concealed behind the centuries of plaster and paint. Not the most settling of thoughts. Nell's breathing finally steadied and, relaxing her iron grip on the duvet, she finally accepted the truth: she was obviously a lot further from getting over Ruby's death than she thought. As she stared at the rectory walls, her mind painted the picture of screaming skeletal remains with arms outstretched behind them.

Glancing at her mobile, she saw she had been asleep for less than an hour. At this rate she would be a wreck by dawn. Turning her pillow over, she settled down again. The sound of ticking from the clock in the living room crept under her door, as did another sound she didn't immediately recognise. As she sunk back into sleep, her mind painted a picture of what she was hearing: the slow rocking of the horse on the landing below.

25

22 December – Dawn

The first morning after the winter solstice dawned dark and below freezing. Anything living should seek warmth, thought Nell as she tucked the duvet around her tighter. Sunrise was due at 8.10a.m.. Checking her weather app again she saw that the sun, if it ever made an appearance, would set not long after 4p.m. when the northern hemisphere would be plunged into another long dark night, but not quite as long as the night before. It was at sunrise that Nana had asked for her remains to be scattered. At the base of an ancient yew tree. In a graveyard. Good grief, fretted Nell, was that even legal?

When she had picked up the ashes, she had been given paperwork that must remain with the box, and she vaguely remembered being told that permission must be sort if she wanted to scatter them somewhere. There had been rules about scattering in a river or water course, she remembered that bit because she had thought of swans or ducks getting bits of Nana stuck in their beaks. Nell glanced at the jute bag in the corner of the room that held the surprisingly heavy remains. She had better drag herself up.

The Old Rectory Guest House was certainly atmospheric, with its uneven floors and tiny windows. But a lurking damp coldness seemed to hang like cobwebs in unexpected places, and Nell had found herself checking the radiators in every room. Yes, they were on, and after all her twisting and fiddling when she had returned from ghost hunting, were now painfully hot to the touch, but unless you were leaning against them their heat did not seem to reach the centre of the room. A clang and a hiss answered her thoughts. The heating was on but goosebumps pocked her skin when she crawled out from the duvet. Her eyes felt gritty, her head ached, and as she switched on the kettle, she resigned herself to a very long and emotional day. The clock caught her eye, its hands still clamped together at midnight, or midday. A memory from last night wriggled out, of hearing it tick, but she dismissed it; she had probably heard her own watch.

Orange flames stretched across the duck egg blue sky and despite the occasion, Nell smiled. Nana would have liked this. The graveyard was huge, but as she walked toward the lychgate, Nana's yew tree was obvious. No longer just one tree, it seemed to have split into three twisted trunks with dark bark, blood red berries, and tiny needle-like leaves. The ground beneath it was uneven from the nest of roots that pushed against the frozen ground, and as Nell approached it she tried to imagine its age. Its main trunk was hollow in places and it looked like a cage. Nell read her instructions again.

By St Edmund's Church in North Chase stands a yew tree of over 400 years. At the first sunrise after winter's solstice, please scatter my remains beneath its boughs. Do this alone and send me on my way. Nana x

Nell quickly looked at her watch, and then checked she was alone. No one else was stupid enough to be standing in a churchyard at sunrise so she had best get on with it.

She had expected tears as she removed her gloves and took the bag from the wooden box. Through the thick plastic she could see the gritty, grey ashes. Quickly, she unpicked one of the staples with what was left of her fingernails and waited for the feeling of loss to hit her. The first ashes hit the dark roots like snow on cold coals, and all she felt was peace and amusement. Trust Nana. She would probably get herself arrested for defiling sacred ground. Then she remembered the woman from the funeral director's other recommendation: 'If for some reason you forget to seek permission, make sure there is no one around, *and* take note of the wind direction, just in case.' Nell had smiled at this; at the thought of scattering ashes in the wrong direction and getting covered. The whole demeanour of the funeral director had been one of warm professionalism, and perhaps some might have taken the remark as disrespect, but Nell had found it helpful. She had dreaded picking up Nana's ashes, but the woman's gentle warmth and humour had really helped.

Now the ashes were flowing and had started to form a small mound. She swung the bag slowly, giving it a little shake, and made a wobbly ring. Nell jumped as the air was ripped open with a crash of the church bells. Eight different notes in a smooth chime as the last of Nana fell in the middle of the circle. The bells continued but had somehow gotten out of sequence, so instead of a melodic descending, there was chaotic clanging like a cat walking on a piano. How fitting, mused Nell. Then a thought struck her: that was twice now she had heard church bells ringing out of sequence. Once while she was with Austin after her swimming lesson, and now here with Nana. Was it some sort of sign? It was deafening, anyway.

Light was beginning to flood the churchyard as the winter sun rose.

'There. All done, Nana, as requested.' Glancing at the flaming sky, she whispered, 'Sorry about that God awful row. Safe journey. Love you forever and thank you for giving me my life back. I promise not to waste a second of it.'

The wind picked up, stirring the ashes, and a few leaves scurried across the ground. It was done. As Nell turned to go, she noticed the robin. It perched on a stone angel and just watched her. 'How long have you been there?' Nell asked. It hopped down to the base of the yew tree.

'I just scattered my Nana. Look after her for me,' she said, and with a small smile turned to leave.

William Montague watched her walk back to the rectory and extracted his notebook. Yew trees, winter solstice, it was exactly as he had hoped. Over the past few years he had begun to trace their family tree. The Montague side was interesting, but it had been when he started on his mother's side that the history teacher in him had stood to attention. Half-forgotten memories from his childhood had started to make sense, and when he had begun the renovation on the old house, which had been in the family for centuries, more pieces began to fall into place. He had found out so much by himself, but with Tilly on board he was making remarkable progress. She had been so shocked when he told her he might be related to one of the oldest families in the town, and he couldn't wait to show her what he had found hidden in the walls last night. He could barely believe it himself. And now his hopes had been realised and he had seen Eleanor here this morning. It all felt right, like they had shared something sacred.

He withdrew his mobile and sent a quick text to Tilly, and smiled when it was immediately returned with a brief, *'On my way now.'*

Will had been watching Eleanor for a little while now; first as she came and went at the penthouse and a few times in Barncroft. He had just wanted to know what she looked like, whether he would recognise anything of the skinny little girl he remembered. Seeing her now, at such a poignant moment for them both, he finally felt the connection he was looking for. And later they would meet face to face. Would she recognise him from yesterday? It had been quite a shock to come out of the site and see her walking past. The first time he had been so close to her that he could see the pain in her eyes. She was no longer the little girl he remembered; she had grown up to be every bit as strong as her grandmother. The doubt reared its head again. Perhaps this would be the start of their new life together, if she could ever forgive him for leaving her. If she couldn't then his dream of reconnecting with her would be finally dead.

He watched her fumbling at the door. She dropped her gloves, bent to pick them up, and for a second she seemed to be staring straight at him. But he was securely in the church porch, so confident he was out of sight. It was interesting that she had booked the old rectory to stay at; almost as if she knew it was connected to their family history.

26

22 December – Morning

A gloomy drizzle was falling. If Nell screwed her eyes up tight it almost looked like sleet, but the droplets on the diamond windowpanes were having none of that. She made a mug of tea in the icy kitchen and then decided to head back to bed while it might still retain some heat. Now she felt cosy and found herself drifting off to sleep again. Or was she? She could hear the church bells ringing, and in the long pauses between peels, the whine of a power tool. The radiator was clanking and somewhere a dog began to bark. She was so comfortable and exhausted after the events of last night. Nana's remains were now safely scattered, so that was a good job done.

She began to dream of the time she and Nana had turned up late to the Christmas Eve service at their local church. Not normally churchgoers, Nell had got it into her head that they should start a new Christmas tradition after seeing it in a dozen festive films that year. So, stifling giggles, they had crept into the back of the church and sung their hearts out. It had been fun, but a little long, and very cold. Nell remembered the even colder walk home afterwards. But they had sung again to keep their teeth from chattering and Nell remembered it fondly as a very Christmassy Christmas Eve.

Was she awake? Surely not because it sounded like her bedroom door had just opened. Knowing how prone she was to vivid dreaming, she decided to stay still and keep her eyes closed. There were no footsteps and already memories of her childhood were beginning to come back into focus.

Then something jumped up onto the bed. She could feel

143

light purposeful footfalls around her own feet, and then they began to move upwards. Towards her head. A deep rumble began as the cat plonked down, rested its soft head against her shoulder and began to purr. Just as she was thinking about springing up, she sank into an even deeper sleep.

Her mobile woke her. She fumbled for it but recognised the number as a particularly persistent caller who would ring once a week about the car accident she had had that was not her fault. She dropped the phone back on the bed, and it was at this moment she remembered the cat. She played it back over in her head for a while. It had seemed real but the bedroom door was still closed and there was clearly no cat, not even cat hair on the bed. A dream, then.

A siren ripped through the air as Nell finally crawled out of bed for the second time that morning. The drizzle had thickened and was looking more sleet-like now as a police car turned the corner and then disappeared. She had planned to meet Max for breakfast, though it might be more like early lunch, and then it would be time to meet her dad. How strange that sounded. She was meeting her dad at two after having lunch with Max. What a very sociable time she was having, but then after today it might become horribly quiet again.

If she had not straightened her pillow, she would never have seen it. A strip of fabric no wider than a ribbon, decorated with delicate embroidery. She simply stared at it for a moment and then, because she didn't know what else to do, picked it up and brought it to her nose. It smelt of herbs, like cooking. Rosemary. Well, that was decidedly odd. Scary? She should be scared, but instead she put the ribbon on the dressing table. Still, the wrongness of everything that had just happened, the strange dream of the cat jumping on the bed, and the ribbon, snagged at her mind and made her nervous. Not again, please. No more weirdness. Then a thought brightened her: she had brought her own pillow with her so perhaps the ribbon had fallen out of the old bedding when she had moved it. She was clutching, she knew she was, but decided to believe it and get on with her day. No more ghosts, please.

She found herself looking at the black and white print again. But this time it wasn't the children that caught her eye, but some dark pencil marks which dropped off the edge of the print. Bold strokes that looked like they belonged to a long dress or cloak, as if a woman stood on the edge of the picture, hidden from sight by the heavy frame, with just a section of her cloak creeping out. The urge to dismantle the frame, to reveal if a woman truly was hiding on the edge of the print, was so overwhelming that Nell had to remove it from the wall and push it under the sofa.

The text came when she was dressing.

'Your father sends his apologies but please can you make it tomorrow at the same time and place? Try not to be too disappointed. Do something fun with Max before she returns to London. Austin.'

Relief initially flooded through her, but it was soon chased down by crushing insecurity. He was going to back out altogether, she knew it. But surely if he didn't intend to meet her, he would simply have been a no show. Don't overreact, she told herself sternly. Another day to prepare and at least she would have a clear head.

William was nodding, but it was the first time Tilly had seen him vexed.

'I think delaying your meeting for a day is for the best,' she soothed. 'I mean *your daughter* will be emotional and it just might not give you the best chance of a reconciliation. You do agree, don't you?'

The truth was that after he had dropped *that* bombshell this morning, she needed time to think. Burying a live cat in the walls of a new house was a barbaric but common occurrence in medieval times, apparently, but it was the print next to it which had roused William's interest and sent Tilly in a tailspin. Faded and fragile, it bore the name of possibly one of William's ancestors, and in brackets after the surname had been written *Maundrell.* If the witch's blood had truly returned to the town then the Corberley heir could be in mortal danger, and she didn't mean from the silly letters the simpletons had written; from something older, something evil. She would do anything she could to prevent William meeting his daughter and finding a reason for them both to settle in North Chase.

Daisy picked up her cold coffee and took a sip. She stopped, listened, and then sighed. Silence. Oh, thank God. Ava was her little angel, but bloody hell could she ever scream. Despite what Mark said, she was certain it had only started when they had moved into this creepy old mansion. Moved back, in Mark's case. She knew it was his beloved ancestral home but it gave Daisy the creeps, and she was sure that Ava felt the same. But Mark wanted his child to grow up in his childhood home, and clearly had plans for filling up all the bedrooms with brothers and sisters for Ava. Older than her by over twenty years, she knew that he sometimes made decisions which affected them both without consulting her. She just wanted to make him happy, but Ava was only nine months old and more than enough for her currently. They had not even gone through teething yet.

The fresh scent of fir lit up the room, seeping from the naked Christmas tree standing forlornly in its pot in the bay window. Surrounding it were antique boxes which contained the Corberley tree decorations. Daisy had placed her contribution, purchased that week from an artisan shop in town, next to them. It was petty, she knew, but she felt her personality, her soul, was being dampened down and folded away in this mouldy old relic. Compromise was the order of the day, and if she must live here then she would at least try to decorate it for Christmas in her own style. She contemplated making a fresh coffee before starting on the tree, but now she was sitting down she just couldn't find the energy to move again. Her breathing settled and before long, her eyes closed. The baby monitor flickered, a rainbow of lights, and a soft humming noise drifted through the white plastic, too low for Daisy to hear in her weary state. Her breathing steadied further as she drifted into an exhausted sleep.

A loud bang woke her. She blinked, dazed for a second, and then without any more thought, raced to the nursery.

'Ok, baby girl, mamma's here.'

Maybe she had spoken too soon and Ava was teething, that would explain a lot, and she made a mental note to discuss it with her baby group. Their helpful tips on getting her settled into a sleeping routine hadn't really come to anything, but teething was a whole new subject.

For a moment she just gazed at the empty cradle, her fraying brain unable to comprehend what her eyes were telling her.

'Ava?' She picked up the blankets and looked again. 'AVA?'

Mark saw his wife's name on the mobile and sighed. Now what? Realising that it could be about their daughter, he took the call.

'Darling … no, slow down. What about Ava?'

As he sped down the road praying that he didn't meet any other traffic, his wife's tearful voice cut into his brain.

'Her cradle is empty. She's been taken.'

He threw open the heavy front door and flew upstairs.

'Daisy?'

As he rushed into the nursery, the first thing he heard was his daughter screaming as Daisy sobbed into her blonde curls.

'Hello, Ava. Daisy, what the fuck?'

'She was gone. The cradle was empty. I went downstairs to ring you and then I heard her screaming.'

He sighed to control his anger. 'You're making no sense.'

'—and she was just back.'

'So, she was never missing.'

'No, no, she was. I looked and there was no sign of her.'

'She is a baby, for Christ's sake, she can't play hide and seek.'

'Why are you shouting at me? She was gone, I tell you, and then she came back.'

'Give her to me, you're scaring her.' He took the furious bundle into his arms and fought to keep his temper. 'Mummy had a bad dream, didn't she poppet, and scared you.' And terrified me, he thought.

'I want her back in with us.'

'Not again, Daisy.'

'NO. I'll move her cradle myself, or ask Seb to help me if you won't.'

Together they carried the antique cradle down the hallway and into their bedroom while Ava gurgled, happily strapped to Daisy's back.

'I am not going mad. She vanished. This fucking house is haunted I tell you,' Daisy insisted. 'Once you've got the money for that land, can't we move back to London? I hate it here.'

Mark's mobile began to vibrate. He glanced at it and then back at his tear-streaked wife, her blue eyes sparkling with emotion.

'Right. I'll cut you a deal. Once, and only once the money is through, we'll talk about it properly. But not London, I like my job at the academy and I'm not changing it but … no, don't get excited, I just said we'd talk about it.'

Her tears soaked through his shirt as she hugged him close. Ava peered up at him with the same blue eyes. Something in his heart caught painfully against his ribs and he felt the panic and pain rise to the surface.

Later, as he ran down the back stairs and out to his car, he wondered if he should just keep driving and vanish. Run away from the threats, away from this damn house and the almighty mess he had made of everything. Again. As he turned the corner, he saw Tilly emerge from the kitchen gardens. She gave him a cheerful wave and he felt it catch in his throat. Damn her and all the other women who had him trapped here.

Tilly watched his car disappear, then dropped her hand and her smile. Well, that had been rather successful. Lordy had told her about the staircase that summer. With her help, he had pulled aside the wall hanging, fitted the big heavy key into the lock and then, with some brute force, opened the door. They had smiled at each other like two conspirators sharing a secret. Lordy recalled how he had played there as a small boy, had hidden from his nanny, because she wasn't let in on the secret. Mark knew about it too, why wouldn't he, and it was one of the reasons she was sure that he had been reluctant for Daisy to use it as a nursery. Sebastian had told her this juicy bit of information, but of course he didn't know the reason why.

As soon as she heard that Mark was moving back, she had grabbed the key from Lordy's desk, thinking about how she would creep into the house and torment him sometime. Or torment Lady Daisy. It was spiteful but so simple to pick up the brat, slip down the staircase until she heard the screaming

and crying move downstairs while Daisy rang for help—
because you couldn't get a signal in the nursery for some
reason—and then so simple to replace the child back in her
fancy cot. It took minutes, but was oh so effective. The idea
had been just to mess with her head, a spot of gaslighting. But
she would take the baby further next time. Mark knew. He
knew what she had done, but there was absolutely nothing he
could say without dropping himself in the colossal pool of
excrement she had him suspended over. Then the smile faded;
everything was accelerating faster than she was comfortable
with, and after the shock of Will's news this morning, she knew
she would have to act soon.

Tilly would have her revenge, one way or another, but no
one must ever suspect she was behind it. One thought troubled
her slightly: just before she had unlocked the secret door, she
had heard a sound that couldn't have come from the child. Just
her imagination, obviously, or the wind, but it almost sounded
like whispering. The child had been twisting her neck to look
at something in the corner of the room. For one moment, Tilly
had frozen and thought it was Daisy standing there, but of
course there was no one. Still, the door had bumped shut and
woken up Daisy sooner than she had planned. As she walked
back to her cottage, she couldn't shed a strange feeling that
something had happened in that nursery that she hadn't quite
understood.

Back at the house, Ava slept soundly while her mother watched
her tiny chest rise and fall. A little winter sun shone through
the window and in the corner of the room someone else
watched, from behind the wall.

27

22 December

'Did you know that the word 'yule' comes from the Norse word 'Juul', and the 'Juul' log was burned as a tribute to the Norse god Thor?'

Nell took a bite of the vegan pasty and let the words sink in.

'Max, why is that even remotely interesting …?'

'But it *is* interesting. Just shows how so much of our Christmas festivities have their origins from Pagan days, and from other nationalities. The Romans worshipped the winter solstice with something called Saturnalia, which …'

Nell lifted her face to warm it in the weak winter sunshine. 'Ok, enough of the Christmas history lesson. Do you want to look at the rest of the stalls or shall we get a coffee and mince pie from that place you saw?'

'And mince pies were originally made with minced sweetmeats and were crescent shaped to represent …'

'How do you know all of this?'

'How do you not? It's history, the origin of Christmas. Don't you find it fascinating to know that little things like hanging a wreath on a door has hundreds of years of history attached to it? And don't get me started on the carols we sing.'

Nell nearly choked on the pasty. 'You're not going to start singing again, are you?'

Max just smiled and muttered, 'You wish,' before she spotted someone in the crowd.

'Ric, Seb, how you doing after last night? Ric, you work in a restaurant, don't you? I bet you know the history of mince pies.'

Nell winced. 'I am so sorry, Max is giving me a history lesson.'

Ric and Seb's eyes lit up with enthusiasm and before long they were sat together.

How strange, thought Nell, that she didn't think anything of sitting outside in the cold at a Christmas—sorry, Solstice Festival—but wouldn't dream of it normally. With her hat, gloves and scarf securely wrapped round her, and with the lights sparkling, it was very festive. Ric, Seb, and Max were still talking history.

'Here's one for you both,' Ric continued. 'Did *you* know about the annual North Chase Christmas pie competition?'

Max was in her happy place, talking food with someone as excited about it as she was. But Nell was happy too. She felt lighter after scattering Nana, and if her dad turned up tomorrow at least she would have a clear head. It had all worked out for the best.

'Those mince pies you tried last night are my mum's trial run,' added Seb. 'She has been going through a load of medieval recipes she found somewhere and is bringing them up to date. Some, she reckons, date back to the plague days, which I think is totally gross.'

'Cooking is creative; an edible art form.' Ric was clearly trying to fight her corner in what seemed to be an old argument.

'It's putting ingredients together so we can eat it,' said Seb.

'No, it's a blending of flavour and texture that needs to not only taste good but look good too. It is emotion, comfort, awakening the senses. Good food is art.'

'Well, I don't always understand art. I mean, I enjoy taking photos but that's all.' Seb was clearly trying to kill the conversation, but Ric was not letting go.

'Then I'm not sure I can really explain it, but cooking is more to me than just … well, cooking. You can change someone's whole mood by just putting the right plate of food in front of them. When I was little, Mum would cook a special pudding for me when I was upset. She would pour crème anglaise over it and add whichever fruit was in season. Now, whenever I am down I make that dish and I am instantly comforted. My dream is to open a restaurant that not only feeds the stomach but the emotions, the soul.'

Seb's face had puckered. 'Umm … what the hell is cream ong … whatever you just said?' he asked, to Max's obvious amusement and Ric's chagrin.

'Crème anglaise. Custard.'

'Pudding with custard can cheer you up?'

'Yes. Don't look at me like I'm mad.'

At this point Max, who could never keep her opinions to herself for long, decided to interrupt.

'Actually, it has been scientifically proven that our mood affects what we eat, and vice versa. You just have to look at the relationship that food cravings have …'

'Really? That sounds like the rubbish people spout to make money from women like my mother.'

'Shut up, Seb. Thank you, Max, I'm glad someone understands me.'

Finally, thought Nell with amusement, someone who interrupted as much as Max did.

'I trained in mental health. Food is important for physical and emotional wellbeing.'

Seb put his hands up in surrender. 'All I'm going to say is that when you live with a mother like mine—who is currently on a low FODMAP diet, and before that it was something else that involved a blender, and whatever she put in it always turned out puke green—then you would wish people just saw food as food, and not a way to cure the world of all ills.'

Fragments of Nell's dream floated by again, of a sickly child being fed human flesh, and when she shivered this time it had little to do with the wintery afternoon. She let the happy chatter lap over her and tried to imagine what they looked like to an outsider; four friends sitting together, laughing, enjoying a Christmas catch up. Max and Ric were now talking tattoos and trying to show each other the more visible ones, and discussing whether Max should dye her hair the same shade of green as Ric's when Ric flinched.

'Oh God, Seb, your mum is over there. Shall I hide under the table?'

Seb just laughed and waved at a smart woman in a long coat, matching hat, and immaculate hair and makeup. Her face split into a tight smile when she saw Seb, then collapsed into a grimace when she spotted Ric and Max, but her expression changed again when she saw Nell. As if her jaw was broken at the hinges, her mouth fell open and her eyes reflected first disbelief and then something else that Nell couldn't quite name.

'Seb, I think we scared your mum,' commented a concerned Max. Seb laughed and said something about her always looking like that. But for Nell it was the ghost tour all over again, when Lord Corberley had first seen her, and from the looks that she was receiving now from Ric, she wasn't the only one wondering why.

'Are you going to ask them?'

Ric shook her head and seemed to have found something interesting on her boots. Nell felt curiosity stir its head, but was far too respecting of other people's privacy to ask.

'Ask them what?' Max clearly didn't have the same boundary awareness.

When it became clear that Ric wasn't going to answer, Seb responded.

'Not only has Ric been hearing ghostly laughter, she also thinks there are ghosts in the house next door to her.'

'Bloody hell, Seb. Now I sound like a right idiot.' But Ric saw Max's face light up and explained, 'Whatever it is has being going on a few weeks now. Bumps and whispers to start with. But once the family next door moved out and I still heard it, I knew something weird was happening. And it has got louder and is almost every night now. I'm not saying it's ghosts.' She shot Seb a filthy look. 'I don't normally believe in all this stuff, but it is something odd.'

'Actually, I think I heard something the other night,' said Seb, trying to earn himself a pardon.

'No, you *did* hear it. The little children …'

Now Max's eyes were practically luminous.

'He thinks I'm being stupid, but how can there be voices next door and the sound of people running up and down the stairs, when there is no one next door to do that?'

'Ric, you do know what Max does, don't you?' Nell asked.

'You said you were trained in mental health.'

'I am, but I also have what people call second sight. Well, it's all been a bit quiet on that front since we found ...' A glare from Nell stalled her for a moment. 'Not had so much as a fuzzy moment until I arrived in North Chase.'

'I didn't know that, Max,' said Nell, and immediately felt selfish. She had been so wrapped up in her own drama that she had not stopped to wonder how Max was.

'I mean if it's gone for good then that is ok, but if it suddenly comes back when I least expect it, then that will be nasty. Thought the ghost tour might have given it a jump start.'

'So you can help Ric?' asked Seb.

'We can certainly give it a go. What time does it usually all kick off?'

'After midnight,' admitted Ric.

Oh no, another ghost hunt, thought a mutinous Nell. Was she the only one thinking of getting a good night's sleep tonight, especially after last night's events? She supposed that Max was used to working stupid hours, and Ric and Seb looked like they were still teenagers so probably survived on adrenaline.

'Look everyone, I'm shattered after last night so maybe count me out.'

'But ghost children respond better to you. Please come with us. You're up for some more spooks, aren't you?' pleaded Max.

'Am I?' said Nell, then yawned pointedly.

'I think so, and Ric needs our help. You can lie in tomorrow and I'll take you for a massive breakfast.'

With that everything was arranged, and Ric seemed reassured, presumably because they were taking her seriously.

'You sure you can stay another night?' asked Nell as they walked back to the rectory.

'Dad won't mind me turning up tomorrow morning instead. I can leave for London straight after breakfast.'

'You can crash at the rectory if you want.'

'Actually, I've already asked the shepherd hut people if I

can stay another night.'

Now Nell had spent time with Max again, had acclimatised to her, she realised that she wanted her to stay, but was relieved not to have any witnesses if she suffered any more nightmares later. And somehow she had no doubt that she would.

'You know what just occurred to me? I love being a nurse, but it's not all that I am. We found Ruby, and Emily. I think you and I were put together for a reason, and it would be great to help someone else.'

'Ric and her noisy dead neighbours?'

'Well, she seemed relieved. I wonder if it is connected to anything at the manor house.' There was always something rather unsettling about Max when her brain was racing. Then, as if a coin had dropped, the wide joker smile was back. 'And, I might have not been entirely honest about something.'

It was Max's tone rather than the words that made Nell turn to her.

'What do you mean?'

'My dad. He said my brother was dropping in to see him tonight, so I might be eager for an excuse not to make it until tomorrow.'

'Didn't know you had a brother.'

'No, I forget myself most of the time, and I'm sure he does too.'

'You don't get on?'

'Put it this way: he cast me in the role of disappointment, failure, weirdo, a long time ago and now seems to permanently have something wrong with his lip when he speaks to me. Can't quite look me in the eye, sneers a lot. Patronising. Does that paint a picture?'

'Oh yes.'

'Dad always says that he and I are cut from the same cloth. A cloth that my perfect brother wouldn't wipe his arse with. But he adored my mum and so pays Dad a charitable visit twice a year. Usually stays the night before an early morning flight for his jolly family holiday with perfect wifey and precocious brats. Dad says I'm too sensitive but I—'

'Don't want to spoil your Christmas by having to put up with him?'

Max thought about this for a moment. 'It's not only that. I'm getting too old to feel uncomfortable around family members, you know? No one else thinks I'm a joke so why should I let him put me down? Anyway, something is telling me that I should be here, that I'm supposed to be here.'

Lucky Max, thought Nell, to have surplus family to waste, but then she softened at the thought that confident, bubbly Max could be belittled by her own flesh. Then another thought struck her.

'Maybe we are both supposed to be here,' and as soon as she said the words more formed in her head; she *belonged* here.

28

'You'll run your batteries down, leaving your fairy lights on like that, Nell.'

'I didn't. I never do.' As Nell followed Max into the apartment she was met with an array of pretty coloured lights. 'No, don't look at me like that. I know I didn't. It's probably faulty wiring or something.'

'Or *something*.'

'Not everything has to have a paranormal connotation.' The moment these words had left her lips, the snow globe sprung into life.

'Wow. Well, Nell my lovely, I think we have company.' Something caught Max's eye. 'This is cute, did you buy it especially?'

The little silver tree was exactly twelve inches tall.

'It was Nana's. I used to take it to the home on Christmas Eve and we'd decorate it with all the old decorations, well, what was left of them.' The memory gave the room a soft glow.

'Is that the first time the lights have gone on by themselves?'

'First time for the lights,' Nell admitted.

'Oh?'

'The snow globe. That was on when I got back from ghost hunting last night.'

Max was pacing slowly, deep in thought.

'Maybe something from the haunting followed you back here.'

'Oh great. Who do you think it is? The witch or the walled-

157

up nun?' For a moment, she remembered the feeling of being watched last night. From behind the wall. Which then brought back the dream. More dreams, nightmares; no wonder she was always tired.

'A few odd things have been happening here. Max, why aren't I more scared?'

'No need to be unless it escalates, but you did choose the most haunted looking old place to rent out at Christmas. And you do have a history of attracting ghosts, and I don't mean last night.'

'The only ghost was Ruby, and whatever that was with Emily.'

'Yeah well, you now have the 'Yule Ghoul."

'Oh, aren't you clever?'

'Yes, I rather like that myself. *Yule Ghoul.*'

It was homely, thought Nell. She tentatively suggested watching *A Christmas Carol* and was delighted when Max asked which version. Hearing the familiar sounds of her favourite film stir into the room and watching the lights twinkle, Nell was hit with something she thought she wouldn't feel this year. It was beginning to feel like Christmas, for real. Aware that she might not feel this way again, depending how things went with her dad tomorrow, Nell was determined not to miss a second of it.

'Max. What was Christmas like for you when you were little?'

Max looked at the little tree for a moment, and then smiled. 'Christmas was always in two parts, Mum and me, and then Mum, Dad and me. He always had to work some part of Christmas. He was still in uniform then, and would appear mid-morning or afternoon with his eyes twinkling and his radio crackling unintelligible conversations that only he could understand. But it was great, you know, I always loved Christmas.

'Then later, I would often work Christmas Day myself, so those with children could have the day off, and then either drive home on Christmas afternoon or, after Mum passed, Dad would come to me. We had Christmas lunch in the hospital canteen once. No, seriously, it was lovely; Dad said it was the best Christmas lunch he had had since Mum was alive, and it really was. Everyone, staff, patients, and relatives, making the day special in some way. Children running around and the place was all decorated. And whatever you think, hospital food in my experience is super tasty. There is something quite Christmassy about a hospital. Everyone would rather be somewhere else so it is sad, but a bit like it must have been in the war, I imagine. When people were in the shelters, spirit of the blitz and all that. People are even kinder, and full of the Christmas spirit. It can be fun.'

'But not this year?' asked Nell.

'No, I feel like my personality, my character, oh how do I explain it, my *soul* perhaps, is being buried in work. I need a break. And being here, right now, is setting me up nicely. Once I get to Dad's tomorrow morning I will be totally chilled. What about you, or is that too painful still?'

Nell smiled.

'Magical. Making decorations with tissue paper at primary school. Learning carols for the concert. Tinsel wings, a bent coat hanger for a halo, and my arms aloft at the nativity play.'

'Oh, *you* got to be an angel.'

'Naturally,' answered Nell with a small smile. 'Why, what were you?'

'As the tallest in the class I—'

'Wise man?'

'Wise man.'

'You got to wear a crown and hold a present, though,' Nell pointed out.

'I guess. Always wanted to be an angel, but carry on.'

Reminiscing should be sad, thought Nell, but like reading a good book, she was being magically transported back to happier times.

'I think we went to Nana's for Christmas dinner when I was small, so unwrapping presents then having to leave everything, get dressed out of pyjamas and go out into the cold. But Nana had a huge tree and there were more presents. We had a few sad ones after Dad left and Mum died, but then it settled down again.

On Christmas Eve, Nana would finally let us decorate the

hall, living and dining room. Never a day before Christmas Eve though, she was strict about that. We would troop off to the woods to collect holly and ivy, even mistletoe if we could reach any. I wore gloves so as not to get sore hands. We would always go back to the same holly tree, Nana would find it year after year and greet it like an old friend and comment on its abundance of berries.

'Why the Christmas Eve tradition? No idea, but Nana was horrified at the idea of it coming into the house any earlier. The tree might get delivered a few days before but it would not pass the threshold until the 24th.

'My room would have been decorated for weeks. A jungle of paper chains and broken garlands. Cards from school friends hanging from strings. Usually, on the night before Christmas there would be a rustling and everything would collapse onto my bed, but I remember the fantastic shadows they all made on the walls and ceilings. I even had coloured lights taped around the walls. That too usually needed repairing a few times before Christmas Day.

'Occasionally we would go to midnight Mass or the community carols, which were earlier. It was lovely. All candlelight and booming organ. We would play a game called 'the three spirits of Christmas'; there was always someone in the congregation who would be drunk and desperately trying to disguise it, they would be number one. Someone would sing too loudly and be a beat behind everyone else, they would be number two, and the final was my favourite, the enthusiastic singer who was filled with the spirit of Christmas but would be totally out of tune, making everyone laugh. Then, when we finally got home, cold, and tired, there would be hot chocolate and one present before bed.'

'Oh, you too, then,' remarked Max.

'Nana's friends would come around on Boxing Day and it was lovely, like you had disappeared into a cocoon away from the world. Even visiting Nana at the home was fun. Amazing decorations everywhere, visits to the panto, they would have entertainers perform in the lounge. Visits from donkeys, and they even had a model railway set up in the hallway with snowy houses and trees. Really incredible. Nana and I loved it.'

A mantle of pleasant memories settled over them both like soft snow. Then a thought surfaced: wherever Nana was, she now knew the whole truth about Gary and the hell Nell had been through. Knew that Nell had reached out to her dad. Knew Nell was rebuilding her life. Maybe the lights and snow globe were Nana trying to give her approval. She had a choice here, Nell decided; she could either see the paranormal occurrences as something trying to scare her, or something nice trying to bring comfort.

Max looked around the high-ceilinged room. 'Are you planning to decorate any more in here?'

'Maybe I could bring in holly and ivy on Christmas Eve. For Nana. And I have one last box of decorations.'

Many of Nell's decorations had been hastily bought in the discount shop along with packets of AA batteries, but the rest were Nana's, and therefore now her decorations. Mercifully, they had been packed in a box labelled 'Nana' and been stashed in the black cab when she had made her escape from Gary. Other bits and pieces were still in his attic. Would he bother this year? Would some other woman open that box of memories and decorate the tree which was also stashed in the attic? Aware she was in danger of bringing up upsetting memories, Nell gave herself a mental shake. The ornaments that mattered were from her childhood and were in the box in front of her. Everything else could be left behind, in the old life she had escaped.

The box was filled with polystyrene balls that had once been used to package glasses Nana had ordered. It had become the perfect vessel for the glass ornaments which spanned over 60 years. But not all were glass. Trends over the decades were represented in the silk thread baubles, plastic balls decorated in Victorian street scenes, Disney characters, a series of felt figures which had once smelt of baby powder. Wooden decorations from the German Christmas markets and some plastic stars which had been all the rage in Nana's early years of marriage. Each year it had been Nell's tradition to give Nana a new ornament, picked up from her travels, or most recently, painted by herself on wood or ceramic. She examined them now and remembered the creation or purchase of each one, and the hanging on Nana's tree.

'How can people decorate their trees in themes with all new decorations each year? A Christmas tree should be a collection of memories from Christmasses past; this has always been the most important part of Christmas for me.'

'Very true,' said Max. 'Now, let's finish watching that film of yours. I love *A Christmas Carol*, and all this reminiscing is getting me in the right mood for later.'

Oh yes, thought Nell, suddenly nervous. Another ghost hunt and this time they wouldn't be part of an organised professional investigation. Before she could internally grizzle any further they settled down to watch Ebenezer battle his last ghost in Victorian London.

29

Ric's cottage turned out to be a short distance from the old rectory, just on the other side of the church. It looked like a Christmas card with its thatched roof and tiny windows. Christmas icicles hung from the eaves, and a holly wreath set off the front door perfectly. In contrast, the adjoining cottage was dark. No twinkling festive lights and no warm light seeping through the curtains. Feeling like she was intruding, Nell followed Max through the front door and into the narrow hallway. Cosy was the first word that came to mind; her muscles seem to soak up the heat from the kitchen range, and as she relaxed she wanted nothing more than to curl up on the sofa again. She had nearly missed the end of the film because of exhaustion, but Max's singing had soon woken her up.

'I'll get some coffees on the go,' offered Ric, but Seb had other ideas.

'Let me do that, you show Max and Nell where you hear the phantom children.'

She swiped at him, clearly detecting sarcasm that was lost on Nell and Max, but took them to the staircase. Had Nell felt warm a few moments ago? Now a ripple of gooseflesh spread across her back. Old cottages were always draughty though. A little like old rectories, she thought ruefully.

'He doesn't believe me, but I usually hear something—'

She got no further because Max had held up her hand and laid her index finger gently to her lips in a plea for silence. Ric exchanged a worried look with Nell as Max gently placed her hand against the wall and closed her eyes. From the kitchen,

163

Seb was whistling as the kettle boiled, and then under it all Nell heard a different sound. It could have been pipes cooling under floorboards, she reasoned. She had read that somewhere. People thought they heard footsteps, but it was just wood or metal changing temperature. But it really did sound like the soft tread of steps on the staircase next door. Still, she reasoned, it was very late and she would probably mistake stomach rumbling for growling.

Tap tap tap.

Nell's head spun round. Why the hell was Max knocking on the wall? That was surely asking for trouble. Silence, and then the distinct sound of small palms slapping the wall next door. Nell's chest ached and she was aware she was holding her breath.

There was the faintest of giggles, and then tiny feet began to patter up and down the staircase.

'That's it, that's what I hear.'

'I think there are two of them,' said Max. 'And I think they are quite tiny.'

They all jumped as a door opened above them.

'Mum, I am so sorry we woke you.'

The portly woman in a floral dressing gown that was now padding down the stairs in her slippers just shook her head.

'How long have they been back?'

'Mum, I don't think it is the neighbours—'

'I never thought it was. You should have told me.'

Seeing Nell and Max for the first time, Ric's mum nodded hello and then disappeared into the kitchen, muttering to herself about dolls. 'You two are here to help, I take it,' she shouted over her shoulder.

Max and Nell exchanged a look.

'Ric asked us to come. We aren't experts, but we do have some experience of this sort of thing. Whatever this is,' said Max with growing confidence.

'Good. You both come with me. Erica, bolt the door after us.' She seemed to see Seb for the first time but said nothing.

'But, Mum.'

'I'll see if we can send them back.'

'Send them back where? Oh my God, what are you setting

light to?'

'Sage. It worked last time this happened.'

Max was clearly on the verge of asking a million questions, but instead followed her orders to open the front door as Ric's mum reached up to a beam and pulled out a long key. With that, the three of them left the cottage, headed down the path and opened next door's gate.

Ric's mum poked the key into the door, turned it, and then attempted to kick the door open with her foot. The door held firm.

'Back door,' came the order, so they followed her floral back, bouncing torch beam, and flickering sage through the long-frosted grass, around the side of the house and along a wall. There was a crash of plant pots and then the beam found the stable door. Just as they went into the damp hallway, two thoughts chased each other in Nell's mind. First, she wished she had stayed at the rectory. The other was something Ric's mum had said, when she was in the kitchen, that had made no sense initially, but now, with images from one of her nightmares weeks ago shuttering in front of her eyes, did.

'Someone has moved the dolls again.' Now all that Nell could see in her mind as they entered the dark house were two antique dolls slumped in a miniature rocking chair that was tipping backwards and forwards all by itself.

Max was only aware that she had been holding her breath when her lungs took a huge gulp and the stench of damp and mould stung her nostrils. The cottage had a lonely feel to it with its tiny, cramped rooms devoid of furniture. And now also devoid of paranormal sound. The patter of slippers on the wood floor led them into the hallway. In front lay the staircase where moments ago they had heard footsteps and laughter. Now nothing. Give it time, thought Max, and she purposefully let her focus drift. Her mind calmed and, concentrating on her breath, she felt the cold silence build around her.

'Did you hear that?' Nell arrived at Max's elbow.

'I don't hear anything anymore. Only you.' How vexing, thought Max. She could hear nothing, feel nothing. The burning sage had blown out during their dash to the back of the house and had been dumped on the grass, but its throat itching stench still lingered and accentuated the cloying damp. This was what she had wanted, to create the correct atmosphere for her gift to return. Surely she should feel something. There had been another strange buzz from Ric earlier when they'd met up at the festival, but that had either fizzled out or she had just got used to it. It certainly hadn't developed. She glanced at Ric's mum who was halfway up the stairs.

'Well, whatever it was has gone.' Then Max saw it, a small ball drifting like a soap bubble down the stairs. An orb or just a fleck of dust? Probably just her imagination, she thought sourly as it seemed to drift around Nell and then disappeared.

'I could have sworn I heard footsteps when we first came in.' Nell was clearly not ready to admit defeat just yet. 'Down here somewhere.' She was looking at the understairs cupboard. Ric's mum gave the handle a tug.

'Good, it's locked from this side.'

Well, that was that then. But Max remembered something her dad always said: 'You have more than two senses. You don't just see and hear.' She took a deep lungful of the thick air, trying not to choke on the stench, and then it reached her. Tobacco smoke.

'Can either of you smell that?'

'The heating is off and these old cottages get damp really fast.'

'No, something else. Like a roll up.' But despite some spirited sniffing, it was clear that only she could smell it.

'The front door is bolted from the inside. No wonder we couldn't get in,' said Nell.

'It can't be. I checked for post yesterday and I used the front door. I always do.'

Now Max felt it, as though her own heart had moved to her head and its beat was pounding in her ears.

'You sure no one else has been here?'

'Absolutely.'

'I don't understand. Why is that important?' asked Nell.

'Because if no one has been in here but me, how did the front door get bolted?' said Ric's mum.

'Ghosts?' ventured Nell. 'Max, you're psychic. Do you feel anything here?'

'Actually, I don't feel anything. Yet again.'

It was as they trooped towards the front door that Max felt the first shiver of unease. She found her eyes resting on the locked under stairs cupboard again, and recognised the unsettling feeling that she was being watched. As they went back into the fresh icy air, she sent up a silent prayer of gratitude that the cupboard door had been locked, because whatever was causing the feeling of disquiet had felt more of this world than the other. It had felt dangerous and very real.

Coffee was poured, and Seb and Ric were told of the empty and silent house next door.

'Maybe we chased them away,' said Max half in jest.

'Or maybe they got what they wanted,' said Ric's mum, and before they could ask her to expand, she asked, 'So, how was the manor house last night? Erica didn't really tell me much.'

Ric recounted the events at North Chase Manor, with Max chipping in. Then, with wry amusement, Ric admitted she was keeping one ear open for any noises from next door, but there was none.

Max was just finishing off another large coffee and was beginning to gather up her coat when she realised just how quiet Nell was. She was cradling her empty coffee cup and brushing its smooth surface against her bottom lip, eyes fixed on the hallway wall.

'Nell?'

'Hmm?'

'You ok?'

'Tired.'

Max thanked her hosts and promised to share any interesting footage from the ghost tour. Nell had one arm in her coat when she suddenly said, 'What did you mean when you said, "someone has moved the dolls again?"'

Ric's mum looked at Seb for a moment before answering.

'Somewhere in the manor house there is a secret staircase that leads outside. No, Erica, it is not just a story, it is fact. Probably built to help priests make a hasty escape in medieval times. During the Second World War there were barracks built by the lake and the main house was used as a hospital. One of the patients was found hiding two dolls, centuries old, and wouldn't say where he had got them. The vicar took them to the rectory for some reason, and apparently the next night several children went missing. Most of them were found the next day in the woods, shaken and confused, but two young boys were never found, and the soldier said he'd had a dream telling him that the dolls should be returned. These cottages were used by some of the doctors and they reported that they'd heard children playing on the stairs late at night. They thought it was the two missing boys, but of course there was no one there. In fact, across the town people reported hearing children playing and singing and laughing in the middle of the night when their own children were safe in bed.

'The soldier returned the dolls from wherever he had taken them and the hauntings stopped. I've lived in this cottage since I was a child and I heard those footsteps myself. My mother lit a bunch of sage, woke up our neighbours and cleansed the house. She used to work at the manor and said that there had been some building work going on there at the time. I don't know, but I wonder if something got moved accidentally.'

'Maybe the dolls are locked in a box or chest and it got moved unintentionally,' suggested Seb. 'Daisy says she hates it up there, that she hears footsteps at night.'

'Yes, maybe when they moved in something was knocked. The sage worked last time; I only remember one night of noise.'

'You've never told me this before, Mum,' said Ric quietly.

Ric's mum gave them both a shifty look. 'No, well, I hoped I wouldn't have to. There is already too much superstitious rubbish about ghosts and witches in this town.'

Nell was paling by the second, her lip quivering slightly.

'Nell? You ok?'

'Max, you know I told you that the nightmares are back?'

'Yes, nasty eating dreams.'

This earned her a shocked look from Ric's mum.

'But I didn't tell you about the other one. To be honest, I had forgotten it until the last few days. But it involved two dolls with cloth faces and real hair, sitting on a child's rocking chair.

That was rocking all by itself.'

'Oh, why didn't you tell me your dreams were back before last night?' said Max.

'Because I wanted you to think I was getting past what happened in September.'

'I think it is going to take us both a long time to get past that.' She was aware that they had a very interested audience and, like Nell, had no wish to discuss recent events. Time for a subject change.

'Come on, let's get back.'

'To the rectory?'

Nell's obvious concern was not lost on their hosts who exchanged looks.

'Be careful, over there,' said Ric's mum. 'Don't go picking up anything that you find *left* in strange places.'

'Like ribbons or strips of embroidery? Too late for that.'

As Max trudged back down the dark road, she wondered how a night that was supposed to be fun had turned into something so unsettling.

'Are you being left presents or tokens?' she asked. 'Be careful.' For the first time she wondered if perhaps her suggestion to visit Ric's had been rather ill advised. She couldn't get rid of the idea that somehow they were being played. She thought her gift had gone, and tonight would have happened with or without her, but she also felt adrenaline coursing through her body and her mind was tingling. She felt alive, properly alive for the first time since September.

You can't help her this time, and you shouldn't try.

Oh, bollocks to that. Her gift was trying to wake up again, she could feel it, and if Nell was experiencing her nightmares again and being targeted by spirits, well it had nothing to do with her. On 1st November she hadn't even booked last night. But the qualm of guilt wouldn't go away as she looked at Nell's pale face and large eyes reflecting the dim porch light.

'I'll make you a cuppa.'

Nell was shaking her head. 'I am so exhausted that I will probably be unconscious as soon as my head hits the pillow. A whole gaggle of ghosts could dance on the bed and I wouldn't hear.'

'Gaggle of ghosts?'

'Or your *yule ghoul*. Anyway, you promised me breakfast, or brunch, or whatever. Don't you leave for London without seeing me first.'

A little colour had returned to her cheeks. Max waited while Nell opened the heavy door and then waved goodbye.

Halfway through the doorway, Nell stopped. 'Oh, and Max?'

'Yeah?'

'About last night. It really was a good Christmas present. The ghosts are always with me, I think I will just have to get used to that, but it is so much nicer, safer, when I'm with other people. I mean it, thank you.'

'See you at breakfast, then.'

The mist appeared as she headed back on the quiet roads to her shepherd's hut. Through it she could just make out a building sign advertising 'Maundrell Mews, luxury family homes coming soon'. Not the name Max would have come up with, but then everyone seemed to be cashing in on the plague story. Perhaps North Chase was a junction of ley lines and the whole town had magnetic or magical properties underground. Max was surprised the local spring water wasn't being bottled and advertised as a cure for all the ills of the medieval and modern age. Whatever the truth was, North Chase certainly seemed to be on the up, and getting a facelift and some extensions into the bargain. Now she was here, and having the time of her life, she felt like she would be leaving the party early if she headed for London tomorrow.

Later, as she snuggled into her bunk, her mobile buzzed. She smiled, expecting Nell, but it was a message from Austin.

'How are you both; having fun?'

'I'm not sure. Last night was great, as I told you, but tonight was a bit weird.'

'Is Nell alright?'

'Yes, don't worry.'

'I will try.'

Then a thought struck her. 'Found out that there is a secret staircase at the manor, it leads outside.'

The reply came back quicky.

'Just as I thought.'

As she tried to settle down to sleep, a thought kept playing in her mind. Somewhere in the big manor house there was a secret passage. What if it went somewhere else and not just outside? When she had been a student nurse, she had completed a stint in a secure unit which had previously been a Victorian asylum. In the basement, bricked up, you could still see the outline of passageways that had led to other parts of the hospital, under the public road, and even to the nearby railway station. In the days when the mentally unstable must not be seen by the public, it had allowed a safe way for their movement without troubling anyone or upsetting the patients themselves. There had been a house just outside the grounds which was used for alternative therapies and one of the passageways apparently led there. Max had never been inside, it had been boarded up and abandoned decades before, but one of the older nurses remembered hearing footsteps leading up to a door on the lower floors. Old hospitals always had ghost stories, but as she finally began to drop off all she could see was the door under the stairs in the cottage, and the unsettling feeling that it was easily large enough to conceal someone hiding.

30

23 December – 1.30a.m.

Daisy's bare feet hit the cold floorboards before she was fully awake.

'Hush baby, mamma's here.'

But Ava was snuffling contentedly in her cradle. Daisy stared dumbly at her for a moment. What had woken her? A creaking floorboard outside their room gave her the answer, as did the empty bed and the missing mobile phone from Mark's side. Her husband was on night manoeuvres again. Damn him; this was all supposed to stop once they moved here. As she opened the bedroom door, his voice drifted from the gallery. What was it this time; some seedy website or an online game? He would normally have slunk into his study for something like that.

'I'll meet you by the old chapel.'

Oh, a delivery then; pills.

A large house just meant even more space between them, more excuses for him to disappear out of sight. In the London apartment, they had been cramped but so much happier. Then Ava had come along, the old lord had died, and everything had gone to shit. Neither of them was sleeping well, and having Ava in with them wasn't helping, but Daisy needed her close by and Mark seemed to be coping by relying on pharmaceuticals.

Now other voices reached her, voices that whispered and giggled. Slamming the bedroom door shut, she realised too late that she had woken Ava.

'Sorry, darling. Mummy is just being stupid. Go back to

sleep angel girl.' Large blue eyes watched her as she stroked Ava's silky curls, and then, with a flutter, her eyelashes returned to rest against her petal soft skin. Daisy resisted the urge to scoop her up, instead she settled herself back onto the bed and listened to her daughter's snores. Doing so meant she was tuned in again to all the other noises, and in this damn house there were plenty at night. What was worse, she wondered, the creeping footsteps as her husband went to get his drugs, or the giggling of the ghostly children that haunted this relic? Paranormal investigation, what a laugh, they should have stayed with her, then they would have heard all the ghosts they wanted. The children weren't too bad generally, but in the last few weeks there had been another presence; one that felt malevolent and seemed to scare the children away. It certainly scared her and Ava. So far she hadn't seen any of the ghosts, and that was the only reason she hadn't packed up and left. Whispering, soft footsteps, giggling, and now this icy draught and a sense of being watched. The old nursery had been filled with such an evil presence Daisy could practically choke on it, and now it seemed to have moved in here. With Ava. Because of Ava.

Should she write another letter? She had been sure that the last one would scare Mark enough to take them back to London. He said they would talk about it after Christmas, but how could she explain that the closer they got to Christmas, the more paranoid she was getting? If this had been her house, if he would only listen to her ideas, they would kick Tilly out, move into the cottage themselves and market this house as a wedding or conference venue. Seb was showing promise as a photographer, Erica could do the catering, and she and Mark could oversee the business. And one thing Daisy knew how to do was organise a top-end party. But no, he wanted to scuff around playing Lord of the Manor, getting in everyone's way at the academy and upsetting the locals. He had been furious when he'd discovered the opposition to his building plans, and now the local lad who had been one of the main ringleaders was missing and there were posters up in town asking for news of him.

Daisy's eye drifted over their wedding photo. Marry in

haste, regret at leisure. Is that what the old people said? Well, she didn't regret marrying him. She knew he might not be perfect, but she had what she wanted; a home, a name, and a beautiful child.

A draught made her shiver and her eyes shot to the door. The handle was turning, slowly. First one way and then the other. Testing the door. The temperature dropped further. Soft whispering started again. This time it was inches from her ear.

'Go and haunt your fucking lord,' she hissed, and went to sit next to Ava's cradle, her arm across it.

'And bring back Ava's ragdoll.'

The door handle was given one last violent twist, and then feet pattered away.

Someone, or rather *something* in this house wished Ava harm. She could feel it like only a mother could, and she was fully prepared to do anything to protect her child. If that meant packing her bags and walking out on Mark just before Christmas then so be it. The evil was getting closer and closer, bolder and bolder, and she was receiving their warning loud and clear.

31

The winter sun was strong and pure, but sections of the grass were still crusted in ice where the trees blocked its power. After so many days of gloom the park was filled with visitors again, dog walkers, children on bikes, families who were walking off a large breakfast. The festivities were just days away now and there was a feeling of holiday in the air. Muddy looking swans basked in the sunlight and pecked at the grass as a small boy was warned by his father not to go near them for fear of broken limbs. Further up the river, a chocolate Labrador was hard at work sniffing the bushes, then as he got closer to the water he began to bark excitedly.

Hours later police tape fluttered like festive bunting in the sun and the waterlogged grass was carved with deep muddy tyre tracks. DCI Kowalski stared down at the body which lay tangled, half-submerged in the tree roots. Why couldn't this have happened either last month or next month? Why did it have to be right before Christmas? The waterlogged body below her was someone's son, boyfriend, perhaps even husband. There would be presents under the tree with his name on, and now this Christmas and each one after it would be blighted forever by his death. No Christmas would ever be looked forward to again because first his family would have to get through the anniversary of his death. DCI Kowalski looked up at the sky and wished that whatever this was—accidental death, overdose, murder—that it had not been today.

Three miles away, Finn's mum was scrolling through Facebook, reading messages of support as yet another day arrived and still there was no news of him. Deep in her heart kindled a small spark of hope that he had just buggered off to a mate's, had too much wacky baccy and would turn up on Christmas Eve smelling like shit and nursing a hangover. Then she read something that turned every drop of blood in her body into a sharp icicle. Something was kicking off in the park. A massive police presence. And she read the words she had been dreading: an unidentified body found in the river. The roar which erupted from her mouth was half anger, half despair, and an old woman pushing an equally old pram on the rough pavement outside stopped when she heard the sound, and turned to face the house it had come from.

Every daydream Nell had ever conjured about reconnecting with her dad now bubbled to the surface of her consciousness. The gush of love that ended in them running to each other, crying and hugging. Him asking for forgiveness and her saying how much she had missed him. Whatever the script, and it had changed over the years depending on her age and her need at the time, it always ended in her feeling that a key had been turned, something finally unlocked, and suddenly her life would become complete. It wouldn't bring Mum or Nana back, but she would be part of a family again.

As she walked into the pub, the moment had finally come. He pushed his chair back on seeing her, mouth open to speak, a moment of confusion while he looked behind her, and Nell, who was suddenly paralysed, realised that she would have recognised him anywhere. He was older, obviously, shorter than she remembered, with more lines and greying hair, but his eyes and the expression in them dropped memories of being a child again from a great height. While she stood and stared, she waited for the tsunami of love and happiness to flow over her. Instead, she just felt a cold rage starting in her feet and making its way up to her heart which began to beat erratically, and not in a good way.

'Eleanor? Oh my God, it is …'

'It is Nell. No one calls me Eleanor. Which you would know if you had bothered to get to know me over the last twenty-three years.'

His smile faltered.

'Oh, not what you expected? Did you not think I would be angry? You've known where I was all this time and you didn't bother to get in touch. You didn't even bother to turn up at your own mother's funeral.'

To her chagrin, her voice wavered at this point and mutinous tears pricked her eyes.

'I am sorry, Nell. Sorry for all of it.'

'You just walked out and never came back. Who does that? Who leaves their wife and daughter without a word?'

Something flickered in his eyes as he looked down. Nell's mouth was still open, the magazine full and ready to fire with over twenty-three years of hurt and anger, but she was stalled by the odd, shifty look in his eyes.

'What? Did you try to get in touch? Because I don't remember that you did.'

He pulled a face, but seemed reluctant to put his thoughts into words. Or was still trying to think of a good excuse or lie, thought Nell.

'Well?'

'There are things you don't know—'

'Clearly. Let's quantify that, shall we? I know absolutely *nothing.*'

Something seemed to have shifted in his head, and decision made, he looked her in the eye again and motioned for her to sit down.

'Your mother and I weren't getting on and she asked me to move out for a bit to give her space to think.'

This was news to Nell, but now the information was flowing she knew to keep quiet and let it continue.

'We had talked about moving to Canada at the end of term. We'd filled in all the forms and they had even offered me a teaching job in Vancouver.'

Canada? Never had she heard her mother or Nana mention emigration.

'But your mum's health issues were causing concerns and it looked like it would be just me moving to start with. Your nana offered to take you both in while things got ironed out.'

Nell still wasn't sure how much of this she believed, but

177

she could decide that when she had heard the whole story.

'We had a big row and she told me to go to hell, to Canada, to wherever I wanted. So I stayed in a hotel that night, and then over the next few days I heard on the news that Ruby Morgan was missing.'

Now he was looking at his feet again. And the expression on his face made Nell think of only one word: guilt. But he hadn't had anything to do with Ruby's disappearance; it had all been a coincidence that they both disappeared at the same time. So what was going on here that she didn't understand?

'Look, there is no easy way to tell you this, and if I'd had it my way you never would have needed to know.'

Suddenly Nell didn't want to know, but it was clear that he intended to unburden himself, for his own mental health and to hell with hers.

'Ruby's mum and I—it was years ago, before I was serious with your mum—well, she and I ...'

At that moment two things happened: she became conscious that her stomach contents had frozen over and were leaking acid over her lungs and heart, making breathing painful. Then a swarm of black spots filled the room, blinding her.

'Sorry, I shouldn't have blurted it out like that.'

Nell flinched at how close his hand was to hers. 'Are you ok?' he asked.

'Just say it,' she snapped.

'Ok. Ruby's mum and I had an affair. But I swear I didn't know she was married. Not at all. I only found out about a week before Ruby went missing that she ...'

'Oh my God.'

His expression changed as horrific realisation flooded Nell's veins.

'Don't tell me Ruby was my *sister?*' Her words fell into a sharp cold silence and the man in front of her looked like he'd been shot. She was aware that a siren was screaming through the street outside, and then as if a spell had been broken—

'No, absolutely not. But her mum tried to hint that she was mine. Look, it was a terrible mess. She must have been pregnant with Ruby at the time and then tried to blame it on me. Then she realised I was Ruby's teacher and ...'

178

'Did *she* ... did Ruby know?'

'It was all lies, remember. Her mother was a piece of work.'

'But she died next door to Nana's house.'

'Look, I didn't know anything about that. I didn't know who that Aaron bloke was, or why they were there. Her disappearance had absolutely nothing to do with me.'

'So why did you run?'

'I was leaving anyway. And when I told your mum what Ruby's mum was saying, she kicked me out, so I took the chance to go to Canada as I'd planned. I just went a little earlier. I thought they'd find Ruby, and that your mum would calm down, get her head sorted, and then you'd both move over with me.'

A thought struck Nell.

'Did Nana know all this? Where you were?' The look in his eye told her everything. 'Of course she did. The solicitor told me that you were a 'separate matter.''

'Yes, she left me her old house in her will. I know she left you the penthouse. She also intended to leave you her jewellery and—'

'Oh, of course. I saw you yesterday, didn't I?' snapped Nell. 'Why didn't I recognise you ... why didn't you tell me who you were?' He was looking uncomfortable again. 'Oh, so you obviously recognised me ...' Then the pieces slotted into place as she remembered his initial confusion. 'Did you think I might bring Austin with me? Be grateful I didn't.' The flies were beginning to gather again so she took a deep breath, imagined Austin was indeed with her and switched to safer ground. 'So, tell me about the house.'

He looked grateful for the change of subject. 'Yeah. She knew I'd retrained in the building trade and thought I'd like something of hers to do up.'

'History teacher to builder? Bit of a change.'

'Yes, well, I found I'd sort of lost my love of teaching. I wanted to do something physical, and I'd always been interested in construction. Took me years, and I'm still learning, but it's what I love. But I'm teaching again too; a few hours a week at Cedarwood, and some private work on the history of North Chase, so I should be able to afford to get some of the tricky bits done by the professionals. Your nana used to talk about this house when I was little. It was her grandparents', so your great, great ...'

'Yeah, I get it.'

'Ok.'

'But I still don't get how you could just leave Mum and me like that. She was so sick. She got worse. Bloody hell, she died, and I had to live through all that.'

'I know, I'm sorry.'

'But not enough to come back and comfort me. To take me to wherever you were.' Nell's voice began to rise as the anger bubbled up again.

'I couldn't come back to Wiltbury.'

'No, but you could have taken me with you. Or sent for me. Nana could have flown over with me.' The injustice of it all was making Nell shout now.

'Your nana said you were settled, and anyway you can't just take a child overseas like that.'

'I wasn't settled. It was so hard. You have no idea. Mum just fell apart when you left. Got sicker and sicker, and then she was gone and I had no one.' What was it that he didn't get?

'You had your grandmother.'

'Yeah, thank God. She has been better than both of you put together. I mean she was ... You should have come to her funeral.'

Finally she saw the sadness in his eyes.

'She wrote to me when she was diagnosed and told me not to come. Said that she would make sure you were well taken care of in her will. You'd have some of her property and, of course, her jewellery box. Let me see, I remember pendants, rings that had been handed down through the family.' Nell shot him a look of disgust. 'Anyway, like I said, I couldn't come back. By then things had got more complicated with Ruby's dad. He was still looking to blame me.'

'You do know it was me that found her body in September, don't you? I'd had these horrible reoccurring nightmares about her since I was a kid. I saw her that Halloween night, you see. Saw her go down into the basement of Butlers Yard and never come back up. And I saw him, the boy in the long leather coat and Halloween mask, but I was too young to realise exactly what I'd seen.'

Silence. In Nell's head she was back in her nightmare, but then she found herself standing in the stale cellar with Max as the key she had kept in her scrapbook for twenty-three years was slotted into the lock and the door was finally opened. Instead of the pile of clothes on the floor which encased what was left of Ruby, she saw Nana's face the last time she had seen her alive. Eyes as wide as a child's, searching the room in confusion, birdlike fingers clutching and plucking at the hospital blanket.

'This was a mistake.' Nell stood, collided with a table, then dashed blindly for the door.

'Nell, please.'

She let the slamming door answer him.

Brushing the tears away, she marched down the street, bolting for safety. The pavement was narrow so she stepped onto the road to overtake a woman with an oversized handbag and uncomfortable looking high-heeled boots. Along with the *click click* of her stiletto heels, something was also jangling rhythmically from her bag. Nell could tell how close behind her the woman was because of the noise she was making. It was like being followed by an alpine cow with its ringing bell.

The next person she had to overtake was a young man in a fraying denim jacket. He was easier owing to the severe limp. Now she had the clicking and clattering, and a shuffling sound behind her. But still she could hear her father's voice, his real voice, saying, 'there is no easy way to say this.' Was Ruby her sister? And then as the next obstacle in her path forced her on to the road again, a thought surfaced in her churning emotions: was it just nightmares that had led her to find Ruby, or had it been the same as Emily? Had she been picking up her distress signals, but in Ruby's case from the grave? Was that because they were related? She'd lived with Gary long enough to know when someone was desperately backtracking into a lie, and she was almost certain that this was what she had seen her father just do. No, not her father, her real father belonged to her past. From now on she would just think of him as William.

'Sorry. I'll walk in the road, shall I? Get myself run over, shall I?' she snapped as an old woman stopped abruptly in front and Nell nearly knocked into the pram she was pushing. For a second her ears blocked out all sound as she looked at the jumble of knitted toys, dolls, and bears in the pram. On the top lay a beautiful rag doll which looked oddly out of place and strangely modern. Shame washed over her for being so unkind, but the old woman had turned off into a narrow alleyway between the houses.

'Sorry,' whispered Nell, and then fury rose in her again as a couple walking hand in hand forced her off the pavement again. Good thing there was little traffic here because she was spending most of her time in the road. Then a car blasted its horn and screeched to a halt behind her. Walking on defiantly, she hoped it wasn't her father chasing after her.

'Nell, what the hell?' Max took one look at her face, and then gestured to the passenger seat. 'In. Now.'

Like an obedient child, Nell scrabbled into the car, put on her seat belt, and stared at the windscreen wipers as they swept away the dusty pellets of snow which had started to fall.

'You don't need to tell me anything. I was just on my way to see you—we didn't say a proper time did we—and then, there you are in the middle of the road?'

'I just met my dad,' Nell blurted out.

'Oh? *Oh*. I mean, was it planned?'

'Austin found him. Nana came from here originally and I scattered her ashes yesterday morning. And *he* is here because Nana left him a house. Austin arranged for us to meet but I was just so angry. I shouted a lot and then I walked out.'

They were parked at the back of the rectory now. The snow had turned to sleet and was sucking all colour from the sky. Finally, she turned to find Max's eyes full of understanding.

'I've just totally blown it. All these years I waited for this moment, and then I go and wreck everything. But he was saying stuff about Ruby's mum and him.'

'Nell, he walked out on you. You've bottled up a lot of anger in that time. He is going to have to let you purge first before you two have any chance of reconciliation.'

'I don't know what to do,' Nell wailed.

'Don't do anything. Let everything settle and then decide whether you want to meet him again. You are here for the next few days, and if he lives here now there will be other opportunities.'

'No, there won't. He'll run a mile from his mad daughter. He'll think I'm crazy bonkers like my mum was. And anyway, he said he'd had an affair with Ruby's mum and she thought Ruby was his.'

'Holy shit.'

'He then said it was rubbish, but I'm not sure I believe him.'

Max took a deep breath. 'Well, that really is a lot to have dumped on you. All those empty years between you, you might just have to draw a line and start again. But don't do anything for now, and I doubt you've blown anything because surely he expected you to be angry.'

Nell wiped her eyes on a paper napkin she had found in her coat pocket.

'Ok. I don't have to do anything?'

'No. Apart from make us a cup of tea. And you're not crazy bonkers, just bruised.'

Sirens ripped through the air. 'Is something going on?' asked Nell as she opened the car door. 'I've been hearing them off and on for hours now.'

'Yeah, well, I got a little held up on my way over here. The police are all over the park. I think they found a body.'

Nell froze in the act of turning the front door handle. 'Actually, I don't think I want to know, Max.'

'No. I think you have enough to deal with.'

It was soothing to hear Max's voice booming in the hallway again. On heavy legs, Nell climbed the stairs and outside her door, dropped the key.

'No, let me.'

Tears fell like melting snow, and Nell let Max steer her to the sofa, sit her down, and then start banging and clattering in the kitchenette.

'Thank you, Max. I'm sorry I am so pathetic.'

The apology was swept away.

'I'm a nurse, I mend people. Can't help it. You fall over and I'll want to clean you up, put a plaster on it. Burst into tears and I'll give you a shoulder to cry on.'

Nell tried to pull herself together.

'Oh, this is nice.'

Max was holding what looked like a posy of dried flowers.

'Is it?' attempted Nell, while a thought rose uninvited that she had not seen it before in the apartment, so it was clearly another unwanted offering from the haunted rectory. 'I'll put it with the ribbon and antique embroidery, shall I?'

'Interesting. Rosemary, for remembrance,' said Max softly. Tea made, she brought it over and, grabbing a wooden chair, sat down. 'Now, tell me about meeting your dad, but only if you want.'

'Actually Max, I don't think I can. Can we change the subject? Talk about something else.'

Max looked across at the posy of rosemary and took a sip of her tea.

'Right, let me see. Oh, my father rang me today, said he's got tickets for the ballet tonight. My miserable brother's gone home, so it's just me and him. Oh shit, I'm an idiot. You've just had the most horrendous day, family wise, and I'm bleating on about my dad and moaning about my brother.'

'It's fine, I did say I wanted a subject change—'

'No, it isn't. It's Christmas. My goodness, is that more decorations?'

'Last few. I kept these back, thought I'd hang them after I met … him. They were Nana's, and possibly my grandparents' before that. This one was always my favourite.'

A little felt angel, with an embroidered face and lace wings, twirled from her finger.

'I remember Nana mending this when I was a little girl. She used new felt, and lace from an old handkerchief that had a huge hole in it. I always hung it on the tree each year, she wouldn't let Dad do it, said it had to be one of the Montague women.'

'Exquisite.' Something in Max's voice made Nell look at her again. She was staring at the angel with a totally blank look on her face.

'Max? Max?'

'Hmm? How very strange, that little angel gave me quite an

odd sensation then.'

'Odd how?'

'Not sure. Like a shadow passed over me or like something ringing loud in my head. It has gone now but it was quite strange.' The blank look was still blotting Max's face.

'It is very old.'

'Yeah, that's probably what it was. I got a sense of all the people who had touched it over the years. I think it may have only been a Christmas decoration for a short time.'

'Well, they didn't have Christmas trees until Victorian times.'

'It reminds me of a poppet.'

As soon as Max uttered the word, Nell felt as if North Chase had been hit with an earthquake. First, she tilted one way, then the other. All she could see was the pram of dolls from her dream, and then the pram she had just seen in the street. A sensation of floating attacked her, as if she was floating above it all.

'Low blood sugar, that's what that is. No, keep your head between your knees. Do as nurse Max tells you. Good thing I saw you wobble and then caught you before you crashed down.'

Nell took some more steadying breaths. 'I think it was because you just said one of the words that we shouldn't say for some reason.'

'Take another breath, you sound like a cat when someone accidentally treads on their tail.'

Nell was remembering how the same thing had happened in Launton when Max had said the word 'starving'. It had all been quite innocent, but it had triggered something in the universe, like a pull on a line or something, that had sent a huge ripple to them. That time it had been because of poor Ruby.

Poppet. She even felt nervous saying it in her head.

'Why do things like this always happen around us?'

'Well, we have gone hunting for ghosts twice since we got here. I've been working too many nights and your nightmares are back. Neither of us have had much restful sleep recently. Oh, and I am still psychic and you … well, I don't know what you are, but you do seem to collect hints of things going on that then reveal themselves to you in your dreams.'

'Max? That word that we are not going to say out loud again. No, don't say it. Yes, that one. What exactly is it? I mean, I think I know but—'

Max frowned to think. 'A doll, really. Nothing more sinister. But there are some thoughts that witches might have used them.'

'Like a voodoo doll, for sticking pins in?'

'Do you know, I'm not sure? May I hold the angel again?'

'Here.'

Max's eyes closed as the small decoration was folded between her long fingers. 'My God, it's like one of those cat toys at the ghost hunt. It's practically flashing at me.'

'Are you seeing anything?'

'No. but I've just got a sense that it is … home.'

'Home?'

'Yeah, it doesn't make any sense to me either. But now I've said it out loud, I know that the word is right. It is where it came from. What's inside it? It's very heavy.'

This threw Nell. 'Is it?'

'Yeah, feel.'

As Nell lay the small angel in the palm of her hand, she realised that the weight just didn't make sense.

'I have absolutely no idea, I've never really thought about it.'

'Look, shall I ring my dad and say I'll be late.'

Nell smiled and shook her head. 'No, you need to go, but thank you for everything. For both ghost hunts and for listening to me. I can't imagine trying to deal with all of this on my own. Thank you for being here.'

'That's what friends are for. And we are a triad, though I'm not sure where Austin is, he hasn't responded to my text.'

'Triangle?'

'No, triad, it means … three.'

'Like a triangle?' laughed Nell.

'Yes, well, I'm the psychic; Austin has no moral compass so is the brute force, door breaker; and you …'

'Yes, what do I do?'

Max smiled kindly. Well, you, girl, seem to attract all kinds of spooky shit, so we just charge you up and let you loose. They find you, don't they; the living and dead who are in trouble. Not physically, but astrally.'

'Why do I always feel like I need a dictionary when I'm with you.'

'Like Emily. You saw her, but she was still alive. Doppelganger, remember?'

'I wish I didn't.'

Max grimaced. 'Look, I've got to hit the road, but if it all gets too much, hop on a train, and come to London. Don't suffer alone.'

Max's professional smile slid off her face the moment she got behind the car wheel.

'Austin? Call me when you get this. All hell's let loose and Nell is not ok, and I've got to get back to London. Wish you'd warned me that she was seeing that father of hers today.'

As she crawled through town, an unbidden vision hit her of the little felt angel. She had wanted her gift to come back and now she could practically hear it stomping up to her door. She turned a corner and drove past the field with the dead tree, its boughs pointing to the sky like fingers fractured by an iron bar. Max slammed on her brakes as the image smacked her in the face, of fresh blood on white skin glistening in firelight. Closing her eyes just brought it closer until she could hear the snap and screams.

Oh God, not like this. Her mouth filled with bile and her burning eyes began to water. She cared about Nell, worried about her, but this Christmas she needed to take care of herself too. She turned on the radio and flicked until she found something festive, but still the stench of blood plucked at her guts. Grabbing the air freshener hanging from her gear stick, she breathed in the bubble gum fragrance. She had to get out of this town and away from the miasma that lurked here. Ignoring the angry car horn behind her, she headed back to the main road, the road that would take her to London.

32

Nell flicked through the book on the myths and legends, but then threw it aside. The ghost hunt had passed, and Max gone. Her fairy lights twinkled coloured beams against the paintwork and her tree sparkled with its decorations, but this only brought memories of Christmasses past to the surface, of happy times with people who were gone forever. Voices from the other apartments seeped under the door, and again she felt the solitude. Alone again. The walls seemed to weep oppression, almost as if the room was holding its breath before letting out a scream. It felt like it was watching her; waiting. This was supposed to be an exciting adventure. It had been good so far, but then she realised it was because she had been busy with people around her. Now Max had gone, Austin wasn't replying, her dad would probably never want to see her again, and the wave of loneliness paralysed her.

But she was used to being alone and she had options. Trains left for London every few hours, although her pride wouldn't let her take up Max's offer. Better to be alone at Christmas than be a charity case. She'd met her dad, and maybe she had expected too much from the first meeting. This cheered her a little. Perhaps she should ask Austin to send him a message. Then her cheer was snuffed out. Austin hadn't replied to her last few texts. Perhaps everyone was just tired of her drama. It was Christmas and they didn't want her bringing them down. Even she wouldn't want to be with her.

She had been prepared to come here to spend time by herself, but then she had met up with Max and Austin, and even seeing Ric and Seb yesterday had been fun. Now they had all gone. Party over. And she was alone, without a family, and no closer to becoming the Nell she wanted to be, that she dreamed of being, when she had finally escaped Gary. However, a feeling of being in the right place at the right time still nudged her. Perhaps this feeling of misery was nothing more than her changing gear in her life, the uncomfortable phase of leaving the familiar and entering something new. The first time she had stepped foot in the penthouse, it had felt like trespassing, but now it was home in every sense of the word. She needed to take control.

Grabbing her sketchbook and pencils from the side of her case, she began to write a list.

Date	Nightmare
1 Nov	Something about flames and a crying baby.
5 Nov	Dolls on a rocking chair & plague mask.
7 Dec	Children without faces and porcelain doll climbing out of an old pram.
20 Dec	Cannibalism.
22 Dec	Walled up alive with hag.

Clearly evidence of a very disturbed mind. She read back over her list and began to doodle down the side. Large wheels, a hooded carriage, and an ornate handle. Her pencil scratched across the paper as she concentrated on the finer details of the antique pram. The sound was calming and muffled all the other noises around her; the squawking crows and the irritating alarm of a lorry, which apparently felt it was necessary to explain repeatedly that it was reversing. The radiator decided to join in, and then, drifting up from the street below, she heard the unmistakeable sound of humming. Startled, Nell rushed to the window, but it was just the old woman pushing her pram of knitted dolls again. Nell felt a pang of guilt for shouting at her earlier. Just a poor eccentric woman who had probably once been a nanny, or perhaps lost a child, and here she was being nasty just because she seemed to be wherever Nell was.

There had been doll therapy used to great effect at Nana's home, and although it was sad to see some of the patients with severe dementia cuddling their stuffed toys or pushing their dolls in their three-wheeled walkers, there was no doubt that they gave a great deal of comfort to those who had them. Nell was reminded of how she had once seen a small boy in the hospital waiting room comforting his toy dog, when it was obvious he was the one who was frightened.

A prickle of unease started between her shoulder blades as she watched the spokes of the pram turn. There was something pitiful and unsettling about the dusty pram of old toys and the shuffling woman. The unease increased as the woman rounded the corner and disappeared, and Nell's heartbeat filled her ears. She couldn't bear it a second longer. Grabbing her coat, scarf and hat, she flew out of the apartment, ran down the stairs and erupted onto the street below.

From the shelter of the porch, all felt quite nice. The late afternoon sun was warming and promised above zero temperatures, but as Nell crossed the road, the wind hit her like a vast wave and her eyes began to water. She realised that there were gaps in her warm clothing, between her gloves and jacket sleeves, her scarf and jacket neck, and somehow her hat didn't seem to be sufficiently covering her ears.

Skirting around some icy puddles, she made her way to the path that led to Church Field. A cloud stole across the sky and blocked out the sun. The landscape was leached of all colour, like someone had tipped their glass over a watercolour. The sky held a diluted hint of salmon, but otherwise everywhere was shades of grey and brown.

The temperature dropped and showed its true character. Nell's lungs were reluctant to breathe in the icy air, and although she had wound her scarf across her mouth and nose, her lungs still seemed to be shrinking. It was as if they had looked at the sky, shivered, and then begun closing the shutters. Best walk more slowly, and she patted her jacket pocket to double check she had her inhaler.

A faint track led across the field and past the dead tree in its middle. Now she was closer Nell could see items had been placed around its trunk, like presents around a Christmas tree. Posies, scrolls secured with ribbons, even a small, knitted doll. It felt sad; abandoned, and Nell hurried past. As she crunched over the frozen grass and muddy ruts, the full force of the wind hit her. It would be better once she was in the shelter of the woods, and she had a mission to fulfil. In the haunted woods. Hopefully before the sun set and it got dark and spooky. A pattering sound startled her and, looking up, she saw the first small hard snowflakes coming down. The wind was so strong that before most hit the ground, they were thrown back at the sky again. Small and dry, they floated and raced like tiny winter insects before larger ones hit her straight in the face.

A robin appeared at the edge of the woods, and Nana's voice filled her head. 'When a robin appears, a loved one is near.' Only there were no loved ones for Nell anymore; just a pile of ash scattered under some splintered yew trees. The robin opened its beak and filled the air with the sweetest of music.

'Hello. Are you coming with me?'

How could such a tiny bird produce such incredible sounds? It was like a full wind section of a heavenly orchestra.

'Keep an eye out for me, won't you?'

The robin hopped onto a branch just inside the woods, and Nell saw that it had pointed out the path. Just like in *The Secret Garden*. Clearly a sign that she should walk on. The snow had got the hang of it now and realised that if it threw down bigger flakes, and more of them, that they had a better chance of reaching the ground. So, while she could still feel her fingers and face, she followed the robin into the woods.

A sweet smell met her. 'Lush' was the first word that came to Nell's mind. Although sodden and barren, the soil smelt so wondrous and floating above it somewhere were the lingering notes of a bonfire. The well-trodden path became muddier as she went further in, and as Nell approached a fork ahead she realised that if she was to follow her instincts, she must take the least popular path. There were no mountain bike tyre tracks here, nor hoof nor boot prints. The trees and bushes were overgrown and tugged at her hair and arms as she walked. A black and white print came to her mind, of a path leading to a house in the woods. Hansel and Gretel had always terrified Nell as a child. Why was she suddenly remembering that now?

It was darker here, under the brooding canopy of skeletal

ash, oak, and beech trees, and ahead a holly tree blazed red berries like blood splatter. She was just contemplating retracing her steps when she heard it. Far enough away from the main road now, all she could hear were her own footsteps, her breathing, and bird song. And what a chorus it was. Every bird in the woods was surely singing, their pure voices weaving in and out of the trees, invisible yet so close.

A robin landed on the path ahead. She stopped.

'Hello again.' A stupid thing to say really, because of course it wasn't the same robin, but it tilted its head to one side and flew on ahead, leading the way. It was true what they said, she thought, you needed to get out in nature, to really listen. Mindful walking, and there was something so magical and intimate about the woods. Her evil mood had vanished almost immediately as she had taken her first breath. As if her fragile mental health was taking a rest from all the emotional drama she'd been subject to recently. Inhaling deeply, she wondered if this was forest bathing. She certainly felt at peace. Her horrible year was nearly at an end and it surely had nothing else to throw at her. Everything had already been broken, lost, or ripped from her.

At least she was not facing another Christmas with Gary. She had climbed a long way out of the dark pit and the thought suddenly made her dizzy. She had created a new chance in her life. A chance to reconnect with her dad and to start her life again. Scary and uncomfortable, but Max had said all the shouting was to be expected. That they needed to draw a line under the past. But that was for another time; right now she was safe and calm in the middle of a beautiful winter wood. A few flakes were managing to break through the canopy of empty branches above her, so she took a deep breath and let the freshness spice her blood. The smile was just building when a twig snapped behind her.

She span around. No one there. Fear slammed into her chest; she was alone in the middle of nowhere at the mercy of any weirdo, thug or creep who could have followed her in here. The birds had stopped singing now. All except for one. A crow, or maybe it was a rook, it was something large and black. It cawed insistently, like a fingernail slowly tapping on a window.

Nell's breathing was deeper as she jogged along the path, her mobile in her hand. No signal. Of course there was no signal. The crow cawed again, but now it sounded more like a slow cackle, a rumble of mirth.

She ran into an opening. It was as if the circle had always been there, long before trees had grown. As if they had known not to violate the ground here. A perfect circle where the grass was short and the setting sun reflected in the pool of water at its centre. Fiery red, it looked like a puddle of lava and for a moment the brightness stung her eyes. By the pool stood a pile of stones. No, not stones, rocks. Carefully arranged in another circle, and at its centre were placed a jumble of objects. Coins, strips of cloth, a posy of dead flowers, and what could once have been perhaps a letter, now reduced to grey mush. Her breath caught again against her ribs, so she quickly pulled out her inhaler. In her haste, she did not notice something else had also been pulled out. Fumbling through her gloves to remove the lid, she took a long slow breath in. The normally sharp click as she sucked in the medicine seemed muted somehow, as if the eerie atmosphere was hushing it.

'I should not be here.' She had said the words out loud and she realised just how quiet it had become as the clearing filled with birdsong again. It got louder as she backed away from the fiery pool and the altar of offerings.

A pheasant roared close by, making her jump. And then she heard it. A whimper; a cry. Coming from somewhere close but out of sight. Many things could sound like a child, she reasoned. A fox, or the wind moving through a broken branch. Then movement caught her eye, and between the slender trees she saw a figure. Another lone walker, just like herself. As if aware of being watched, the figure stopped and turned. Nell froze; ready to run, but they took one look at her, turned, ran, and then disappeared. The feeling of wrongness was back, of having strayed into the wrong garden, so she retraced her steps, back past the pond, and didn't slow until she was on the main path again.

What was that strange clearing? The jumble of items left by the stones looked like offerings. Much like she had seen by that dead tree in the field. Ric and Seb had called it the hanging tree.

193

What a cheerful thought. Then she realised the items were not unlike those that had turned up in the rectory.

She looked at her mobile. Barely sunset. It felt so much later, as if she had walked in the woods for hours, and she had forgotten to collect holly and ivy which had been her sole purpose for coming here.

A text appeared on her screen.

'Mr Austin gave me your number. Please don't be angry with him. Or me, though you have every right to be angry with me. But it was so lovely to see you. Can we meet on Christmas Eve? Love Will.'

Tears stung as they tracked down her face. She hadn't blown it. Perhaps this was the unconditional love she had always heard of, that she could throw a tantrum but he still wanted to see her again.

'Come to the rectory and I'll cook us lunch. Love Nell.'

She began to type 'It was lovely to see you too.' But something stopped her. As an afterthought, she deleted the *'Love Nell'*. It sounded too much like a plea to her long absent father to care for her again. They didn't even know each other; it was stupid to think there would have been any attachment. It would take time and careful steps, just like the steps she hoped would bring her out of the woods. Nell finally felt a glimmer of hope. Her Christmas dream had been dropped, kicked, and was now a battered mess at her feet, but it wasn't quite Christmas yet and anything could happen.

Back at the clearing lay the folded square of sketching paper that had fallen from Nell's pocket. A slight breeze nudged it, and now it lay within the stone circle, along with the jumble of other wishes, prayers, and spells.

'Hello girl, where did you come from?' Seb greeted the overexcited lurcher who was skipping in circles around him.

'Isn't she lovely,' enthused Tilly. 'Margaret from church has gone to visit her daughter over Christmas—you know, the one with all the problems—and she couldn't take Millie, so I offered to look after her. It's only for a few days.'

Millie danced around them on delicate legs until Tilly ushered her in to the utility room where she immediately knocked over a pair of wellingtons and sent a laundry basket skidding across the tiles.

'Yes, well, I'm not exactly prepared as you can see, but we'll soon adjust,' trilled Tilly. 'Oh, wait, I have her things in the car. Yes, come on then, darling, we'll go and get them, come with Auntie Tilly.'

Seb watched on in amusement while his mother grappled with a large dog basket and a bag of dry food.

'Well, don't just stand there; her bowls, toys, and goodness knows what else is in that shopping bag.'

'Come here, gorgeous. Yes, yes, I love you too,' laughed Seb as Millie gave him kisses.

'You don't mind, about her, do you?'

'Not at all. You always said I could have a dog when I was a bit older.'

'Very funny. It's just for a few days. Poor Margaret. She was so worried about her.'

'Saint Matilda, the guardian angel of all townsfolk,' laughed Seb.

Tilly rounded on him. 'Don't be facetious. I'm just trying to be a good neighbour.'

'Funny how you never went to church before we moved here, though.'

'Well, no. I didn't really feel very neighbourly before. Anyway, I feel like I've made some real friends in North Chase. I wish we had moved here when Mark and I were still married.'

'Yeah, and you would be Lady Corberley now.' Seb smiled and caught his mother's eye.

'Well, never mind all that. He's with Daisy now,' Tilly spluttered, fussing with a dog bowl.

'Oh, look at your face. You really can't bear her, can you?'

'She's perfectly lovely, for a human unicorn. All rainbows and frills, and that silly little voice. That habit of screwing her eyes shut repeatedly when she talks is ugly, and I just love to see her prance along like a little pony on those stick thin legs.'

'Oh dear—' mocked Seb.

'No, don't laugh at me, you disloyal boy. She'll totally ruin him. He needs a strong woman by his side to play the role of Lady of North Chase. There are charities in town that need a patron, committees to sit on. She could be such an asset to this town. I take it she won't be making an appearance at the community carol singing.' With a sharp look, Tilly added, 'I can rely on you to come, I hope. You can bring Millie.'

'I think Daisy plans to take Ava. And *you* can take your new daughter. Millie can have a howl, can't you, girl?'

Tilly's mouth dropped open. 'Taking the baby out in this cold, whatever is she thinking? She honestly is a total simpleton.'

'If she pisses you off—'

Tilly winced. 'Please don't use nasty words like that, darling.'

'As I was saying ... If she *annoys* you that much then perhaps we should move away.'

'Perhaps. In the meantime, I am perfectly prepared to compromise my pride and sanity for the sake of your relationship with your stepfather. Ex-stepfather. Oh, whatever.'

Seb had heard this too many times before.

'I'm quite happy as I am. I don't want his money.'

'Well, she's certainly ripping through it for him. What does she need that huge vehicle for, anyway? Ava's not a baby hippopotamus.'

'Seriously Mum, we could move into town. You could still flounce about doing your charitable works and I could still see *Dad,* but it would put some distance between you and Daisy.'

Tilly rounded on him again. 'Has he said something to you?'

'We don't speak about you.'

'Oh very good; I almost believed you.'

Seb knew this was dangerous ground so quickly continued, 'I could get a job, or I could do that advanced design course I saw.'

'Design? Taking photos, you mean. That profession is saturated. However talented you are, there will always be someone who has the right surname, or went to the right school, who knows all the right people. They will be successful before you are.'

'Well, I'll think of something, and in the meantime I'll continue to take photos.'

'No, I won't have a son of mine turning into an entitled waste of space. You will learn a trade, get a job, or do something.'

'Perhaps the navy.' The words had fallen from his mouth so casually. Perhaps this *was* the perfect time to tell her.

'Oh, stop it. You would never do that to your poor mother, surely. I would be worried sick for you. What is wrong with being a teacher, or an accountant like me? People will always need help with their finances.'

'Boring, boring.'

'Well, it puts food in your tummy.'

It would have been so easy to change the subject, to have been his usual flippant self. 'Actually Mum, about the navy, I've been thinking about it for a while. I've even spoken to—'

There was a crash from the kitchen.

'Oh dear … Darling, go and see what she's done. Then we'll get ready for church.'

Seb sighed as his mother disappeared upstairs. He wasn't sure if she had heard what he'd said, but sooner rather than later he knew he would have to break his mother's heart.

33

23 December

The little mouse wore smart black trousers and shiny red shoes and braces. It was also standing in the middle of their bedroom. As Mark looked on in horror, its eyes began to flash and it raised its tiny arms in the air. Mark's foot caught in the rug as he backed out of the room, but then the hideous toy started to shuffle forward, towards Mark, beating its drum. The rattling increased and the eyes now glowed demonic red.

'Get that evil thing out of this house,' Mark hissed.

'What?' Daisy's face fell. 'But it is charming, and Ava loves it. Look how she claps her hands as he drums.'

'If you won't stop it—'

But Daisy had scooped the mechanical toy up in her arms. 'Don't. It's Seb's. He said his father gave it to him and he thought Ava might like to see it. What's wrong now?'

'Seb's father?'

'Yes, apparently. Well, that's what Tilly told him, anyway. Now, look what you've done.'

Ava began to wail.

'But he didn't know his father.'

'Oh, for goodness sake, Mark. Does it really matter? I think it was lovely of Seb—'

'And that hideous, evil thing used to belong to *my* father when he was a child.'

Daisy kissed Ava's soft curls. 'Look, I don't care. You've upset Ava. She likes it, so why don't you leave us both alone.'

She turned away from him and bent to wind up the toy again, but before she reached it the mouse's eyes flashed, and it began to advance on Ava's cot again, beating its drum faster and faster. Ava laughed and clapped her hands in delight, and from the corner of the room someone else laughed too.

Mark just made it to the bathroom in time. There had to be an explanation. Perhaps Tilly had found it, or his father had given it to her. He washed away the bile and swilled out his mouth. Yes, that must be it. But something nagged at his brain about the first time he had met Tilly. He had been visiting one summer, and Tilly had been invited along with some other single mums to a charity children's party on the lawn. Their attraction had been instant, and he had been so surprised when his father had encouraged him. The old lord had always been so fond of Tilly and Seb, and Mark had just accepted it.

Last time he had seen that toy it had been in a room no one ever visited, no one even knew about. And when he had slammed that cursed door shut he had locked it himself. For the first time, real fear raised its head in the pit of his stomach. He listened to Ava laughing one more time and then, decision made, he went to find Tilly. Time to find out what else she was up to.

34

A thin curl of wood smoke drifted through the trees. Austin changed direction in response. Too far to be coming from the manor house, or the cottage, so it was definitely worth investigating. So many things were hidden in these woods. It was rather nice; the hunted and the hunter all together, and Austin was definitely in hunter mode.

The van had been parked there so long the trees had claimed it as their own. Glossy ivy snaked across the roof and covered the windows, but a vent in the roof and the light seeping through the leaves gave it a warm, cosy glow.

'Bit late for a country ramble, isn't it?'

Austin stifled his instinct to pivot and punch. Instead, he slowly turned to look into his accuser's face. Young, unshaven, and from the smell of him, he had been living rough for a while.

'I might say the same thing to you,' he replied amiably. 'And I would love to know where you popped up from.'

Austin had been spending his time researching archives, completing background checks on the key players, and listening to the village gossips. It was this gossip which had led him to check out a remote part of Corberley Estate. Despite the rustling trees, he prided himself on having an acute sense of hearing. And for knowing when he was being watched. So where *had* this scruffy young man come from?

'You haven't answered my question. What are you doing wandering around Lord Corberley's estate?'

Austin was just about to reply when realisation dropped. 'I

think you and I might very well be doing the same thing.'

'I don't think so, mate.'

'Mark mentioned to me that there had been some unpleasantness lately. That he is worried for his family's safety.'

'Well, not from me. I'm keeping an eye on her for him.'

'*Her?*'

The young man just nodded over his shoulder.

Quickly, Austin gathered up his mental data and ventured a play. 'His ex-wife?'

'Yeah, she's had it in for them ever since they moved back. And that mummy's boy of hers. I thought he was ok, but I reckon he's worse.'

'So, you are Mark's security?'

'Which brings me back to my original question.'

'Oh yes. Hello, I am Austin, the private detective. I presume you are Finn.'

Finn was all smiles now and soon Austin was perched in the van, accepting a mug of black tea. 'Now her ladyship knows about me, she's been bringing me supplies. I used to pop up to the house, but she reckons if she can spot me then so can the ex.'

'But surely your presence has not gone unnoticed?'

'No one goes near this part of the woods. Well, some local lads were close by a few weeks ago but they were ...' He glanced at Austin. 'They had their own business to mind. It would have been ok if they had seen me though, Brett and Jordan are good lads. Keep their mouths shut.'

So local news had not reached him yet, thought Austin.

'Do tell me. How *did* you creep up on me?' Austin continued conversationally.

'That hazel hides an old passageway. They used to store ammunition in it during the war. There's another one that goes into town, hundreds of years old. Some of the old families know about that one, but they probably think it's boarded up. Well, it isn't. And *this* one had a cave in at some point. Just enough room left for a skinny lad to keep out of sight.' The boy smiled proudly, and Austin felt a stirring of amusement. 'I keep it well covered, but I heard your car and thought I'd wait it out.'

201

'The town think you are missing.'

The smile faded. 'Yeah, well, I had a barney with my mum and just needed some time to calm down a bit. Bit of family bother. Came out here and his lordship said I could stay if I promised to keep an eye on the place. But only until Christmas Eve, then I must go back home. He said it wasn't fair on her.' The boy seemed on the point of saying more, hesitated, and then glanced up at Austin again.

'I didn't mean to upset everyone, just had to get away. And things are simpler, safer, when people think you are gone. *She*, the ex, knows that local lads use these woods, and I've seen her and that bloody big vehicle of hers in parts of the estate that don't make sense. I've seen other things in these woods that make even less sense, but a few ghosts don't scare me half as much as *she* does.'

The urge to question the boy further was compelling, but Austin knew when to let the words flow naturally. Sometimes it wasn't what was said but the order in which they were said that really mattered. He sipped his tea and listened to the trees stir around him. This was something he could understand. Solitude allowed a person to think, to listen, to heal. Allowed you to reconnect with your true self. After his wife's death, he had thrown himself into work, kept going, as if grief was a snarling dog that he must escape. But it just meant that when it had finally caught him, he was too mentally and physically exhausted to travel through the cycles. Nell was using the five stages of grief as a safety rope, with the hope that it would eventually lead her out the other side. She was allowing herself to feel whatever she was feeling in the safe knowledge that it had a label on the cycle, that it was normal, was to be expected. His boss had referred him to a counsellor who had tried to guide him through, but Austin had simply hidden behind a mask of coping. It had got him to work every day, but behind it he had been slowly crumbling. It had taken him years to heal from the deaths of his wife and stepdaughter, and although he recognised that the Austin who had survived was colder, harder, alone, he was lucky to have friends who accepted him.

Having Nell to look out for was a comfort he had never expected. He understood Finn disappearing into the woods, going to ground while he made sense of the world. Austin preferred to work alone, relying only on himself, but he was never too old to learn new tricks. Locals had probably poached on these lands for centuries and passed down their knowledge. This job had stopped being about who wrote the threatening letters a long time ago. There was real danger here. Time to pool resources.

35

The peace that Nell had found in the woods, and from Will's text, started to wane within minutes of returning to the rectory. Her Christmas lights had all turned themselves on in her absence, and shadows seemed to dance in the tall mirror. She hastily switched on the main lights just as a clock chimed on the floor below. A creeping cold reached out from the walls, so Nell wrapped herself up in a throw and curled up on the lumpy sofa. Closing her eyes, she listened to the sounds of the house. Doors opened and closed, and one of the stairs on the flight below her creaked, twice.

There was shouting from the street below. The festival had packed away last night, but a few people had begun gathering near the church for the imminent community carol singing. However, this didn't sound like the good-natured shouts of people greeting each other. Then one word penetrated her sleepy brain. *Witch*. Against her better judgement, Nell stepped over to the nearest window and poked through the musty curtains to find the gap.

Flaming torches illuminated the scene unfolding below. A man was dragging a chained woman through the streets in front of a jeering crowd. A stone was thrown and she fell heavily. Immediately, a young girl ran to her side, pleading for mercy. It was at this point Nell realised that she must have fallen asleep on the sofa. Don't catch their eyes, she thought, because the moment she did, she would become either the woman being dragged or the weeping girl. Instead, she closed the curtains and began to pace up and down. It was beginning to be too easy to slip from reality into these dreams, or hallucinations, and again, she wondered if there was a medical term for it. Crazy, bonkers, mad.

Immediately there was more shouting.

'Stop fucking about, Jordan.'

She stopped; that sounded real.

This time, as she peeped through the curtains, she saw a group of teenage boys raging outside. Relief that she wasn't dreaming soon turned to fear. One had found themselves a 'for sale' board and was threatening the others with it. Then it got nasty as they were blasted by a taxi trying to get through. The boy smashed his board at the taxi door. With a screech of brakes, the driver shot out and punches flew. The boy's friends melted away from the trouble.

'I know who you are, and I know where you live. Remember that. Shame it was your mate and not you pulled out of the river this morning. Maybe the witch will get you next,' bellowed the driver. Nell tensed, expecting the boy to retaliate, but all the fight seemed to drain from him. He dropped his sign and walked away.

'Fucker,' concluded the driver, and wiping his face, he yanked up his jeans and squeezed back behind the steering wheel.

The encounter had shaken Nell, even though she was separated from it by thick walls, the windows had suddenly seemed very thin. It would be a while, she realised, before she could witness violence and not feel it was about to rain down on her. Not for the first time, the acronym 'PTSD' came to mind. But at least it had been really happening, not another hallucination from her mad mind. Being alone was not good for her, and despite the chill from the glass, she settled down on the window seat. In a parody of the horrific scene she had dreamed a few minutes earlier, a woman now walked down the street with a small child in her arms. Minutes later more people began to drift towards the church lychgate. Dressed in their Christmas best with warm hats, matching scarves, and long coats, they looked ready to pose for a Christmas card. A couple of families even sported flashing antlers and their dogs, cosy in their quilted jackets, sniffed and greeted each other.

This was a real Christmas, realised Nell. Families with children, or groups of friends. It was the bonfire night all over again, and once more she was the outsider looking on. She should join them, make an effort, and then she saw Seb trying to make an excitable lurcher sit. He turned to a tweed-jacketed woman in a feathered hat who smiled and frowned in equal measure and Nell recognised Seb's mother. Her mouth seemed permanently open as she chatted and waved to the growing crowd. Then her lip curled as Seb beckoned to the beautiful blonde with a small cherub in her arms that Nell had just seen. Not everyone was friends, thought Nell ruefully. Her mobile chirped to reveal a text from Max.

'*Arrived safe. Enjoy your evening.*'

Nell shivered; everyone *was* enjoying their evening. They had things to do and people to be with. Max was off to the ballet, and she'd heard nothing from Austin so presumably he was packing for the airport. A small reminder bobbed up that she had rashly invited Will for lunch tomorrow. She should be planning a menu, popping out to the supermarket. But it felt fake. And anyway, he would probably cancel in the morning.

Outside, the first carol began, triggering memories of Christmasses past, and Nell found her eyes had strayed to the child again. She was straining her neck to look around, and then her eyes spotted Nell spying from her window. Her mouth made a small 'O', and she lifted a small hand to point. Nell felt a sudden pain, as if a blade had ripped through her stomach and her organs had spilled to the floor.

It was all too painful; she turned away from the window and, switching on the television, she stabbed at the remote until a black and white film caught her eye. A dark wood where two small children huddled in the snow. Not very cheerful. She stabbed again, but the film continued and in the background she could now see a hooded figure creeping up behind them, carrying a basket of bread. She slapped the remote and when that failed, she marched towards the television and switched it off at the socket.

Back at the window, she watched the flickering candles and happy faces. Nana would have loved this. The stinging tears burned her face as loneliness caught in her throat. Carol number two started, and one voice seemed to rise above the choir. A voice pure and delicate like a fine thread of gold being pulled through silk. It was a medieval carol of such longing and sadness, but instead of intensifying Nell's misery, it seemed to reflect and then offer comfort. For the first time ever she really listened to the words, listened to a mother trying to sooth and comfort her baby. She imagined holding the little girl from outside in her own arms, of that chubby hand reaching for her face as she rocked and comforted her.

There was a sharp click. The television had switched itself on. Then slowly, so slowly, as if it was almost not moving at all, the apartment door began to open. Dark from the corridor outside spilled in as the crack widened. Nell's breath caught and it felt like something heavy was pressing on her chest. There was sudden movement from the tall mirror, as if it had reflected the closing of a heavy curtain, and then the draught from the open door hit her. Nell's gasp turned into a dusty wheeze, and the grandfather clock suddenly chimed. The broken grandfather clock with its hands permanently stuck at midnight or midday now filled the apartment with a shuddering death knell. The window seat dug into the back of Nell's legs as she stared at the gap in the door. She was dreaming again, she had to be. The asthma attack gained ground, but her inhaler was in her coat pocket, hanging on the back of the door. She couldn't breathe. The clock chimed its last and singing filled the apartment again. As Nell gasped for breath, the shadowy figure of a small child appeared in the doorway.

'Good afternoon, Lady Corberley. I see you've got Miss Ava wrapped up warm.'

Tilly's head spun round, only to spot the reverend smarming up to dippy Daisy. Wrapped up warm indeed, the child looked ridiculous in her red velvet cape and hat. But not as ridiculous as her mother who appeared to have totally ignored the importance of the community carol singing and was dressed in jeans, high-heeled boots, some sort of moth-eaten poncho and shocking red lipstick. Tilly straightened her scarf and turned to fuss with the table of song sheets. Now the reverend had spotted someone else.

'Hello and welcome. So glad you could make it. Let me introduce you to Tilly … Corberley who has arranged so much of this today.'

The confusion at the surname was evident as the man looked first at Daisy and then back at her. Once they were out of earshot, an amused Sebastian said, 'Mum, you should change your name.'

'Actually, I was giving that some thought myself.

'You could go back to your maiden name.'

'Or I could change it to something new entirely. Like Maundrell.' The words, spoken in spite, had the effect she wanted.

'What?'

'Imagine. I could open a shop in town. *Tilly Maundrell's Maison*. I could sell things with a witchy theme. Make a fortune. And we could display your photos.'

'You're not joking, are you?' Seb smiled.

'I'm not sure I am.' Then she noticed Daisy waving.

'Hello Tilly, hello Seb.' Oh God, now she was prancing over to them. 'I just wanted to say thank you again for that lovely toy you gave Ava. It seems to terrify Mark, but Ava loves it.'

'Toy?' snapped Tilly, and then tried to soften it with a smile. 'What toy is this?'

'The little drumming mouse. I'll make sure she doesn't break it, because I know Seb's dad gave it to him. Funny, Mark said that *his* dad had one just like it when he was little. He got quite cross about it.' And then, clearly unaware of the bombshell she had dropped, Lady Daisy trotted away.

'You don't mind, do you, Mum? She'll probably get bored of it by Christmas and then I'll take it back. I wonder why Mark doesn't like it, but then he seems to have got jumpy since that ghost hunt.'

'Where did you find it?'

'Oh Mother, you *know* where I found it.'

She needed to think, think quickly.

Daisy for chatting happily to the reverend again. 'No, Mark is still at home. Won't be able to make it,' she chirped.

Unforgiveable, spat Tilly; with all the trouble he had caused, he should absolutely show his face. Then an idea bubbled up. Could this be the chance she was looking for? She desperately needed something to stop Sebastian leaving home, and if Mark guessed her secret then time was running out.

The singing started, and gradually Tilly drifted to the edge of the congregation.

'I'll just check the tea urn is switched on,' she informed one of the other helpers, and then strolled into the church. There wasn't much time, but if she put her foot down it might be possible. Excitement bubbled up in her chest as she dashed to the crypt entrance, disappeared inside and then, grabbing a torch, hurtled to the very end. But it wasn't the very end, there was a small door if you knew where to look and had the key, which took you down a steep staircase and into the hidden passageway under North Chase. At one time all the staff at North Chase Manor and, of course, members of the church would have known about it, but as years passed, and it was no longer needed, it drifted into folklore. Just like Mother Maundrell. Just like the hidden staircase at the manor. At one time it had just been her and the old lord who knew about it, but recently there had been different scents, and an empty beer can left by the manor entrance. The bicycle she hid at the bottom of the steps lay untouched, so hitching her skirt and switching on the lamp, she prepared for the cardiovascular workout of her life. She pedalled fast, past the door which led up to the cottage next to Erica's house, and on until she reached the end.

She hated the abandoned chapel in the grounds, and hated the crypt even more, but she was now well within the estate grounds. The icy air took her breath as she pushed open the heavy door. She stopped to listen, but there was no one around. Cursing her tight tweed skirt, and resisting the urge to check her watch, she marched up to the house.

Because there really wasn't much time and she might not get another chance.

36

'I thought we'd get some supper on the way.' Max smiled at her dad's words. *Oh good, more food.* The journey into London had been unremarkable, and somehow the simple act of driving—of negotiating lanes of traffic, of queuing on and off the motorway—had settled her. As she opened her dad's front door, the smells of home hit her: mulled wine, fresh pine, and cigar smoke. Now showered, dressed, and feeling totally festive, they headed to the tube station. Her velvet dress left her legs cold, but after months of only being dressed in uniform or jeans, it was blissful to be wearing makeup and her best clothes. Perhaps the purple biker boots were a little heavy for the dress, but this was London, and despite the tubes they had a lot of walking to do.

God, she'd missed London. Smelly, dirty, grey, but it had a pulse that you could feel coming from the buildings and traffic like the purr of a mythological beast. London felt like home; the beautiful and ugly architecture side by side, the modern sitting on the ancient. It was a living, breathing creature, and she felt herself come alive as she walked its streets. The underground reminded her of magical ley lines linking the modern city to its primitive roots. Whenever she was back she acknowledged just how fast the months were flying by while she worked and slept and made no progress in her life. Like the heavy Thames, she was slowly flowing, but for her the scenery didn't change.

She had escaped from here after a bad breakup, and

Launton had seemed like a healthy place to lick her wounds and recover. At first things had been great, she'd been in a new relationship and putting down new roots, but she and Di had been over for too long now and still she was going to work, coming home, and sleeping. Did she miss being in a relationship, though? To be honest, she wasn't sure she really had time for one. She'd make time for the right woman, though, wouldn't she? As they waited on the platform, a couple walked past arguing fiercely. Maybe she would have this conversation with herself again in the New Year, but for now she loved the easy company of her work family, Austin, and Nell, and, tonight, her dad. Then it hit her: she was a selfish person who loved being in charge of her life. She had to make no compromises and was free to do whatever she wanted. After Christmas she could hand in her notice and move back here if she wanted. Or to New York, or even Brisbane. She wasn't lonely; she was free.

The underground station displayed posters for an exhibition which had just opened. The great fire of London in 1666 was a familiar piece of history, so after glancing at the poster Max dismissed it. Then the smaller text underneath caught her eye. Also included was an exhibition on the great plague of London which happened the same year. Not a good year to be a Londoner, thought Max. If by chance you had survived the plague, you would probably have burned to death in the fire.

The tube doors shut and they were whisked into a tunnel. The train's screech turned into a scream. Max's head whipped round to locate the source, but the grimy windows just reflected her own face. Her skin erupted into gooseflesh as a familiar icy sheet wrapped around her. Something, out of sight but very close, was no longer alive. Max began to fuss with her bag. Sometimes when she had an awful vision or paranormal sensation, she would withdraw her attention and energy, and simply wait for it to fade. She had wanted her gift to return, but not like this. The screaming stopped and the tube began to slow. Tentatively, Max glanced at the people around her as they pulled into the next station. They jolted to a stop, the doors opened, people got out, people got in, and the doors closed.

Another jolt, a grind of metal, and they moved off.

Different advertising posters flashed by, and then as they were swallowed up by darkness, she saw her own reflection and that of a woman sitting quietly next to her. Hands in her lap, her hair loose and, hiding her face, a beaked, leather mask.

When she had been a student nurse they had visited a museum of medical artifacts. The plague rooms were fascinating, and it wasn't until Max had returned home that the unease started. Something she had seen in those glass cases hadn't been right. That night, as she closed her eyes to sleep, she saw it again. And just now, in the reflection of the woman sitting next to her, she had seen it once more. Behind the eye sockets of the beaked plague mask lay an evil darkness which was watching, and waiting. As she looked, she felt her mind disappear along a dark line of time, back through the centuries, back to the plague days of 1666, and there she saw something that froze the blood in her veins. The creature next to her raised its hands and slowly began to remove the mask.

'Maxine? What is wrong?' Her father's strong hand reached for hers and she felt herself pulled back to the present. 'Are you alright?'

'Not really, but I don't think there is anything I can do.'

An arm wrapped round her shaking shoulders and she hid her face in her dad's jacket. No need to explain to him. He was her dad and he just knew. Fishing her mobile from her bag, she sent a quick text.

'Austin. Don't know where you are but get to that haunted manor house.' She forced herself to remember what she had just been shown. *'And keep Nell away from rivers and lakes.'*

As they joined the crowds that spilled from the stuffy underground and up to the street, Max shivered in the sharp cold. The psychic had been right, in part. She *couldn't* help Nell this time.

Then, as they waited in line at the night food market, she sent one more text, in answer to one she had received earlier from Nelson and Stan of Spooky Spots.

'Thank you for the kind offer. I would love to accept the job.'

37

23 December – Late afternoon

The cold air hit her face before Nell realised she was outside. What the hell was going on, and more importantly, where was she? She was just raking over the last thing she could remember when the sound hit again. A bark, a cough? Something or someone had stood in the doorway. Quickly, she looked at her hands and was relieved to see her inhaler cradled there. *The child.* But all she could remember now was the horrible film, and how one of the huddled children had seemed to appear in her own apartment. From the rectory porch, the community singing was loud and real, but lingering above it was still this strange noise. Stopping and starting like an old engine turning over, the voice rang out over the town. Nell slammed her hands over her ears, but it only made the voice seem louder.

Icy fear rippled over her skin which rose in response. Horror movies tried their hand at the cackle of an asylum, but this was something else. It was quieter now, almost a giggle, and this was somehow worse. The giggle of an evil child with blood on its small hands. Like the small child who had stood by the door. Suddenly, a cold breath hit her as if someone was stood right beside her, giggling an inch from her ear. The image from the television screen hit her again, of the tiny children shivering, and the figure creeping up on them. The dreams she had endured all spoke of children and dolls. If only she could understand them. Whatever they meant, or didn't mean, her body was drowning in adrenaline and she knew someone, a child, needed her help. As she crossed the road, the community singing drifted over her and a few words stuck, *'All children young to slay.'*

The lurcher stopped dancing around Seb's legs and began to growl. The giggling in Nell's ear turned to screaming again, and the small cherub in the beautiful blonde's arms went rigid, eyes wide. She twisted her neck, and in her eyes Nell saw flames. The hanging tree was on fire.

Tilly let herself in through the kitchen door, extracted what she needed from the locked cupboard inside, and then went to hunt down Mark. She found him stomping around in the gallery upstairs.

'Hello, Mark. I think it's time for that little chat.'

She recognised the shifty expression on his face, one that she used to think of as his spoilt brat look.

'How dare you just let yourself into my home.'

'That's not very friendly.'

'And what's all this rubbish about that bloody toy? Seb gave it to Ava, said it was his father's. It belonged to *my* father. I've decided, after Christmas I need you off my land. Seb can move into the manor if he wants, but *you* need to go.'

'Oh? I don't think so. The board at Cedarwood would be very interested to know who went bleating to the press about poor missing Hugo. I hope the money was worth it.'

'What? Do it. I'm sick of the blackmail, and the threats. I've promised Daisy that we are going to sell up, start again. I should never have come back. Seb is welcome to come too. Before he joins the navy.'

The rage that flooded Tilly's body was stronger than anything she had experienced before and frantically, she worked out her next manoeuvre. *She* was calling the shots here, not him.

'I'm not sure Daisy would be so keen to go anywhere with you if she knew the truth about your *tastes.'*

'Oh God, you're never going to let this go, are you? That was years ago, when I was married to you.'

'I must say, I did wonder why poor Hugo was hanging around *your* woods. Was he looking for magic mushrooms for you? I know how you all used to enjoy those special tea parties. So many waifs and strays that suddenly disappeared, but normally no one even notices. *I* had to get rid of Hugo. But that druggy boy—Finn was it?—I wonder where he is?'

'Leave Finn alone, and Hugo, I have no idea what you are talking about. Yes, you know about the drugs and those dinner parties, but I've never harmed anyone and that was all years ago. I love Daisy; she's all I want or need.'

Tilly bit her bottom lip and smiled; balance restored. Mark was pushing his glasses back up his nose, a sign he was agitated. Well, so he should be; Tilly knew far too much about him and his occasional tastes. How he had liked to experiment and push the boundaries of decency. She had never discovered who else had sat around the table at the private dinners, or how many times it had happened, but she was sure they had all been old blood, repeating barbaric practices that had been handed down through the centuries. And none of this was a problem until the son of one of the dining guests had recognised Mark at the academy and begun to ask questions about acquaintances that Mark wanted to remain hidden. In a moment of panic, Mark had confided in Tilly and he had clearly been regretting it ever since.

She had used her time wisely at the manor, learning about the Corberley history, and discovered that it wasn't just the breaking of a taboo that had originated as protection from a curse. And she had someone very precious who needed that protection, now more than ever. The practice of eating human flesh had been conducted by the head of the Corberley family for generations to secure their futures. She had protected Mark for so long, cleaned up his messes, got rid of that obnoxious brat who just wouldn't take a hint. She had discovered a talent for the kill, and rather enjoyed it. And now he treated her like she was not needed; she was unwanted, replaceable. The rage cooled as suddenly as if it had been doused, and she saw clearly. Time to end this; *one more kill.*

'What did you just say?'

'Oh, silly me. Did I say it out loud? Time for one more kill.'

'Oh my God, Tilly. What have you done?'

'What had to be done to secure the Corberley bloodline and to protect you until Sebastian was older. Even after you kicked me to the side, I've still maintained the legacy for those who come after you.'

'Ava doesn't need your help.'

'Oh dear, don't you know? Surely not even you are that stupid. Ava's not yours. Your own father said he doubted she was yours.'

'Enough. How dare you?'

'Get a DNA test if you don't believe me. It's really easy; you just need a few hairs, pop it in the post, and then the truth is typed out in black and white for you. I seriously suggest you do it. I did.'

'No.'

'And you *still* don't get it, do you? I did this, all of this to protect the *true* Corberley heir.'

Mark's mouth opened, but coherent words were beyond him by now.

'Did you never feel played? Didn't think it weird how your own father introduced us? He needed a spare to the heir and had no wish to remarry after your mother passed, so he found another way. With me. It was his idea that I should marry you, to keep you and the spare together in one place, and when you die, Sebastian will inherit. It's no good swearing, the letters are with the solicitor to prove it.'

'You really are a slut, aren't you? A gold-digging whore.'

'Now, now. You should investigate your own family history. You'd be rather shocked. It is all there, diaries, letters, stretching right back to the plague days of the reformation. Did you never read the contents of your own library? No good now, I've got all the important paperwork safe, but it really is damning.' All her secrets were out now, and it was so enjoyable to see his face twist in pain and anger.

'Father told me rubbish about human sacrifices to keep the witch's curse at bay.'

'Oh no, it is not rubbish. An offering was made for each child born in the Corberley family, to keep them safe. Any generation who did not do this always suffered a premature death.'

'Yet somehow the Corberleys have always survived,' Mark retorted, smugly.

'Only because there was a spare waiting in the wings, and

trust me, the mistake wasn't repeated. A blood offering was always made, and you are so wasteful, Mark. Pleasures of the flesh?'

'What the hell are you talking about, I've never touched …'

'You use them and cast them off like used needles without a thought for the true value of their flesh. And I'm talking about the flesh from the old families of the town. But Lordy taught me well, Sebastian will flourish after your death. I thought he'd be so proud of me when he realised I had brought back the old traditions. The family recipe for the Christmas pie mentions *pure* meat. I bet you can guess what that means.'

Mark stared at her mutely with another expression she recognised.

'My God, your father looked just like that when I told him what I had been doing with the flesh. I think the shock might have brought on the stroke that killed him.'

Mark made a lunge at her, so she showed him what she had procured from the locked cupboard downstairs.

'That was my father's gun, put it down before someone gets hurt.'

'As I said before, your father taught me well.'

Despite her bravado, she realised that she had never hit a moving target before, and certainly not one that was rushing towards her. The blast was deafening, and as her ears rang and her shoulder jolted, she saw Mark's expression change as he slid down the wall. Blood seeped between his fingers, ran down his shirt and pooled between his legs. Was it enough? She took a step towards him just as they were plunged into darkness.

Never had she stood in the house in such blackness before. As her eyes adjusted, the gallery seemed to shrink around her, but then the clouds outside parted and cold moonlight flowed through the bare window. Mark was panting at her feet, eyes locked on her face. Then they widened as he stared at something behind her. Tilly's own breath was sharp and shallow, then another sound reached her. Someone was whispering close by.

The clouds returned, and so did the darkness. Tilly frantically turned to scan the entire gallery. Someone was here and had seen everything. Soft footsteps slowly approached her, along with a sound like heavy fabric being dragged across the floor. Tilly raised the gun again, but all was darkness. The moonlight returned and she saw them; two little girls in long white nightdresses, standing hand in hand.

'Help me, please.' Mark's voice was broken.

Tilly stared in horror as the girls smiled their reply to him.

With a scream, Tilly ran; down the gallery and towards the back stairs. Total darkness blinded her so she pulled her mobile out and, using the torch, hurtled down the corridor, down the stairs and back towards the kitchens. The back door was now locked so, cursing, she ran back to the main hall. The advent candle stood on its table by the front door as it had every year since Tilly could remember. So little of it left now, it was always lit for a short time each evening when the family was home and it was sitting in darkness now. As she ran to the front door, there was a loud hiss and it burst into flame. Tilly wrenched open the front door, slammed it shut and with Lordy's best hunting gun still in her hands, ran as if the little girls were at her heels. In her haste, she did not realise that the gust from the door slam had knocked the candle. Had it merely fallen to the stone floor then no harm would have been done, but it rolled until it was stopped by the heavy curtain. Wax spilt, the small flame found a new wick and the curtain soon blossomed and roared with a cheerful light.

Tilly ran to the chapel, the vision of Mark's crumpled body and the little girls blinding her. Vaguely, she remembered a very young Sebastian talking about two little girls he used to play hide and seek with in Granddad's house. She would tease him about his imaginary friends. Could it have been a trick of the light? She could still hear the swish of fabric on the floorboards, see the cold light from their eyes.

She still had the stupid gun, so dumping it behind some ivy, she pulled open the crypt door. As she rode back along the passageway, she glanced at her watch. Stupid; she'd been too long *and* left his body. But there hadn't been time, and there was too much blood to clean up. Again. Really, drowning was so much cleaner.

What a mess. Never in all the years of the Christmas sacrifice had anyone made such a pickle of everything. Perhaps she'd just have to leave this body for the police and bury the gun on the grounds, or leave it in the passageway as she had with other surplice body parts once she had butchered what she needed from them. She needed an alibi.

As she climbed up into the crypt at St Edmund's, she checked herself for blood splatter, smoothed her hair and listened. She'd been too long but there was nothing she could do now. The church was still empty, so she slipped out of the door and joined the singing again.

'You were ages, Tilly. Everything alright?'

'Call of nature.' Tilly smiled. 'Tummy trouble.'

Ava had screamed all the way through 'The Coventry Carol', and didn't seem much happier with 'Away in a Manger', so kissing her crumpled forehead, Daisy started to rock her from side to side. Opposite them, Tilly was singing with great enthusiasm. Then she glanced over at them with such venom that Daisy shuddered and squeezed Ava tighter in her arms.

'Look, Ava, Millie's not crying,' said Seb kindly. 'But I think she could be brewing for a woof.' Daisy smiled down at the large dog.

'Is Ric not coming?'

'Too busy, I just checked. Between you and me, my lady, I don't think this is really her scene. Oh God, Mum's giving me evils again.'

My lady was Seb's nickname for her and it always made her smile.

'Your mum vanished just now. Was gone absolutely ages.' She hoped that this would pass on some of the unexplained fears she had felt when Tilly had reappeared with creases in her skirt and mud on her coat.

'Look, I'm going to take Ava back. I don't think anyone appreciates her contribution to every carol. You staying? Yes? Ok, bye bye doggy.'

As she fastened a now quiet Ava into her car carrier, she spotted Seb making his way across to his mother; whose eyes were still fixed on Daisy. The singing sounded rather lovely now she could hear it properly, but then another voice reached her. A voice that was laughing, and not in a happy way. Ava's eyes shot open. She stared at her mother's face, and then began to scream. Daisy slammed the Land Rover into gear and put her foot down. She should never have left Mark tonight.

As she drove past Church Field, she saw a slight figure hurrying towards the hanging tree.

'We need to get to Daddy, poppet.'

A flash of orange and red filled her rear-view mirror; the hanging tree was aflame.

But still the laughing continued.

38

The top branches of the hanging tree blazed in the frosty field. The flames reflected off shiny objects hanging from its dead branches lower down, and as Nell got closer she could see ribbons, necklaces, scrolls, even dream catchers made of bright wool.

Why were they all still singing? Apart from the baby girl and dog, no one seemed to notice the drama in Church Field. She must be dreaming again. The heat from the tree warmed Nell as she crossed the field, and she suddenly realised that she wore no coat, hat, or gloves. A cry came again from the tree line, and the feeling of urgency flooded through her once more. Someone needed her help. Twenty-three years ago she had heard a cry for help, but been distracted and a young girl had died. She would not ignore the cry again, even if it was just a dream.

And if you hear a child cry near the path that leads into the wood, don't you follow it. Don't you go in there. All you will find is death at the hands of a witch who was hanged over three hundred and fifty years ago.

Had she read that in her book? Dreamed it? Why couldn't she wake up? When she did, she would dress warmly and join the singing. Be among real living people again. She was allowing herself to be sucked into these hallucinations far too often than was healthy. It scared her to realise that it was happening more and more, and getting easier and easier for her to do it. She could remember moping in the rectory, and then the creepy black and white film had brought on a vivid nightmare. The cold air was making her sinuses throb, but someone was in trouble, someone needed her. Austin or Max would know what to do, but all she had in her hand was her inhaler; her mobile was back in the rectory. Then she realised that this was her problem, she was always trying to wake up from the nightmare instead of seeing it through, listening to the message behind it. Perhaps if she faced her demons then she wouldn't have to repeat the nightmares so often, and they wouldn't start creeping into her waking hours.

Nell ran, no longer caring if this was a dream or not. She would follow the voice into the woods and face whatever was waiting for her. Otherwise, she would probably find herself here again tonight. As the woods swallowed her up, sirens split the air, and over it all the low giggling continued.

Sirens broke through the last chorus of 'Hark the Herald Angels Sing', and one by one the congregation stopped.

A first responder and then a fire engine tore through the narrow streets, filling them with harsh blue lights.

'Mum? Look.' Seb was staring over the treetops towards the manor house, where a blush of rosy light and thick cloud was blocking out the crisp twilight.

'That's smoke. From the manor. Quick. Mum.'

'Oh no,' Tilly said, pulling her smile into a frown. *What a stroke of luck.* In her head, she quickly worked out the sums, the insurance would cover everything, and hopefully they would blame Mark's attacker, or whoever it was that had been sending those juvenile threats. Fire would cover all her tracks. Fixing her face into what she hoped was a worried expression, she headed to the car park, turned her 4x4 in the direction of the house, and prepared some suitable phrases of condolences in her head.

Finn's mobile vibrated. Frowning, he gave it a quick glance, and then clearly relieved, answered it.

'Hello.'

Austin could hear a familiar voice but the tone sent his mind into action mode.

'Shit. Hang on, we're coming.' To Austin's enquiring eyes, he said, 'It's Mark, my dad. The bitch has shot him.'

'Emergency services?' Austin shouted as they ran to his Mercedes.

'He called them, but he thinks he can smell smoke.'

As they thundered over the broken road and emerged from the trees, the twilight sky was bright with flames.

Austin's mind flicked through the floorplans he had memorised of the manor house, trying to work out the fastest routes.

'Where did you say he was?'

'The gallery. Front entrance is no good. Secret staircase will be quickest. Follow me.'

As Austin followed Finn across the kitchen gardens and down to a forgotten corner of the house, he realised that his suspicions had been correct. The ivy covered door opened onto a narrow spiral staircase, which led them past a tiny windowless room housing some old toys and a chest. Austin glanced at them as Finn struggled to unlock the door. Austin kept his torch steady but Finn was clearly panicked by the smell of smoke drifting under the door.

'Power's off,' shouted Finn as he disappeared through the door. The air was fresher now as Austin chased after Finn who easily negotiated the many corridors and backstairs until they emerged in a long room at the top of the house.

The sharp stench of blood reached him and, pushing past a now stationary Finn, relief filled Austin. He'd seen enough gunshot wounds to know that this was nothing more than a nick.

'Thank God. Are we on fire?' whispered Mark. 'I called an ambulance and the police. Stupid woman left me with my mobile.'

'May I see?' Austin passed his torch to Finn, lifted Mark's shirt, and was relieved to see an exit wound. 'Did you see the gun she used?'

Mark's eyes widened as he tried to remember, then he barked a short laugh. 'Father's old air rifle. Used it on the pigeons. Christ that hurts.'

'The pellet has travelled through, just a graze from what I can see, but I'm no expert. You've lost blood and I don't want you moved.'

'What about the fire?' asked Finn who was pacing by the windows.

Then the sound of sirens reached them.

'Finn, go and fetch them, and close all the doors firmly behind you. Inform them that the shooter appears to have gone. Yes? Go now. Good lad.'

Pulsing blue lights splashed against the window frames as Finn raced off. As he slammed the door behind him, an insidious waft of smoke entered.

Mark shifted his gaze from the door and stared at Austin.

'Did he tell you? Finn? Why he's in the woods?'

'I believe congratulations are in order. You have a son.'

'I didn't know, you see. Found out when I moved back here. His mother isn't happy. The look she gave me ... well it told me everything, and then I saw Finn again, living rough near the railway tracks, just by chance. Poor chap ... so I offered him a room. He wouldn't have it, but he took the old van. Thought it was safer than the streets, until he could—'

'Try to rest.'

'All those entitled brats at the academy, and my own son, my *heir*, was struggling ... I've always done what I can for the waifs and strays, the young people who lose their way.'

'He's a fine young man.' Austin was still trying to staunch the flow of blood.

'You think so? So do I, and Daisy has become quite fond of him. For a while, I think she suspected me of having an affair, all those late-night calls. She is an angel, Daisy. Truly an angel.' His voice was now so faint that Austin could barely hear him. *Hurry up.*

'Lord Corberley, tell me about your daughter.'

The eyelids flicked open again.

'Tilly said she isn't mine, but she is. Tried to say that Seb is my father's son. She is totally mad. I knew she was vicious, but not that she was evil. Well, I know now, and I intend to destroy her.' Finally, Austin saw Lord Corberley was ready to fight, for his family and for his life.

Tilly pulled over as the fire engine lumbered past them.

'Mummy,' shrieked Sebastian, and Tilly felt a warm glow. He had not called her that for years.

'It will be alright, darling boy. He managed to call for help, didn't he?' This thought chilled her; she had shot him, for goodness sake, she'd seen the blood, so who had rung 999?

As they turned a corner, colour lit up the sky; yellow and reds from the fire, and cold blue from the emergency services. Millie began to bark in excitement, and in the middle, talking to everyone, *taking charge,* was Daisy with Ava still in her arms. Sound drained from Tilly's brain and her eyes were suddenly blinkered from the bright lights; all she saw was Ava.

Daisy turned to them as they approached.

'Mark called them in,' her voice faltered. 'He said he'd been shot.'

At that last word Tilly's plan settled in her brain.

'Sebastian, stay here with Daisy.' Then, holding out her arms to Ava, she said, 'Shall I take her for you?'

Just like that, with tears streaming from her vacant eyes, the stupid little girl handed over her daughter. Tilly made soothing noises as she turned away, muttering about taking her to her own cottage and away from all the fuss and noise.

'Your daddy will be dead by now. I saw to that. How would you like to join him?' Despite herself, Tilly couldn't resist a little giggle.

A shout went up behind her ,and over the noise she heard the words she was dreading.

'Quick, Mark's in the gallery. I'll take you.'

Tilly turned to see a lanky lad staggering from the direction of the secret staircase.

'She shot him.'

Tilly did not wait to hear any more, she slipped behind the fire engine and headed for the woods. Still alive, she could feel danger creeping up on all sides.

'YOU'RE A FUCKING LIAR!'

Sebastian's words hit her with a stabbing pain. Away from the lights, she walked fast with the impossibly heavy child in her arms, until the trees swallowed her up and hid her from sight. Tears blinded her but she shook them away impatiently. If the game was up then so be it. She had always known that one day she might have to sacrifice herself for her son. But on this special night, she wouldn't go alone.

'You need to arrest Tilly Corberley for attempted murder.' Finn gulped in the fresh air before rushing over to the paramedics.

'You're a fucking liar,' wailed Seb, wrapping his arms around himself. 'You don't understand.'

Finn turned as a thin hand grabbed his arm.

'She's got Ava. SHE'S GOT AVA!' The scream pierced through the sirens and the voices. Shaking his head, Finn pushed Daisy away and led the ambulance crew into the house.

Doors crashed open and heavy footsteps approached.

'Ah, the cavalry at last,' quipped Mark feebly. 'Late as usual.'

'Over here,' shouted Austin, and then moved out of their way.

Finn grabbed his attention. 'Tilly was outside with Daisy and Seb, but she's gone now. Daisy says she's taken Ava.'

'Finn, is there water close by?'

'Water? What do you mean? There's a big lake by the academy.'

'No, something smaller.'

'The pond? Why? Never mind, follow me.'

'No, you need to stay here. Show me.'

Finn pulled up an app and pointed. 'Look, it's here, use the what3words app and type in *fire, challenge, church*. That will take you straight to it.'

Austin ran, hoping his sense of direction would lead him through the maze of corridors to the stone staircase. If Max's warning was wrong, or his usually acute instinct off, more than one innocent life might be lost this night.

39

Six months ago

If she had been stronger then he would not have made such a mess. This vexed her because it had not been part of the plan. She sighed and wiped her hands, then dropped the cloth in disgust. More mess. Her plan had been beautiful. Almost erotic. His pale face getting paler, and his blue eyes growing larger, filled with realisation, then terror. He had struggled and she had not been strong enough. So her beautiful choreography had descended into farce, with him rushing to the kitchen door and her grabbing a knife in panic and jabbing at him from behind. That had floored him, so she had taken back some control and held the knife to his throat.

But then it was all wrong again, with his eyes screwed up tight and his face all flushed. Finally, in frustration she had thrust the knife into where she thought his heart might be, felt it snag on a rib, and then it was all over. And she had this bloody mess to clean up. She almost wished she hadn't bothered.

Then her positive nature kicked in; there were lessons to be learned. She had underestimated how strong a teenage boy could be when someone had a rope around his neck, and now his blood covered her normally spotless floor and her blouse was absolutely ruined. Best put this one down to experience and plan again. Practice made perfect, and perhaps she should attempt something much smaller next time. Like a toddler. But the opportunity had presented itself today with such favourable signs; no one knew he was here, no one was due home, and the urge to try something so tremendous had got the better of her. Also, he was a troublemaker, one of the brats from the academy, so he shouldn't be wandering about the woods, calling for Sebastian. *Her* Sebastian. It was a mother's duty to protect her child.

Had it lived up to the expectation? She had often imagined the life literally leaving a person and the eyes becoming empty. She had expected intimacy which she had not truly experienced since her own son was born. The exquisite moment when a new life came into the world, made from her own flesh. So powerful, God-like power, to create life where none existed before. How much more powerful would it be to *take* a life, to be the sole reason that a person, with all their character, hopes, dreams, loves and hates, was suddenly just not there anymore. All because she had chosen it.

Looking at the heap of dead meat at her feet, the sly spreading pool of blood across her tiles, she sighed. No, it was nothing like she had imagined, not at all. But then, she reasoned, she hadn't wanted blood. Stinking slippery stuff. Perhaps a drowning next time, and the thought of golden curls floating peacefully underwater made her smile. Yes. Much better. But now she had a body and a mess to clean up. Once more she looked at the ruin of her best blouse. Maybe she had something under the sink that would get rid of blood stains if she soaked it right away. She smiled, there was never so big a mess that couldn't be cleaned up with a bit of elbow grease and the correct cleaning product.

She was just contemplating whether to bring some plastic sheeting into the kitchen or drag the body outside to it when another thought crossed her mind. Yesterday she had passed the butcher and observed with suspicion the rabbits hanging in the window. Lordy was always muttering about poachers on his grounds. It would be such a waste not to take advantage of all this fresh meat and, after all, that was one of the most significant of the old traditions that had been handed down through the centuries. Where would she put the surplus? She looked down at the bloody carcass. The ancestors had used the old crypt; perhaps she should follow their example.

Grabbing a larger knife, she had a little hack at the boy's

arm. Just like mini chicken fillets really, and Sebastian loved his mummy's homemade southern fried chicken strips.

40

23 December – Evening

It was a delicate tune, simple. Just a few notes turning and twisting around each other like a waltz. A lullaby. As soon as Nell realised the simplicity, it settled on her like the wet snowflakes that were beginning to drift from the sky. A lullaby to soothe a fretful child, and bring comfort, but there was nothing innocent about what was happening to the children of North Chase. The snowflakes hissed as they landed on the fallen leaves, and for a moment that was the only sound. Then the humming started again.

Of all her vivid dreams, this was the most real yet. Without coat or scarf, the cold was biting and had frozen around her ribcage making breathing painful. Without a torch, she crashed from one tree to another, but she was making progress, following the creepy humming. This time it felt right. This time she was not running away or hiding from the dream, she was listening to it, following its lead, a lead that would hopefully end in a rescued child, and this one a babe in arms. The snow settled and gave off an eerie glow. Here the woods were older. The barren trees felt like she was walking through the bone-white ribcage of an ancient monster. Then a faint cry dented the scene. The baby.

Running in the snowy woods in the near darkness was a hazardous affair. Her face became snagged by branches, and twice she nearly fell as a tree root or rabbit hole took her by surprise. The snow became thicker, the trees thinned and she was in a clearing. The remains of a house blocked her way, the trees growing out of the ruined walls showing how long it had stood there. Then, just beyond, she saw movement.

'I have one last child for you, Martha,' a woman's voice shouted. 'One more child, for *my* child.'

Nell stumbled around the fallen bricks and saw a pool of water on the other side. By it stood the woman who had shouted, shouted above the screaming infant in her arms.

As if frozen chains had coiled around her legs, Nell found she had stopped. The wet snow seemed to sense her warm feet and began to creep over her boots, then soak through the leather. Now was the time to turn and run, or to wake up, but as the woman shouted out to her and the child screamed, she realised that any hope she had cherished that this might be the most vivid dream ever had just disappeared. *This* was the reason for the nightmares, the hallucinations, the fears. *This* was where she was supposed to be.

For one strange moment, Nell was reminded of a nativity scene with the baby Jesus lifting its cherub arms up to the Virgin Mary, but this time it was to Nell the child reached. Nell felt her own arms lift, but the woman laughed and continued to shout at her. Only one phrase penetrated Nell's consciousness: *you look like her.* Then, miraculously, the wind dropped, the snow stopped, and Nell realised she was inches away from the woman and child.

Nell blinked and shook her head. On heavy legs, she backed away, eyes locked onto the second figure before her; the nanny she had seen pushing the pram of dolls. She was directly behind the woman with the child, which was why she had not seen her before.

Then the woman lifted her head. The scream that had started in Nell's throat erupted from her. Because there was no face. It was not a trick of the light, or a shadow, or a mask. From the black hair down to the chin, there was just smooth skin. No mouth, no nose, no eyes. Yet the hideous figure could see her, of that she was sure, and before Nell could turn, the figure had stepped forward and arms grabbed her. She scratched at the hands, ripping at the fingers that imprisoned her. But it was the woman she had seen holding the child who was dragging her to the water's edge. A shock of icy water hit her legs as her feet pierced the fragile ice at the edge. She fought to keep her balance. Then her breath was gone as she was submerged. The cold water hit her with physical pain as her chest ached. She struggled, but her feet were slipping on the muddy bottom, and she went under again. She was going to die here. At Christmas.

It was peaceful in the woods, away from the sirens and fuss. Tilly had managed to slip out of sight before they noticed her and, from the direction of Daisy's screeching, they were looking in the wrong direction. *Finn? That druggy from town? What on earth was he doing there?* She thought she had scared him off when he had started sniffing around Sebastian. She stopped for a moment to catch her breath. The child was awkward to carry and insisted on trying to free her arms to reach up to Tilly's face, so she wrapped her arms tighter around her. If Mark was alive then she was going to prison, so why not make one more sacrifice. For Sebastian. To ensure his future safety.

'I have one last child for you, Martha,' she shouted into the trees. 'One more child, for *my* child.' Ava was squirming and crying, but she would be silent soon. Sacrifice was such an intimate, sacred event. Just her and the child, and the spirit of the witch. The pond was before her now, its surface like a scrying mirror. Then something appeared at its edge; a figure where none should be. Tilly felt a shot of fear; was this the witch herself come to witness the last sacrifice? There was something familiar about the dark wavy hair and large brown eyes. Then she recognised her; the woman Sebastian had mentioned from the ghost tour. As the woman approached her, reaching out her arms for the child, she realised something else: William was correct about the family connection. For a moment, her courage flickered and she touched the silk scarf around her neck. Perhaps with William's help she would find a way out of this yet.

'Oh, you *do* look like her. Martha Maundrell? There is a small painting of her and her sister, Lady Mary, hidden in the manor house. Yes, they were sisters, but no one remembers that now, and it was Mary who accused her of being a witch. She had to, to save herself and her son. Mark spotted you immediately at the ghost tour. Gave him quite a turn. Funny that you should turn up here, by her pond, and at such an important moment.'

The woman said nothing, but again held out her arms for the child.

Tilly threw Ava onto the bank and flew at the woman. She easily overpowered her and dragged her to the water's edge.

'Did you know that they used to do this as a test for witches? Don't worry, if you are innocent you'll drown. But you're not innocent, are you? Strange dreams that are scarily like the history of North Chase. Oh yes, Sebastian told me all about you. And your psychic friend. Shame I couldn't get you both here.'

While Ava screamed from the bank, Tilly used her weight to throw the woman off balance, then kicked at her legs until she buckled. With her hands still around her throat, she pushed the woman under the water, straining her neck to keep her own face from the thrashing hands. The woman's eyes grew wide. Tilly relaxed her grip, thinking the moment of sacrifice was imminent, but then the woman's pupils seemed to shrink. A grip like a bear trap clamped over her own throat. Her hands, now empty, flew to the leather gloves around her neck that lifted her out of the water and slung her to the frozen ground. Just before her vision faded, she saw a tall figure waist deep in the water, frantically calling a name. *Nell.*

The trick was to not hold your breath when you were under water, but to let it out in a controlled manner. Was she dreaming this? Dreaming of her swimming lesson? She remembered screaming laughter, dashing through the dark woods, and the fear that she would be too late. Too late to save the child. Then mind-numbing cold gave her a moment of clarity before she fell back to sleep. But if this *was* real then it was already too late.

Icy waves, one after another, and a roaring in her ears. She needed to breathe; kick to the surface, but the light above her was too far away. Water entered her lungs and panic ripped through her. The last thing she was conscious of was a pounding on her chest and her name being shouted again and again.

41

1666 - Spring

The fear was paralysing. It gripped around your chest until your breath was naught but a weak, shallow thing that did nothing to ease the pain. As if the pestilence had already found you. Each time she heard a cart on the track, a horse in canter, or a voice she did not recognise, she would call out for her son, frantic if he did not come immediately running.

In the family chapel, there was talk of God's vengeance sweeping across the land again, of how sin was never hidden from *his* eyes and would strike down the young, old, the seemingly pure and devout, without hesitation. The sermon was over so Lady Corberley prepared to take her leave. A sharp cough stopped her. Her husband met her eyes with impatience as he wiped his mouth, but then was struck by another cough, this time wracking, gasping. Reaching blindly for the edge of the pew, he stretched out his other hand to her, but it found nothing but dusty air. Her son winced as she hauled him along the aisle and away from that fetid place. Once in the soft warm air, she filled her empty lungs again, deaf to the entreaties coming from behind.

'My lady?'

'Take John to his chamber and let no one in but myself.'

Terror had a smell as well as a sound, thought Lady Corberley. The acrid stench of vomit and vinegar as the hideous swellings had erupted on her precious daughters' bodies like foul toadstools. The sound was that of retching, of groaning that got fainter and fainter, as her frantic prayers had become hoarser and hoarser. Some survived the poison-filled buboes, but there was no mercy if they had the other contagion, which started with a cough and ended with the searchers and a bed of lime in the ground.

Her beautiful girls were taken by God's mercy within days of each other, and when she had emerged from their chamber and laid eyes on her son again, she had given thanks to whichever deity was still listening to her that he had been spared. The snows of winter had fallen and covered the burial mounds, but as spring thawed the ground, strangers had been seen again heading for the nunnery. Vagrants passed through the village, and as the sun rose earlier and earlier each day and the frost left the ground, the sound of coughing could be heard. Like a death knell; grating, breath robbing hacking started to be heard throughout the village, from behind cottage doors, and now from within her own walls. Her husband's man helped him to his own chambers, and with what was left of the servants, prepared for the days and nights of the sickbed to come.

'Please let my husband die,' she whispered to the beautiful blue sky. For if he died then perhaps her son would be spared. She was prepared to bargain with God or with the devil himself if it meant John survived. Last year, whole families had been wiped out with no one left to wrap the bodies, so their neighbours had filled the pits with the rotting corpses.

From John's window she could see the crops thriving in the fields, and in the orchard, a shower of apple blossom drifted to the grass below. She could feel it coming. The choking advance of disease, and for a moment anger flared through her that her husband had brought this into their home, probably picking it up from one of the village harlots. John was chatting behind her, asking why he had to stay in his room when he wanted to go riding. He was healthy, a warm glow in his cheeks as he cantered around the room, stirring up the rushes on the floor and leaving the summer scent of lavender in his wake.

Please let it be his father who was taken. His cruel, violent tempers had mellowed for a while when the girls had passed and half of the village was in mourning, but with the autumn fogs and slower death rate, his rages had returned. Between the beatings, the pestilence, and the loss of her daughters, she had to fight the urge to run. For where would she go? If he found her it would mean death, and then who would protect John?

Bird song drifted through the open window and she was about to call for Frances when she remembered her youngest daughter could no longer hear them. How the warm spring sun mocked her with its cheer and hope. The soft air brought with it the sound of coughing from below and, in panic, she slammed the window shut. Nothing must harm John. How many more years would they be punished until the contagion had taken its fill? How many more children had to die, families destroyed?

At the edge of the tree line, a figure walked. Her rich brown hair bounced against her back as she stepped into the kitchen gardens. Picking a few sprigs from the herb border, she placed them into her basket before heading to the kitchens. The widow Maundrell, though her husband had been killed in a fight not by disease. He had been protecting their livestock from robbers, and now she and her daughter, with another on the way if servant gossip was to be believed, made their living alone by brewing remedies and assisting at births. She had been there for all three Corberley children and had brought poultices for the girls when they were stricken.

Was Martha still a God-fearing woman? Lady Corberley knew they had both been brought up to be, but what god watched a man beat his wife and children and did nothing. What god killed innocent and wicked alike with such a plague? She had prayed for hours at the girls' bedside until she could no longer stand. And when praying did nothing, she had sung a lullaby that had soothed them when they were still in swaddling bands. When her voice could no longer sound, she had hummed to them. She could not drop another child into the pit.

There was talk in the village about widow Maundrell and her daughter. Servants whispered that their knowledge of healing was unholy, but still they called them when sickness came or when a child needed birthing. An idea flittered on the edge of her subconscious, but then John began to grab at her hand and from downstairs, her husband shouted for her. She called downstairs to the servant who told her the widow had left herbs which must be mixed with wine. Sorrel, dandelion, and sage could help the body sweat and rid itself of the disease, the servant informed her. Hearing her voice, *he* called her name but she gave instructions to the servants and headed back to John. With a finger to her lips to silence the questioning looks from her woman, she pushed the curtain aside and unlocked the secret door. Closing it softly behind her, she crept down the stone staircase. She listened for a moment until, satisfied that it was safe, turned the key and stepped into the gardens. Steep narrow steps, overgrown and purposefully hidden, led her onto the path and then into the kitchen gardens.

The night was mild and John fretful, so she opened the window and let in the sweet air. Her fingers still bore the scent of the sage she had shredded earlier for John's wine. He had not liked it much, so she let him have the last of the bread to soak in it. Her ears hummed as she listened to his soft snores and that of her woman. The sound of the sickbed drifted up through the floorboards and footsteps trod outside.

'My lady, he asks for you again.'

'I must protect his heir.'

The footsteps withdrew. Her words sounded so weak. She had tried to protect the girls, as if the very strength of her will could keep them alive. The same will that had brought them life, had pushed them from her body into the world, had fed them from her own breast. But she was powerless. Her efforts futile.

'Help me. Someone please help me,' she whispered to the moon. 'Show me what I must do.' She wept then, silently shaking, as she had learned to weep years ago so her husband would not hear her. Resting her head against the window frame, she closed her eyes for a moment, and such was her exhaustion, she slipped out of consciousness.

A dream, it had been nothing but a dream, but of such portent, such clarity she had never known before. She woke to find a cold dawn lighting the room. The moon still shone brightly in the apricot sky and the air was so fresh that, although she shivered, she felt its healing virtues. Soft snores from her son reassured her that he slept soundly still, so she stared at the sky and tried to make sense of what she had been shown in her dream. She had asked for help, for instruction, and perhaps she had received it. *Innocence to the innocent, purity to the pure*, and all to be done in isolation, in privacy. In that moment, she knew how to keep him safe. She would isolate him, safe from people, and ensure that the only nourishment either of them took was water from the spring and meat from the purest source.

'He is gone, my lady,' came the exhausted message through the locked door. So, it was over and they had survived. Still she worried about letting John run free. What if one of the servants, who had so faithfully nursed their master, now carried the plague? The evil miasma might lurk the corridors still.

She gave orders through the thick wooden door for her husband's body to be removed and the bedchamber locked before she gave them all leave to be with their own families in the village, including her own woman. They had been isolated in John's rooms for five days since his father had been taken sick and she knew Jane worried for her parents. Five days, and though she had used the secret staircase to visit the spring and bring back clean water, their supply of bread and cold meats had been exhausted by the second day.

Once she was satisfied that the house was empty, she crept down to the kitchens, but the fire was naught but cold ash and all that remained on the table was a pot of broth that smelt ill. The sparce pantries showed evidence of weeks of plague and lack of servants, and further investigations in other rooms told a similar story. It was as if the normally bustling manor house had been deserted for weeks, but then perhaps it had but for the few who had remained to nurse his lordship. She could walk into the village, but that meant people and she had to keep John safe. No, food must be found elsewhere.

The kitchen gardens showed some promise, and there were abundant herbs, but she wanted meat. *Innocence to the innocent.* The dream drifted back to her, a soft voice whispering in her ear, guiding her as to what she should do, what had to be done.

If the world really was coming to an end then it was all about keeping alive, keeping her son, the new Lord Corberley safe, until they were all judged by almighty God. And she would do whatever was required to do just that.

She found them in the woods, huddled together by the spring, but they struggled to their naked feet when they heard her approach. So innocent and alone. She sang a gentle lullaby and they came to her willingly, perhaps seeing the mask she wore and thinking her a healer who had come to help them. Their small cold hands slipped into hers and slowly she led them back to the manor house. Carefully, one foot at a time, they managed the steep kitchen steps, large eyes peering round at the tables, at the bright pots and pans. Perhaps they hoped for food, for warmth, for safety.

Initially they refused to be separated, clinging to each other frantically, but small fingers break easily and while they were subdued, she slammed the head of the eldest against the wall to stun him. Once he was locked away, she hunted down the smaller child whose gasping cries betrayed his hiding place.

Although she had supervised the slaughter of swine before, she stopped to think through her next steps. Fresh meat was precious and must not be wasted. Once naked, the small child was not so different from a piglet and she managed to hoist him onto the hook with only a little effort. His blood gushed warm and clean into the pail below, and the rich smell made her stomach growl so she took a goblet of it to John mixed with a little mead for flavour.

'Drink, it is medicine which will restore your strength after such a long fast.'

Using two hands to steady it, he lifted the goblet to drink, the richness of it colouring his mouth. She left him and returned to the kitchen where the stout wooden table would be used to butcher the meat. Already a fire spat and crackled, waiting to cook their meal. Perhaps heart could be added to a pot with honey, rosemary, and thyme to make a warming stew while the spit turned. John would dine like royalty.

42

1666 – Winter

The pond? Surely she had not walked that far. It was dark in the woods but here in the clearing, the sky showed the last fire of sunset, although the surface of the water reflected nothing but black. It was so quiet; a gurgle of water nearby from the spring was the only sound. No birds sang, no trees creaked. And then the crying started again. Martha's body jolted; she had almost forgotten what had brought her into this part of the woods in the first place.

'Hello? I am a healer. Do you need my help?'

Martha's voice rang out into the clearing and the pond rippled. The voice was clearly human and appeared to be close, but though she turned around she could see no one.

'*No, NO!*'

Martha ran in the direction of the voice with an icy breath on her neck. In the distance, she saw a dark cloaked figure dragging two small girls. Dragging them towards the pond.

'STOP!'

The figure stopped and turned. Lady Mary Corberley.

'Go back, Martha, and forget what you have seen. You would not help me when I asked, so I am taking matters into my own hands.'

Martha was used to the rough pathways and gained on her.

'You know I could not. That dream you spoke of came from the devil himself. Let me take the children back to the village. It is a wicked cold night for these little ones.'

The blow came from behind, and as she fell to the ground

she saw a slight figure grab one of the children's hands as he helped his mother drag them towards the pond. Whatever unholy practices were happening in these woods must be spoken of. She must tell someone, must stop them. She would run back towards the village and go straight to the rectory.

'If you wish to keep that baby you carry, speak not of this, or I swear I will destroy your family and leave you begging from door to door. It is my charity that allows you to live on these grounds.'

Martha's hand betrayed her then by sliding across her belly.

'Now go before I change my mind.'

She ran then, ran in fear, with her baby heavy inside her, but from behind she could hear splashing and a sharp instruction: 'Keep them under the water until they stop struggling and are still.'

43

1666 - Winter

Martha woke to peace. Silence. Then the insistent trill of birdsong registered. Gently breathing in and out, she tried to remember when she had last felt this free of pain. Complete absence of worries. And then she remembered a pain jabbing in her belly where the baby lay and more memories flashed before her eyes. She remembered shouted for Elizabeth to come quickly, and then the dragging sensation that she had forgotten from before. The fear, the excitement, but soon all she could think of was the pain that came in ever increasing waves. As she lay in her bed remembering, the fear returned. Where was the baby?

'Daughter?'

Immediately there was a bump from somewhere in the cottage and soft footsteps approached. The door opened and all she could see was a small soft bundle in her daughter's arms. A small perfect face, rose bud lips, and a pure, clean, heavenly scent.

'You have a son; and I, a brother.'

The peace washed over her again as she held her baby. The ordeal of birth was over and they had both survived.

'I will name him Thomas, for his father, as he would have wished.'

Her daughter's eyes sparkled with unshed tears, and she turned to fuss with some linen, but Martha saw her hand rise quickly to her face. The warm bundle in her arms gazed at her in puzzlement, and she laughed at the little frown.

'Welcome to the world, Thomas Maundrell'.

Voices from the lane broke into the domestic peace. Angry men shouting and many feet pounding the lane outside. They stopped, turned, and then were storming towards her door.

'Elizabeth?'

Her daughter had no sooner gone to the door when Martha heard her cry out and the bedroom door was flung open.

'There she is, with Satan's spawn at her breast.'

The room began to spin as Thomas was ripped from her arms and she felt herself dragged from the bed. Screaming, shouting, her bare feet ripped on the rough path outside. In shame, she noticed blood bloom on her night shift. *Witch*. She could hear Elizabeth screaming, and then the mercy of God granted her oblivion as she fainted.

Clutching her basket tighter, the woman followed the flickering torch. Down the weeping passageways, thick with the foul stench of human misery, past the reaching hands of lost souls.

'In here.' The warden placed the torch in the sconce and left her. At first she could see no one. Just brick walls and filth. A rat scuttled over her boot and she nearly dropped the basket.

'Mistress Martha?' she whispered. Then she saw, hanging from the ceiling, a single chain, and the ragged, bloodied body before her. With a hiss, she crossed herself and the figure let out a groan. Then the witch opened her eyes.

'I have … brought …' She had barely placed the basket on the floor before she was fleeing back down the passageway.

'Save your prayers for those who deserve it, sister,' said the warden who let her out into the mercifully fresh air. 'Food and comfort are wasted on the witch.'

He stepped aside then, as the men of law entered.

'Has she confessed her sins yet?'

'She has not, and if we inflict more persuasion, she will die with her secret within her.'

'The child?'

'The holy sister just brought it.' The warden pointed out the fleeing woman.

The baby's cries echoed strangely in the prison cell. From

where she hung, the witch cried out to him.

'The devil's words will not help him now. Confess your marriage with Satan or watch him die.' Closing his ears to her cries, the witch-finder turned to the warden. 'Brick him up.'

For a moment, the warden looked at him blankly. 'What?'

'Put the spawn of Satan in the wall cavity and brick him up. Perhaps his dying cries might loosen the witch's tongue.'

The small cell rang with the scrape of mortar, the slap of bricks, and the shared screams of mother and child. Finally, the witch-finder heard her whisper the words he had waited for.

'I will confess, only please save him. I confess to unholy practices.'

It was done. Another witch found out.

'Shall we take the little wretch out now?' asked the warden, nodding to the wall.

'Leave it in there. It will quieten soon.'

'NO, YOU PROMISED. If I confessed … YOU PROMISED.'

'I DON'T MAKE PROMISES TO WITCHES. IT WILL BURN IN HELL WITH YOU.'

Wiping the spit from his mouth, he turned and headed back to the rectory, but not before sending a message to Lady Corberley that her fears had been correct; her sister had confessed to witchcraft and the killing of four village children.

Later that night, he proudly recalled the events to his wife as he finished a good supper and a second slice of bread.

'There are less deaths, and there will be less still when she is dead.'

His wife wrapped her arms around her. 'And the child?'

'There is no need for fear. The child will be dead by now, and she will follow him to the fires of hell in the morning.'

He threw another log onto the fire, watching it flare and embrace the fresh wood. 'I think we might plan a little surprise for her.'

44

The frosted air stung Martha's lungs as she took a deep, juddering breath, the first since her captivity. Sweet and wholesome, the scent of fallen leaves and sharp berries brought memories of home. She kept her eyes on the frozen path beneath her, at the jagged flints and sharp ruts. There was no need to look forward because she knew where they were dragging her. Her arms were pinned to her sides and the cold iron chains dug into her bare arms.

After so long in the darkness even this grey fog seemed bright to her eyes, and she stumbled and tripped on her sodden skirts. Her guards seemed in no hurry as she concentrated on not falling. The path changed and, raising her head, she saw they were passing the church. A beacon of safety, of reassurance, it was in these grounds that her family lay, that she had once hoped to lie in everlasting peace. Now she would be dumped at the crossroads in a shallow scratched hole.

The church field lay just beyond, and she could see a small gathering at the hanging tree. Here she had seen so many wretches, dragged, strung up and left to jig until they hung still. Few people lined the road, but still a few jeers reached her, as did a well-aimed stone. She lurched backwards, tried to right herself, and then fell heavily to her knees.

'Too late to pray now, witch.' The weak ripple of laughter seemed far away as she was jerked upright again. Sharp pain as her bare feet glanced off a flint, but then the cold numbed them into blocks of ice again. A yew bush with bright berries came into sight. Poison. But she was dragged forward again, away from their mercy. She must make a pathetic figure, she thought, her white feet matching the snow that was now falling fitfully on the miserable ground below. As she neared the field, a nervous laugh rippled out again.

'Look up, witch, and see what awaits thee.'

Without thinking, she obeyed. The people watching her gasped as she stared at them; at her friends and neighbours, people who had held her hand and thanked her just months ago. Now they hurriedly made the sign of the cross before turning away. Then she saw it. A weak cry of fright escaped her and, again, she wished she could wake from this evil dream. This could not be real. Her gaze passed the hanging tree, to the small unlit bonfire. Faggots made of twigs and large branches carefully laid, and in the middle, like a candle, stood a large post. A rough ladder was propped against it and nearby, a cloaked figure held aloft a flaming torch.

'No gentle hanging for you, witch.' Jeered the same man as he cackled in glee at the trembling form in front of him.

There were few people out to watch the burning on that snowy morning. A few men in black who wore their authority in their austere garments and grave expressions, and a small number of villagers who looked a little nervous but excited. Then a woman pushed forward, her face to the ground when she spoke. 'Did you kill my girls? They were gathering berries, weeks past, but did not return.'

The little girls she had seen in the woods.

'Gathering on Corberley land? Ask her ladyship. She will know what end they met at her hand.'

The woman raised her head and stared Martha in the face, seeking the truth. She found it there, and with fresh tears hurried away. The crowd was growing now, and from the tree line, she saw a lone figure.

They had to drag her up the ladder, for her legs could no longer support her. Branches of dark yew had been hidden in the faggots and a small flicker of gratitude warmed her for a moment. It was believed that burning yew would omit poisonous smoke. Would this render her senseless before the flames reached her? Was there enough? As she was dragged to the stake and the chains wrapped around her body, she looked once more out to the waiting villagers. The priest was muttering prayers, and fervent 'amens' drifted across to her.

A sudden movement and bright light blinded her for a second, and then warmth trickled down her face. A stone ricocheted off the faggots and landed out of sight. The pain and a wave of nausea crowded her senses as the flaming torch grew larger. Then flames leaped and warmed her face. She must have screamed because bitter smoke entered her lungs along with a fierce heat which scorched her throat. In vain, she struggled against the chains as flames and billowing smoke enveloped her. The heat seemed to be a living thing that roared behind her ribs. Then she saw the figure at the tree line again and something in her seemed to detach.

The smoke became fog which crept across the field, like a crouching beast, to where she stood at the edge of the field, watching herself burn. This could not be the end. She had done nothing. There was still time. Someone would come and they would throw water on the burning wood. She had heard of quick fires when the poor soul was burned alive. But there were also slow merciful burnings when smoke rendered the victim senseless before flames reached them.

Was this how they would remember her? Not that she was a mother of two, had been a faithful wife, a midwife, had helped at the sickbed of half the village. Women, and men, were being murdered across the country, she knew; as the pestilence spread, so did fear. But some were pardoned at the last minute. There was still hope. For a blissful moment she felt a shiver of cold as she watched herself from the edge of the woods. Before she could take a deep breath of the merciful air, she was back in the fire again, straining against the chains that held her upright in the agonising heat. Rage filled her then, and while she still had breath she screamed out her curse to those watching her torture.

A sudden wind cleared the smoke and through streaming eyes, she saw Elizabeth. Her daughter raised her head and started forward as she met her mother's gaze. Then, incredibly, she moved her cloak aside and for one second Martha saw two things: the ring on Elizabeth's finger and the tiny hand that reached for it. How? She had heard his screams as the bricks were slammed on the mortar, encasing him in his cold tomb. At the sight of them, the tears boiled out of her on a wave of sobbing. Her children, her family. But she feared that Elizabeth would be snatched again so, blinking away the tears, she sought to find her again in the crowd. As they exchanged one last look it was as if she knew what her mother wanted; she gave a small smile, wrapped her cloak firmly around her again and headed across the fields, past the lone figure, until the trees swallowed her.

The flames had caught at her damp dress and she experienced the first taste of the agony to come, and with it, the last of her hope was lost. All thinking disappeared and was replaced by the terrifying cage of pain from which there was no escape. Her own screams filled her ears, until her lungs felt they were boiling in the heat and she could no longer use them. There was no time, no regrets, no thoughts, just pain that made every breath feel like a hundred. Just before she lost all sense, an image appeared behind her closed lid; the last thing she would see this side of the grave. It was not of her daughter's soft brown eyes, or the tiny hand of her son, it was of a shivering figure which stood at the edge of the woods, watching with large eyes. Whom she had seemed to change places with for a few seconds. The woman's mouth was moving as if she was talking to someone, or to herself. And then she simply faded away.

Wake up, Nell. She was at the edge of the woods again, where she had seen the robin, but this time looking back at the field where the obscenest execution was taking place. Not a hanging, but a burning. The flames grew higher, but Nell could still see the small figure standing erect in the middle. Blood ran down her face, the only colour in this white-grey scene, apart from the dancing flames that lit the dawn. Blood dripped onto her thin chest as her head fell forward, but incredulously through the roar of flames, Nell heard a hoarse voice shout out.

'Hear me well. For on my innocent blood that you spill this morn, I curse you. On my newborn son's blood, that you slew, I curse you. And while a Maundrell still breathes upon this land, I will one day return and have my revenge on the filth that roams North Chase Manor.'

The villagers muttered and the priest's voice rose higher in prayer, and over the spitting fire, Nell could hear Martha's own voice as she proclaimed her innocence to any who would hear it. Then her voice turned to screams that ripped into Nell's head. She slammed her hands over her ears and closed her eyes tight, but still she could see the figure writhing, bloody matter spewing from her mouth. Time to wake up before she switched places with the poor woman again.

Come on Nell, enough. Opening her eyes, the smoke slowly turned to the dark ceiling above her, but just before she fully awoke, she heard a voice.

'The witch will be a long time burning.'

The stench of scorched hair and skin caught the back of her throat and she turned over to vomit. When she was able to focus again she saw not the bed cover but frosted grass. *Still* trapped in the dream then. Suddenly, a new voice found her. One that was deep and soft; and very familiar.

'Nell, you are safe.'

The voice faded, and she watched dry flakes of snow join the ash that had settled on her cloak.

A light snow fell from the grey sky as Lady Corberley turned her horse in the direction of home. Breaking into a canter, the solitude hit her again. She had no husband to command her, no groom to accompany her, and few servants to watch her. She had no family left but her son. Dry flakes scratched across her cloak, but all she could hear were Martha's screams.

Once when they had been children, they had dared to talk in church and both been beaten severely. She had obstinately refused to cry but her older sister had screamed until she fainted. Sisters; their likeness still hung in a forgotten part of the manor house where their old cloth dolls sat on their toy rocking chair. None of their brothers had survived to adulthood, so on her father's death, her cousin had inherited. Martha was intended for him but she had shamed the family and married beneath her. Mary had been quick to take her place.

A figure suddenly emerged from the woods.

'She said I should ask you. My daughters are missing.'

Mary recognised one of the villagers and, unbidden, the memory of two little girls and their screams crowded her memory. The woman must have seen the guilt in her face for she let out a cry. Mary lifted her whip. The woman fell to the ground, blood flowing through her fingers, and Mary spurred on her horse. The woman would have a nasty scar across her face as a reminder not to challenge her betters.

As she trotted into the stables, a slight figure emerged.

'John. Back into the house. You will catch a fever.'

'Did Aunt Martha——?'

'Yes. It is done.'

'But what we have done, what we did, that was evil too. Those missing children … it was us, not her.'

She glanced round quickly, but there was none to hear his foolish words.

'Do you think I do not know that? But it was God's will that you be spared, and *his* will that she perish. A confession was got.'

'What did they do to get that from her?'

Mary's eyes darted to him in shock.

'Hush now. Back in the house.'

He would not speak to her, refused to eat.

'It is swine, from the farm.'

'Is it though?'

What she had done had been justified. Her son lived, was thriving. Why would such a dream come to her had it not been a message from God? That night, she wrote down her account of what she had been required to do. It was her confession and once done, she sealed it carefully and hid it within the skirts of Martha's doll, confident that none would ever find it.

John woke in the night to a roaring sound. Puzzled, he lit his candle and ventured out onto the landing only to be knocked back by the wall of fire. Frantically, he tried to reach his mother's room but the flames beat him back. As he fled down the secret staircase and into the cool gardens, he didn't notice his mother and aunt's old dolls on their rocking chair in the alcove, or how once he slammed the door shut they slowly began to rock, first back and then forwards as the second soul that day entered them. Two dolls for two sisters who had both perished in the flames of God.

In the grounds, a woman with her face tightly bandaged, looked on with pleasure as the house burned. She remembered the curse that the widow Maundrell had uttered as her innocent life was taken, and vowed on her own daughters' memories that until her dying day, and perhaps beyond, she would protect the children of North Chase from the filth who wished them harm.

45

Nell began to cough, and then vomited. Gently, Austin lay his warm jacket over her, grateful he had removed it before wading into the water. Suddenly, he realised how quiet it was. The baby had stopped crying. With his body still protecting Nell, he twisted his neck to check on the child but all he saw were leaves. Tilly and the baby had gone. As if to confirm his deduction, he saw a flicker of torch light bounce off the trees in the distance. He should have hit her harder.

'Save the baby,' whispered a soft voice by his knees.

'Say again?' Austin lowered his face to Nell's. She was struggling to sit up.

'I'm fine. Go now, before she escapes.'

'Are you sure?'

'Absolutely. I'll follow.'

Austin took one long look at Nell, realised she was being truthful, and then ran after the flickering light.

The darkness was complete save for the moonlight which cast a dreamlike spell over Nell's senses, but she dodged low hanging branches, jumped tree roots, and bulldozed through low bushes until the light ahead brightened. She saw a van in the distance, and a figure pulling at the locked door.

'Give me the baby, Matilda.' Nell recognised that Austin's gentle voice hid a building rage.

Tilly spun round to face him, a knife in her hand. Nell quickly looked around in the gloom, but they were alone.

'You could come quietly,' he said, and again, Nell heard danger. 'You will not get away again.'

'I was only protecting my son, the Corberley heir. Do you have children? Clearly not or you would understand the need to protect them, how as a mother you will do anything for your child.'

Austin took a step closer. 'Now I understand the confusion. You don't know Mark's secret, do you?'

Tilly stared mutely for a moment, and then began to laugh. Nell, shivering in her wet clothes, felt like she had taken another plunge in the pool. It was not just the comment about being childless that chilled her to the bone, but the merriment. It felt wrong, disturbingly wrong.

'You again? You are supposed to be dead,' Tilly shot at her.

'I am supposed to be a lot of things. Where did you put the baby, is she close by?'

'How should I know? You saw her, the woman, I know you did,' said Tilly, but then her voice broke into a sob. 'She was standing by the brat so I presume she took her, took my gift for her. So in answer to your question, ASK HER, ASK THE WITCH.'

The woman with no face, so she hadn't been part of Nell's dream. The visions she had just seen and the dreams leading up to it began to surface. The burning, the baby, the dolls, the broken fingers of the child. Over it all, she could smell scorched hair and blood.

'Did you know where the first Lady Corberley kept the children she was going to sacrifice?' continued Tilly conversationally, as she waved the knife about like a sparkler. 'In the old crypt. It was so the body of Christ could enter them before they were eaten. To make the meat even purer. I read it in her account. Then each and every one was drowned.' If Tilly was trying to shock her, thought Nell, then she clearly hadn't experienced the horror of vivid dreaming.

'Not sure where you are getting your facts from but, trust me, I've seen it all first hand, and that's not how it was done,' Nell answered.

Tilly exploded in rage.

'You are too late anyway; I have already slit her throat.'

Again, Nell shook her head. 'I don't think so. Do you know what happened to Mary?'

Tilly's mouth opened, but before she had time to speak, Nell whispered, 'She burned to death in the manor house the same night she sent her own sister to the flames.'

While Nell had Tilly's full attention, Austin was creeping up behind her, like the witch in the print. But Tilly wasn't finished yet.

'How do you know this? Oh wait, now I understand. Funny how you survived the drowning, isn't it? Not that innocent then, witch.' Tilly winked once, and then with a scream, flew at Nell with the knife. Austin was quicker, but as he was reaching for her, a loud crack broke through the night air and Tilly suddenly vanished. Her sharp scream was cut short by a loud snap. Nell fell to her knees as if in prayer, splashing vomit onto her hands. The silence was complete except for a soft bumping which came from the hole at their feet, but soon that too stopped. Austin carefully stepped forward and looked down at the ground.

'Stay away, Nell.'

'Where did she go?'

'Entrance to an old passageway. Finn obviously didn't cover it properly.'

'I don't …'

She was on her feet, wiping her hands down her sodden jeans. Ignoring Austin's warning, she cautiously peered through the gaping hole where from a beautiful silk scarf, the body of Matilda Corberley continued to swing.

Austin calmly gave directions to the police while supporting Nell with his other arm.

'They are on their way. We need to get you to a hospital.'

Nell shook her head. Both arms wrapped around her, and as she relaxed her face against his soft sweater, she tried to remember when she had last been hugged or felt quite this safe.

'You are so cold.' Then Austin's phone began to ring again and Nell was released.

'Max. Your timing is—'

'Nell?' Austin put her on speaker, and in the background

Nell could hear Tchaikovsky's Nutcracker overture. He quickly filled in the gaps, ignoring Max's whispered questions.

'Keep her warm and get her away from those damn haunted woods. I should have been there. Been with her.'

Nell took a puff from her inhaler and tried not to think of Tilly hanging a few feet away.

'I was in time, thanks to your warning.' Austin looked into Nell's face. 'We are a triad, remember. We work together.'

'But the baby is gone, and we don't know where,' Nell whispered, and the urge to look back down at Tilly's dead body began to pull at her.

There was a pause, and then Max said, 'I think you do.'

'What?'

'Nell, my lovely. Listen to me. All those weird dreams. What is the point of them if not that someone is trying to tell you something.' Had it only been that morning that she had last seen Max? It felt like she had lived through so many lifetimes since then. Fire thrashed in her mind again.

'But they make no real sense.'

'But have any of them been true?'

For a moment, Nell was back in the dream, watching Martha burn.

'They've all been true.'

'In November, I was told by a psychic that I couldn't help you this time and that I shouldn't try. But I think the message was that I shouldn't try because *you* had to do it. You need to face this because I think you are the only one who can find her.' Although Nell wanted to argue with Max, deep in her stomach she knew she was right, and hadn't she said to herself tonight that it was time to stop fighting, to follow her path and face her demons?

'Tilly said that there was a woman by the pond and that she took the baby.'

'Ok, good. A real woman or a spirit?'

'She had no face.'

Austin was staring at her with concern.

'Oh, I know her. She kept me company on the underground just now. I think she is the witch.'

The scenes Nell had just witnessed flooded back.

'No, I don't think so. I've been seeing her all over town. I thought she was real. She pushes a pram full of dolls—'

'Ok, but maybe you have seen a baby in your dreams?'

A voice interrupted.

'Maxine, is everything alright? It's starting.'

Nell grimaced and Austin took over. 'Max, I'll take it from here. Be with your father. We have this.'

'No, I need to help.'

'You have. You've told us what to do. Like you said, Nell needs to do this.'

Panic flushed through Nell. 'But I can't just see this stuff whenever I want.'

'Tell me what you've been seeing.'

It was when Nell spoke of the burning, of the tiny bundle she had seen bricked up alive, but had later appeared hiding safely in his sister's shawl, that Nell began to feel a blurring around her. The trees began to lighten with the eery glow of new snow, and she remembered.

'They walled the baby up alive to torture Martha. But someone must have saved him, must have given him to Elizabeth. A nun visited her and then was later walled up alive herself. Perhaps because she went back.'

Torch lights appeared in the distance, and the voice of a young man telling the police to follow him. As Austin looked back at her she saw his face change to that of a man she had last seen in an underground cell that stank of blood and urine.

The police would have questions, which would detain them, but as Austin hatched a quick getaway, Nell got to her feet and began to walk. Silently, he followed as she stepped swiftly and lightly through the trees as if following a path that only she could see. Grateful to be moving again at such a fast pace, Austin let the trees swallow them up. He had an idea, so quietly made a call.

'Finn, no don't tell them I'm ringing. We are going to find the baby, but I need your help. Where are the oldest cottages in town? Those that are hundreds of years old?'

As Finn gave him directions, Austin realised that right or wrong, Nell was walking straight to them.

46

1666

The baby's frantic cries tugged at the rough bricks, at the empty chains, at the stale damp air. They bled out into the passageway causing the torch to flicker and dim. Then the cries too began to dim until deathly silence fell heavily like a hangman's noose. A new noise filled the empty cell as the chains which hung like entrails from the ceiling began to sway.

Samuel shuddered outside the door. The witch had confessed so she had been moved, he had done it himself, so who was moving the chains? It was an evil business done that night, and he shook his head to think of his own newborn safely at home.

Was the baby still breathing? His ears strained to listen against the damp bricks, but perhaps it was his own gasping he could hear. Then he heard the faintest of whimpers, and soft bumping against the bricks as if the baby was patting its tiny hands, perhaps waiting for a warm finger to wrap its own around. Waiting for a soft kiss on its downy head. The torch flickered once more and threatened to plunge him into darkness. Like the baby was in darkness.

Witchcraft, the devil's business, but he had seen too many in these cells to believe it any longer. The old, the ugly, the alone and confused. They had all been led to these cells to be tortured. One woman's only crime was to be from other shores, and another was just disliked for her popish beliefs. But to murder a babe. The mother had confessed so why should he still die? It reminded him of a scene from the mystery plays, of the slaying of babies by Herod's decree. None of this felt

257

right, felt holy. Soft footsteps approached outside and he was surprised to see the holy sister had returned.

'If you have your confession, I can remove the child?'

She looked puzzled and then horror filled her eyes as she followed his gaze to the wall. She dropped her basket and began to claw at the bricks. This was surely a sign from God, so he pushed her aside and, using his knife, scraped out the mortar. A foul stench met him as he pulled out the first brick. The sister was praying softly at his side as he thrust his hands into the gap and grabbed the soft bundle inside. Something snatched at his fingers and, with relief, he brought the small lad out.

'I'll take him back to his sister,' she whispered. 'Pray he stays silent while I remove him from this foul place.'

They exchanged a glance that said more than they dare speak, that spoke of the danger they would both meet if their treachery was discovered. With a small smile, she was gone and Samuel swiftly replaced the bricks and smoothed down the mortar. Outside in the passageway, the torch danced against the walls and then settled back into a fierce flame. Samuel prayed he would be forgiven should his disobedience ever be learned, but in his heart he knew that he had done God's will that night.

47

'Austin, I think I know where the baby is.'

Nell was cold as a frog and her eyes burned overly bright, but Austin was relieved to see that she had returned to the present.

'Is it far? My car is parked close by.'

'A car with a heater?'

He smiled down at her. 'This way, and I believe I may have a spare sweater for you.'

With the engine running, he returned from the boot with the promised clothes and a rug which he insisted on wrapping round her. Then with the heating turned to max, he slammed the car into gear.

'It was snowing, in my dream. The first dream when I was walking through the woods. I thought it was a dream, anyway, but then I woke up and I saw her, and the woman behind her. Are we too late? Do you think the baby is still alive?'

'Why don't we find out.'

Bumping over the tree roots, he headed back to the main road and into town.

Cursing that she had to work that night, Ric was gleaning all she could of the fire at the manor from punters in the restaurant. There was a lot of speculation which had gotten more fanciful when an ambulance went tearing by. She tried Seb's number once more and then, catching the chef's eye, she quickly slid it back into her pocket.

Her eye fell on the print that had disturbed her a few weeks

259

ago. The figure had gone, but from a wall near the old chapel she thought she saw a faint outline of a person. As if the artist had drawn a woman standing by the wall, had changed their mind, and then failed to entirely erase them so they now looked to be encased behind the bricks. She shuddered; they really needed to get some cheerier prints, and she made a mental note to mention Seb's photographs. Seb; surely someone would think to tell her if something awful had happened to him.

The kitchen door flew open and a tall man marched in.

'I am looking for Ric.'

She raised her hand and he beckoned.

'With me now, please.' The chef began to protest but was waved aside with a brusque, 'there will be explanations later.'

Ric grabbed her bag and coat, and then gestured to the back entrance.

'And who exactly are you?'

He turned and smiled tightly. 'Nell sent me. We did try your cottage but there was no answer.'

Slightly relieved, Ric trotted to keep up with his stride.

'No, Mum's gone out. Why—'

But she was then struck dumb at the sight of Nell shivering in a blanket and a sweater which reached down to her knees.

'Is Seb alright? Oh my God, what's happening?'

Nell just shook her head and attempted a smile. 'Seb is fine but Ava is missing.' She exchanged a look with the tall man. 'This won't make any sense, but I think she might be in the cottage next door to you. Where you heard the children? Can we borrow the key?'

As Ric hurried down the road with them, she heard the man comment, 'We would be in by now if you had agreed to my method.'

'Yes, but this is nicer.'

A thousand questions crowded Ric's mind, but she concentrated instead on not slipping on the pavement which was beginning to freeze.

It was as they unlocked the door that Nell felt her vision begin to flicker. The menace which lay beyond that door, just out of sight, paralysed her and before she could stop herself, she was backing away. In horror films, this was the point when every sane person watching would roll their eyes and exclaim, 'Well don't go in there, you idiot.'

The harsh electric light turned to flickering candlelight. She dug her nails into the soft flesh of her palms to stay present, took a step through the doorway, and then suddenly she saw her. With a click, the lights went out but the image of a woman with long dark hair, who rocked from side to side, was burned into Nell's eyes. All sound faded from her ears as she approached the middle of the room, and as her eyes adjusted to the dark, she saw the woman turn around. Ric's scream hit her like a physical blow. As the woman lifted her head, Nell realised what she had been rocking. The pram with the ornate handle was straight from her dream of the dolls. In the darkness, Nell saw movement.

'May I?' she asked the ghost who stood before her, and as she stepped aside, Nell saw something fly out of the pram. Nell slowly crouched to pick up the small rag doll as Ava began to scream. 'Is this yours, baby girl?' Ava's bright eyes saw her doll, and with chubby arms, she reached for it. Then, thumb back in mouth, she gazed at Nell with interest and didn't protest when she was lifted into her arms.

Nell turned to Ric and Austin, blinded by her tears, and then with another click, the lights came back on.

'Found her.'

48

'But there is so much I don't understand,' complained Max. '*How* did you know she was in there?'

Nell had showered and dressed in her warmest clothes, and now nursed a mug of coffee. She glanced over at Austin who raised an eyebrow in exasperation.

'Max, I saw so much and I haven't put together all the pieces yet, but I think the nanny might have been one of the mothers whose children Mary took.'

'And ate.'

'Yes.'

'Like Tilly Corberley. And I thought they hanged the witch, not burned her? So, history is wrong?'

For a moment, Nell saw the figure of Tilly swinging beneath her, with the scarf around her neck like a noose.

'Max, let poor Nell finish. You really do have the most awful habit of interrupting. There will be plenty of time for explanation when we meet up tomorrow.'

As Nell hung up, she listened to the room settle around her. Austin had wanted to take her straight to London, but tomorrow was Christmas Eve and Nell needed a chance to make amends with her father. Her Christmas gift. Talking of gifts, she opened a cupboard and brought out a bag for Austin.

'Happy Christmas,' she attempted. 'I saw this and thought of you.'

Austin smiled his thanks and withdrew the bottle.

'Solstice flames?' For the first time, she realised she was hearing Austin laugh, a deep rumble that coaxed a smile from her at the irony of it. 'Did you by any chance purchase this here?'

Now she was laughing too. After everything that had happened that evening it felt good, defiant, as if she was showing the world that not even a near drowning, a hanging, and a close encounter with a very scary ghost could knock her off her perch. She shrugged.

'As it happens I did.'

Her peripheral vision caught a movement as something dark drifted by. The events of the night were still taking thin slices from her sense of reality, despite her best attempts, and she realised that there was a very real chance that she might slip back to 1666 at any moment.

'I don't think you should be alone tonight.' Austin had been watching her carefully.

'No, and I don't want to be. The sofa is supposed to pull out to a double bed, but I can't imagine it will be very comfortable.'

Austin just shrugged. 'I can sleep quite comfortably on the floor, if necessary.'

'I have one more important job to do before I settle down, though.' Slowly but purposefully, Nell took down the mirror and monotone prints and placed them in the cupboard.

Her eye fell on the posy of rosemary, the embroidery, and the ribbon she had found just days ago.

'Maybe the children left these for me,' she whispered. '*Rosemary for remembrance.*' She was suddenly aware that Austin was standing close behind her.

'I am not entirely certain of what I saw in that cottage, and I can live with that. But consider this; perhaps *someone* has had faith in you from the moment you arrived here, even when you doubted yourself. *They* had faith that you could rescue the child and uncover the truth, unmask the—' Austin frowned, unable or unwilling to name Tilly for what she was, but Nell could.

'Witch?'

'Killer,' he conceded.

Nell noticed the clock. The hands which had stopped at midnight or midday were now pointing to nine o'clock, the time that Martha had been burned. From deep within its oak casing came a steady tick tock, like a heartbeat.

Nell was exhausted, but couldn't turn off her mind. The past horrors and the very present violence chased around her consciousness and her arms ached. Ached for the baby she had held in her arms, both Ava and little Thomas. Nell's maternal clock gave a dull chime. Did she want children, really? Perhaps. Gary's best friend's girlfriend was pregnant. Quickly, Nell did the maths. The party had been at the end of August and Cindy had been about twelve weeks then, so she would have a sizeable bump now. Her friends would be talking baby showers and birthing plans. For a moment, Nell wondered again who the father really was. She had sneaked back to the house to get the rest of her things a whole seven days after she had run away, and seen high-heeled shoes in the living room that looked like Cindy's, and the lipstick smear on the wine glass had been her shade. Coincidence? Possibly. Probably. She gave herself a shake, who cared about Cindy and Gary and the unborn baby; they were part of a life she had run away from.

Gary had once broached the subject of them having a baby. But at the time she had been wearing a medley of bruises, old and new, across her arms and back, so she had changed the subject quickly. Being pregnant would make her even more vulnerable. She had heard of women having unborn babies kicked out of them, and the thought of his violence harming an innocent child, whether born or waiting to be born, was something she couldn't risk. A baby would have only complicated things. Now the only relationship she was interested in was with Will. Her father. Even the word sounded weird. She had hoped that meeting him would ease the pain of her past, that it would be soothed, and the emptiness she carried inside her like a ghost baby, that fed off her and made its presence known, would mysteriously disappear and she would become whole again. Whole, with a messy past and some psychological scarring perhaps, but on the first steps of her new life.

Still, for a moment, she imagined holding her own child in her arms. Of those innocent eyes locking with hers, and knowing that there was one person in this world whom she would always love more than her own life. Born of her own flesh and blood, forever linked. She thought of Tilly, then, and how she had felt justified in her evil because it was all for her son. As Mary had felt justified because she was protecting John. Why had her own father never felt that need to protect her, above all others? To offer his strength when she needed comfort?

Strange though, when she thought of strength and comfort, a different person came to mind. A person who always listened, and advised, and although was a little scary, was firmly on her side.

49

Christmas Eve

It was Christmas Eve and Nell had plans. She had texted Will to change their lunch to coffee, then she was packing her bags and going to London for a few days with Austin. Their conversation at dawn had lasted no more than a minute, and now there was no sign that he had ever been there except for the faint scent of sandalwood coming from the sofa. She decided to leave her decorations up for now, as a link to her past and a link to Will, but she packed the rest of her belongings.

As she picked up the *Myths and Legends of North Chase* book, she paused. Perhaps she could give it to Will. It slipped from her fingers and fell face down, and as it did, something small fluttered to the floor. A pressed flower, brown and fragile. Opening the book to put it back, she saw it had been pressed against one of the ink block illustrations. A man lay under a door and rocks were being placed on top so that he slowly crushed to death. Oh, bloody hell, she wished she hadn't seen that. Any thought of torture made her feel faint, and she had to steel her mind away from the visions of last night, of the stench of the damp cell. The inscription below said the man was being 'pressed'. How could people do such horrible things to other human beings? She put the fragile flower back into the book and closed it. Pressed flower, pressed person. Of course. Someone thought they were being witty. How tasteless.

Will was due any minute so in anticipation, she walked down to the entrance hall below, giving the rocking horse a stroke on her way.

He looked shorter; his eyes filled with emotion, and he seemed to be as physically wrecked as she was, but he smiled when he saw her waiting by the door.

'Come in.'

Nell stepped aside so Will could step over the threshold. Still smiling he stopped to look around the entrance hall.

'This really is a magnificent building. As old as the church.'

He was not much taller than her, she thought, his greying hair was styled with gel but as he passed, she could see he was thinning on top.

'I've got some rooms upstairs. It is lovely really, but a bit dark. I suppose I've got used to my apartment in Devon.'

An odd look flashed across his eyes, but he smiled once more and nodded. As Nell followed him up the stairs, she couldn't resist, 'But you know about the apartment already, don't you?'

She fumbled with the key and, again, held the door as he entered.

'I kept in touch with your Nana over the years. I stayed at the apartment for a few months when I first got back to England, must be five years ago now.'

Again the flare of anger. *Five bloody years and not a word.* And in her apartment too. But then, she reasoned as she filled the kettle, the apartment had been rented out so plenty of strangers had called it home for a while. And in truth, that was what he was now, a stranger. But if she wanted her Christmas wish, she needed to start with a clean slate. Hanging on to his past mistakes was not going to let them move on to whatever future was possible.

'How do you take your coffee?' She almost felt like apologising for not knowing if her own father took milk or sugar.

'Black, please.'

Something had taken his eye. Her Christmas decorations.

'Oh, I remember these from my own childhood. How lovely that you kept them. But I suppose there must have been lots of stuff from Lark House. Sorry you had to sort all of that out by yourself. Let me think, there were books, paintings,

267

jewellery.'

He had his back to her while he examined her little tree, and when he turned round something in his smile jarred with Nell.

Odd. 'Not really much stuff at all. She sold most of it. Or gave it away. I have her engagement and wedding rings, and her old photo albums. She gave me her decorations when she moved into the home.'

'I remember she used to have a lovely jewellery box. She would never let me near it when I was a child.'

'Given to friends or sold, I'm afraid.'

What was it with the interrogation?

He just smiled and reached for his coffee.

'I am sorry, Nell, for so much. But perhaps we can make a new start now. I meant what I said yesterday.'

'I want that too.'

It was strange, she thought. She had always imagined that the invisible link of kinship, of shared blood, would make itself known when she met him again. That there would be a little tug, an easing of the pain, a filling of the void that Nana's loss had created. Faintly, she remembered the old daydream that he would see her in a crowd, call out her name, and she would be enclosed in the warm hug she remembered from childhood. A memory of Austin's hug last night as they had both been shivering in their wet clothes surfaced and she felt the comfort of it as if he was standing there now. So why did she not feel it with her own flesh and blood?

Perhaps the daydream had really been about the feeling of certainty, that this was her dad, returned to her, and all would be well again. That she would once more be the most important person in someone's life. But she saw it now for what it was: a child's daydream. She had never been the most important person in her dad's life, or if she had, then not for long. He had left her to deal with all the mess that had come next, and she couldn't help feeling slightly angry at Nana too, for keeping such secrets. All that time she would have known he was alive, had left him the house in her will and presumably the money to renovate it. Had she met up with him, talked to him, or was it all through the solicitor? Most of all, she was just angry that her father was finally standing in front of her, had come back into her life, and she felt nothing for him. He was a total stranger. He was admiring her tree again, talking about nothing, so perhaps he was nervous too. Then he raised his eyebrows and tilted his head, and she felt it, the first stab of recognition.

'I don't know what to call you.'

He stopped mid-sentence, and Nell realised she had said this out loud.

'For now why don't you call me Will? I've don't think I deserve to be called dad yet, do you?'

'Ok.'

He must have seen the tears because the next thing she felt was his arms around her, tentatively, and then firmer when he realised she wasn't going to pull away.

The church bells began to ring outside, and Nell closed her eyes and let the last of her reserve drop. They had a long way to go, but they had taken the first steps.

As if realising how precious their progress was, when she mentioned she would spend Christmas in London, he agreed and said it was a good idea. Perhaps they could meet up in the New Year and he could show her how the renovations were going and the progress he had made on the family tree. When he suggested she stay somewhere more cheerful, they exchanged a smile and, again, the awkwardness shifted slightly. There was something bittersweet about Christmas, thought Nell. Happy and sad all at the same time, and instead of trying to diminish the dark or the sad, perhaps the trick was to accept that its very presence was what made Christmas magical.

The stars looked so beautiful because they twinkled in a cold dark sky. The warm fire was comforting because of the bitter cold. Would the decorations on the tree, and those sparkling in the town, have quite the same effect if all was not cold and barren, devoid of life? She looked at her tinsel and ornaments, and they now reminded her of the buds which would appear again in the spring when the bone-like trees would bloom with green.

Yes, trees and flowers would blossom again, and perhaps Christmas reminded us that once we had celebrated these times, listened to these songs, sung carols and watched films, and wished a 'merry Christmas' to people, loved ones, family who were no longer with us. It reminded us that life was fragile and the spiral of time looped in tighter circles at midwinter, bringing our childhoods within a sigh's distance. So close were these memories, closer than any other time. As she watched from the window, Nell saw Will emerge from under the porch and start down the road. He stopped and, turning, looked up at her window to see if she was watching. Nell waved and smiled in answer, and the smile he returned jolted a memory from long ago.

She had met her father and it would be ok. Not quite what she dreamed of but all the better for that, because her dreams could never be trusted and had a nasty way of turning very sinister and coming true. So let the dark skies make the stars shine even brighter, and the cold wind make the fire burn warmer, for the cheer in her heart would lighten the loss and sadness. This Christmas she was learning that balance of dark and light were needed for magic, and for wishes to come true. And every day from now on the sun would rise a little earlier and set a little later until it was time to withdraw and rest again in winter's silence.

'Maybe everything is going to be ok. Nana, I just met my dad, and it was ...' As tears flowed, she realised that she didn't need a word to describe it; her dad had hugged her and it had felt right. The room felt warmer somehow and, despite the terrifying events yesterday, it was as if a corner had been turned and the ground underfoot was firmer. Even the ghosts were quiet today. Maybe that was because they had passed on their message, the killer had been uncovered, and the callous murder of Martha Maundrell had been revealed. The long sigh had only just left her chest when suddenly one of her decorations crashed to the floor. The little felt angel which had given Max a scare the day before. *Crashed to the floor*, Max was right, for a felt decoration, it was overly heavy. She crept to the tree, bringing her newfound optimism with her to fight off the growing unease that had begun to return.

Laying the angel in the palm of her hand, she gently pressed her finger onto its soft belly. Something hard squished underneath. Gently but firmly, she felt from the other side. What the hell was in there? A small weight to make it hang properly? But that didn't make sense. Something was inside; *hidden* inside.

Grabbing the nail scissors from her wash bag, Nell very gently unpicked one of the side seams, and there, nestled in the cotton wool which must have been there since before she was born, was a small metal object. Carefully, she reached inside and pulled it out. Grabbing her mobile, she stabbed in a number and waited. Max appeared, hurriedly moving into another room.

'What time are you leaving? Oh my God, Nell, are you crying?'

'I found this hidden in that angel.' She held it up to her screen.

'Bloody hell. That looks so old. Is it gold?'

As Nell held it up to the light, she thought that somewhere in the old rectory, or perhaps in the street or even in her own subconscious, she could hear whispering.

'Nell, this is serious. Bring it closer.'

Still speechless, Nell pressed the small ring closer to the screen as requested.

'Wow. It is so thick. I mean, look at the difference between my signet ring and this one. Must be hundreds of years old. A family heirloom.'

At that point all the contentment from the last few hours sank through Nell's bones and into the floorboards below. That was exactly what it was; a priceless family heirloom that Nana had known about and hidden. She remembered again Nana's words to her.

'You like this little angel, don't you, Eleanor?'

'It is my absolute favourite. But she looks a bit scruffy, and angels shouldn't be scruffy.'

'Then we will give her a makeover, and if you help me then from this day on, this little angel will be your own special Christmas decoration.'

'For me?'

'Just for you, and only you. But you are to keep it safe. And Eleanor?'

'Yes?'

'Keep it somewhere hidden. It is very special, and I gave it to you.'

She had been thirteen years old; she knew that because it had been the year the school did *A Christmas Carol* at school. She had been an urchin, her enthusiastic, out of tune singing was easily hidden amongst the chorus, but she could dance a little. Nana had found calico to make her costume, and they had used the remnants to restore the angel.

'Now you will always remember the year I gave this to you,' Nana had said.

During her years with Gary, she had kept the angel hidden away. Nothing precious was safe with him. But it wasn't this thought that made her angry now, it was that she finally realised what her dad had been talking about. He had asked about Nana's jewellery a few times and had not seemed happy with her answers. Was this what he was referring to? Did he know about it and want it?

'Keep it safe, keep it hidden.'

'What was that, Nell?' Max enquired

'That's what Nana said to me when she gave me this.'

'She knew what was in it.'

'Oh yes. But she knew I could be trusted to not lose it.'

'I've got an idea.' Max was looking away. 'Stay put, I'll ring you back.'

Such a small ring, but so heavy. Nell took after her grandmother physically and had the same small hands and narrow wrists. The ring easily slipped onto her ring finger as if it had been made for her.

Her mobile was vibrating, a call from Max. 'I've sent you some images I found, take a look.' Nell opened the collection of photos of medieval jewellery.

'Curative?'

'Possibly. Curative rings were given to people to cure them of diseases, apparently.

'I wonder if it did cure whoever was given this.'

'Could date from the seventeenth century. Nell, you should get it checked out. Maybe after Christmas.'

'Thank you, Nana.'

'Yeah, it's one hell of a Christmas present.'

'I think my dad might have been hinting about it. He was here this morning, it was nice, now I feel a bit weird about it.'

She felt disloyal about saying this to Max. Having only just been reunited with him, she was already suspecting him of having mercenary motives. But seriously, who could blame her? At their first meeting he had been talking about Nana's stuff and what had happened to it. About her jewellery. This ring must be worth a great deal just in gold value. He had been left the house and some money to renovate it, what more did he want?

'Look. Maybe your dad did realise. Maybe he just wanted to check that the family heirloom was still safe. I don't know, but it's Christmas Eve and I don't like you being on your own, especially after yesterday. So I repeat, what time are you leaving? Austin has changed his flight to tomorrow so we can all eat tonight, and you can spend Christmas Day with me and Dad.'

Nell slid the heavy ring onto her finger and her world tilted for a second. She had seen it before. Smoke had mixed with mist as she had stared with burning eyes at the figure before her, at the shawl, which was moved aside to show her Thomas, safe and happy, clutching at the ring on his sister's finger.

50

Christmas Eve - London

It was too bright to be a star and wasn't moving so … perhaps a planet? Whatever it was, it shone in the sky like a mythical sign and Nell half-expected to see camels, men with beards, and some shepherds mooching underneath. Anything was possible on this most magic of Christmas Eves.

A cheer went up as the Salvation Army band finished one carol and turned their music sheets for the next.

'One more and then we'll head off to meet Austin, shall we?'

'One more,' agreed Nell.

'Silent Night'. As they began to sing, Nell felt a soft pressure on her shoulder and turning, she saw Austin's reassuring figure behind her. Max, who was singing a few words behind everyone else, waved enthusiastically at the sight of him. Against her will, Nell felt her eyes and nose begin to sting as the timeless music brought back happy memories, and the peace of Christmas washed over her. She wasn't alone.

'Maybe I get it now.' Nell put down her glass and gazed at their reflection in the high windows of the restaurant. Outside, a few flakes of snow were falling and in its softness, the last few pieces in Nell's heart found their place. 'All the happiness, love, feeling of security and wellness that you feel with a parent or someone you connect with, isn't lost when they die. Energy doesn't die, it just changes. That's why you feel like the person is still with you those first few days after they pass. You expect to open a door and see them, take a call, and expect to hear them. It doesn't feel like they've gone at all. Then gradually, as the days pass, and the condolence messages and cards stack up, the tears flow, and you feel the loss. But you were right the first time. They don't leave you, never will. They, and their energy and your relationship has just moved to a new phase where it continues until you also move to the next place. So, love really does never die because it physically can't. It just evolves, as everything does.'

The hug from Max nearly knocked her off her chair.

'That's so beautiful, and so true. You should write it down.'

From the safe place of Max's hug, there was still one person whose approval she sought, and as she looked across at the candlelight flicker in Austin's hazel eyes, she knew she had it. Locked in, she just stared at him, as if seeing him properly for the first time. Now she finally acknowledged that her Christmas wish *had* come true. She was with family.

EPILOGUE

Christmas Day

It seemed that no one could wait for the Christmas service to end before the congregation began to gossip about the goings on at the manor. And of Tilly Corberley. Will sighed; remembering the bright, beautiful woman he had begun to know. Only he hadn't really, had he. Again, he winced to think that it was his present that had caused her death.

A slight hush went over the crowd as they spotted Seb waiting outside. A tattooed girl with green hair went to hug him, but he stepped back, looking behind her.

'Finn; talk to me,' he shouted, but the man behind the tattooed girl shook him off.

'Leave it, Seb. Leave us alone,' spat a woman from behind as she put a motherly arm around Finn.

Seb stood there, lost and miserable, until he spotted Will.

'You don't believe all this bullshit about my mum do you? You were friends, weren't you, so you'd know.'

Seb had known about the two of them; that surprised Will, and worried him. People were turning to him now with renewed interest.

'We were working on a book together,' he offered.

'Yes, and dragged up loads of medieval rubbish that they are now pinning on my mum. She wouldn't have hurt Ava. Mark is telling lies.'

Will shrugged. 'I don't know anything. But this isn't the place.'

A Land Rover pulled up.

'Seb. Come away.'

Will exchanged a glance with Daisy. As Seb shuffled miserably to the open car door, he turned once more to Will.

'All this curse business. She was only trying to protect me. You started it all, doing up that old house. Mum said you were related to the witch.'

Everyone had given up pretending they weren't listening now. Will shook his head.

'It was a long time ago. Half this village is probably descended from the Maundrells. Let it go. I think your mother was just a little confused.'

Seb flew out of the car before anyone could stop him. The punch had little strength, but it caught Will unawares and he fell heavily.

A taxi saw the commotion outside the church and slammed on its brakes. But the driver's foot went straight to the floor and, with a deafening smash, it crashed into the churchyard wall. Bricks rained down on the prone body of Will Montague as people rushed to his aid, and above all the noise, the shouting and the gasps, a humming could be heard. Just a few notes, simple, like a lullaby to soothe, or to *lure* a small child.

ABOUT THE AUTHOR

J A Higgins was born and raised at Porton Down in Wiltshire, and currently works for the NHS in Salisbury. She has always been fascinated by history, crime and the unexplained.

A Long Time Burning is the second book in the Nell Montague Mystery series which explores how horrors from the past are still very relevant today.

Also from J A Higgins:

Three Spells for Christmas - a quartet of creepy Christmas short stories

The Christmas ornaments look sweet, but hidden in each is a paranormal entity, ready to unleash horrors on three unsuspecting strangers.

To break the spell they must each face their fears, or this really will be their worst Christmas ever.

Printed in Great Britain
by Amazon